The Task
and
The Burden

The Task
and
The Burden

Marjorie H. Noon

To Alan
best wishes
Marjorie Noon

VANTAGE PRESS
New York

FIRST EDITION

All rights reserved, including the right of reproduction in whole or in part in any form.

Copyright © 2004 by Marjorie H. Noon

Published by Vantage Press, Inc.
516 West 34th Street, New York, New York 10001

Manufactured in the United States of America
ISBN: 0-533-14639-9

Library of Congress Catalog Card No.: 2003097872

0 9 8 7 6 5 4 3 2 1

Dedication

Theodore W. Noon, Jr., DSC

Captain, Co. G 351st Infantry

*And for those who
left their personal
lives to take up the
task, and who today
still share the
burden.*

Preface

"... easy is the descent into hell
but to recall thy steps and issue to upper air,
this is the task, this the burden."
Aeneid—Book Six
Virgil

The Task and the Burden is for those who have lived long enough
to remember World War II, and for everyone interested in that
generation.

Characters in the book, confronted by interruptions in their
lives, respond to the task. Most of them, but not all, are competent in situations not of their choosing as they cope with the burden.

The manuscript was written fifty years ago. The combat
chapters could not have been written without using details from
my husband's reminiscences. I am grateful for his permission to
include them, for his encouragement, and for his editing help.

It is my hope that you will enjoy reading the story and find
insights into the human costs of war.

—Marjorie Noon
October 2003

I

In the unusual stillness Second Lieutenant Donald Cutler could hear the small sounds of Camp Carver as he walked through the dusk toward the lighted doorway of the Officers' Club on a September evening in 1942. Like the buzz of a giant hive, muted voices came from the barracks. Behind C Company mess, covers clanged harshly on trash cans; and from the darkness came the Zzzzzz of cicadas singing out the summer's end.

Under the street lights the Post was almost attractive at night. The permanent buildings were a mock Spanish style with stuccoed walls and stonework showing through at the corners. At division headquarters there were curved arches over doors and windows; but the rest, the buildings which had been added so rapidly, were of wood, not unlike huge chicken houses. At night it looked like a toy town with the streets laid out in a grid and the barracks buildings lined up precisely in rows. The sentries posted at intervals looked like toy soldiers. As Lieutenant Cutler passed Chapel Number Four with its white spire set incongruously between the other buildings, he felt almost like a toy lieutenant. He played with the idea, finding a grim amusement in it. Colonel Spaulding was a toy soldier, he thought, and Captain MacRae, and even "Eager-Beaver" Duval were toy soldiers, and so was he. They had been picked up from their real lives and hypnotized into acting out parts in the colossal disruption known as the Second World War.

Donald Cutler, sandy haired, with blue eyes and a genial grin, was twenty-three years old. Months of training had given him a leanness which somehow counteracted his youthfulness. Lanky, well-coordinated, and quiet, he took responsibility well and believed in the gradual adding up of effort. His determination showed in his walk. The men found him dependable and accepted him.

As he came up the walk of the Officers' Club, he heard the

orchestra blaring and saw several officers talking together on the steps under the lights. One of them was Captain MacRae, his captain. MacRae nodded as Cutler went by and into the club.

In the far corner of the hall the orchestra played, and over everything was the Saturday night air of gaiety and expectation. The rooms of the Officers' Club were humming with the sounds of many conversations. Uniformed men were everywhere, the older ones with campaign ribbons on their blouses. One could see the Purple Heart ribbon for wounds in action, the stripes of the 1918 Occupation, the bright Asiatic-Pacific Theater, and even a few ribbons representing the Silver Star. But for the most part, the men were young, alert, and clean shaven in new uniforms with only the insignia of rank on their shoulders.

As usual the bar was the focal point of the club. Standing with others waiting were Lieutenant Rusnick and Major Van Tuyl, Lieutenant Jensen and Lieutenant Duval. Jimmy, the mess boy in a white jacket, was doling out drinks as fast as he could mix them; and the officers were ragging him about his speed. The jokes were old to Jimmy but he smiled. His job was complicated by the fact that each bottle was labeled with an officer's name, and it was necessary to locate the correct bottle before he could mix the drink. He had some private filing system of his own by which he could put his hand on an officer's bottle almost immediately, but even so they had to wait. Jimmy's feet hurt. He kept thinking how nice it would be to take off his shoes. As he emptied a bottle, he dropped it into a barrel with the rest of the "dead soldiers." It was going to be another wet night at the club. He'd be lucky to get back to his barracks before two o'clock.

The thing which distinguished Saturday night from the rest of the week was color as much as anything. All week long the men were surrounded with olive drab uniforms, jeeps, water cans, helmets, tarpaulins, even the handkerchiefs. But on Saturday night women were invited to the club bringing color—vivid blue, red, yellow, pink, green. Lonely officers maneuvered to sit next to a woman at dinner; even the duller wives seemed desirable. In this world where the men outnumbered them, they were all belles. The attention was exhilarating, brought out the best and the worst in them, turning imagination to actuality. In this atmosphere each woman became more herself, closer to what she truly was.

Saturday night at the Officers' Club is an army tradition. It is the social center of the week, the dress night, the dance night, the big drink night. It is the time of contacts and apple polishing and upstaging as well as a chance to relax with friends, to get away from routine. To the young officers at Carver, it was a part of their education—for some a first glimpse of a social life neither they nor their families had had an opportunity to sample. It made them feel important to be in this mobile atmosphere where a man could climb on his own abilities.

Second lieutenants outnumbered the others. They were the lowest rank at the Club, but they learned rapidly and knew that in wartime they would soon be pushed up the rank ladder by the arrival of younger, greener men. "Shavetails" were expected to make some mistakes but to learn from them. At the club they were observed. Many of the qualities valued here were important in the field.

Leaning against the bar was a battalion colonel. He was graying at the temples, tanned, and solid looking. He wore the uniform with a certain amount of distinction and dominated the scene around him. No one crowded the colonel. He stood with a glass in his hand watching the crowded room as he observed to himself that it was a perfectly ordinary Saturday night. He watched the eager politeness of the younger officers and saw his wife, overgroomed, playing colonel's lady to her usual court of apple polishers. It all made him very weary.

Colonel Malcolm Spaulding had been in the army since the First World War, longer than many of these young officers had been alive. He had gone through West Point and was sent overseas in 1918, returning with the rank of captain. He married the daughter of his hometown fire commissioner. Her name was Violet and she had been what they called a "real looker." They soon had a daughter and then one more. It was a point of chagrin to Spaulding that both of his offspring were female. Previously he had publicly and loudly proclaimed the superiority of male children. He privately blamed his wife for this inadequacy and let it become a wedge which slowly cracked the marriage. She fell defiantly into the flirtations and affairs which plague any army post

3

in peace time. As the years went by, they were shifted from post to post and Spaulding advanced in rank. The daughters were sent off to a Southern finishing school. When their older daughter had been married at the post, Violet Spaulding had let herself get roaring drunk and yelled after the departing couple as they ran the gauntlet of rice and confetti, "Live it up, live it up!"

The colonel watched his wife dance by with Lieutenant Duval. She was still attractive although fading. She was wearing a tight green dress and already showed the results of her drinks. She also showed, in the slight sagging of her face, the results of too many hangovers, too many arguments, too little understanding; but she had reached that stage which comes at different times to different women when, balanced between youth and age, she was desperately trying to counteract the flow of time. She didn't feel that she owed Spaulding a thing.

Colonel Spaulding's only reaction was ironic amusement. He felt outside of it all, as an observer without power to interrupt or redirect. His wife was acting like a tramp, and he didn't care enough to do anything about it. The hell with it. He felt old and stale as he finished his drink. He wanted to get overseas, and tonight he didn't give a damn whether he ever came back. He turned to the bar.

"Jimmy," he said, "fill it up and make it strong."

As he clumsily barged into the crowd, he banged against Lieutenant Cutler. The drink rose like an amber wave in the glass and slopped over Cutler's sleeve.

"Oh God," said the Colonel annoyed. He pulled out a folded handkerchief and offered it to Cutler who used it to dab at his sleeve.

"Sorry, sir," said Cutler with an embarrassed grin.

"Not your fault," said Colonel Spaulding. "I should have seen you standing there." The colonel had an idea.

"Come with me, son," he said and led Cutler over to where his younger daughter, Alice, was talking. He introduced Cutler to his daughter feeling that he was doing the young man a great favor and then he walked off.

Cutler had known who she was. She'd been jokingly pointed out to him more than once as a high road to promotion but, as

4

yet, not even Lieutenant Duval, called the eager-beaver, had felt that initiative in this direction was worth the risk. She was a pretty girl of eighteen in a fresh pink dress and Cutler was human. He was glad that the colonel had spilled whiskey on him.

"Well, hello, Lieutenant Cutler," said Alice smiling at him archly and turning her head sideways. "Wherever do you come from?"

"All the way from New England," said Cutler.

"Let's see," said Alice, "that must be up beyond New York. We went to New York for the World's Fair several years ago," she added brightly.

"Did you like it?" asked Cutler.

"It was dreamy," said Alice twisting her head again to look at him as she had practiced in the mirror. "Did you go to the Point?" she asked abruptly.

"Well, no," said Cutler. "I'm only a gentleman for the duration." The reference was to the wording in which men were declared "officers and gentlemen" in the ceremony of commissioning.

"That's a pity," she said, missing his attempted humor. "Well, what do you do when you're not in the army?" she asked.

Cutler hesitated. "Archaeology," he said, "history and anthropology, they're interrelated."

"Archaeology!" said Alice. "Wherever did you study that?"

"Harvard," said Cutler wishing he hadn't been asked. Out here he had no desire to play matador with the crimson banner. Even now he felt that some explanation was in order.

"I studied archaeology," he said, "because it's a way of getting at history. Anthropology feeds into the whole thing too—largely determines it I suppose. There is history in all the old remains, and the archaeologist has the keys to it."

"How fascinating," said Alice smiling at him sideways and lowering her eyelashes demurely. "You must tell me all about it." She waited expectantly.

"Well," said Cutler, "I've always wanted to travel to see where things happened, to Peru for instance, or Mesopotamia or Greece. As a matter of fact," he confided, "I was signed up to go on an expedition to Peru when this army found me. What I'm interested in is people and situations and the way the combination makes history."

"Whyever do you want to go to Peru?" asked Alice.

"Well," said Cutler, "I expect it is hard to understand. Perhaps it's because I keep thinking that there's some universal answer to some of life's questions and that if I keep looking I might find it."

"My," said Alice, "you must be a philosopher. Whatever are the questions?"

"The one which comes most readily to mind," said Don wryly, "is what are we here for?"

"That's silly," said Alice. "We're here to dance."

Cutler smiled. "You just could be right," he said.

Captain MacRae's wife, Fran, came back from the powder room with fresh lipstick, every hair in place, and a calculating look in her eye. She stood in the arched doorway, not to make an impression—the room was too crowded for that—but rather to make an appraisal.

As her glance went over the dancers and those who ringed the floor in conversation, she saw her husband at the bar talking with Colonel Spaulding. That was good. She had told him often to make opportunities to know the colonel better. It would help his career. She saw the colonel's wife in a green, slinky dress dance by with her head on Lieutenant Duval's shoulder. *That old bitch!* thought Fran. She saw Lieutenant Duval's face. He looked cowed, a little numb. This amused her. *'Eager-Beaver' is working hard for this promotion,* she thought. She saw the colonel's daughter, Alice, a blond in pink, trying to flirt with Lieutenant Cutler. *Well, well,* she thought, *that's a new combination.* She saw Lieutenants Jensen and Rusnick and toyed with the idea of joining the bachelors but decided instead to help her husband with the colonel. She started across the floor toward them.

Fran was a maverick. Under twenty she had been a little wild and now, at twenty-four, she still bore the brand. She liked a scrap, liked to be struggling for something. Her father had walked out on the family when she was young and ever since she had felt that she could depend only on herself. She had wanted many things which her mother had been unable to provide. She had dreamed of beautiful dresses (she still did) and of going to parties and of being strikingly attractive. When she had met Richard MacRae on a blind date, she had quickly realized that he was the best her limited horizon had to offer.

Captain Richard MacRae was a big man with large hands and feet and a shock of black hair. Although still under thirty, he was older than most of the young officers, a natural leader, well on his way to a Majority. He was happiest out of doors and outstanding in field maneuvers. At the club, he felt somehow constrained, afraid of breaking something or tripping on the rugs.

He was talking to the colonel about target-range practice. They had both seen Fran in the doorway. He was proud of his wife. She was clever and smart, and she knew how to look like a million even though it did cost him plenty. When he had met her on leave, she had singled him out for attention, which had been flattering. She danced well, dressed with a flair, was never at a loss for words. He had never known anyone quite like her. His own sisters and their friends were more predictable, and Fran fascinated him. He couldn't help himself. She told him about her childhood and her parents' divorce and said that she liked him because he was steady and dependable. The idea that she needed him made him bold. When he asked her to marry him, she had insisted that they elope immediately.

As she came across the floor to where he stood with the colonel, there was a pertness about her, a cockiness which still intrigued him as much as it ever had. He watched her greet Colonel Spaulding, draw him into conversation, flatter him, make him laugh. When the colonel turned briefly to get her a drink, she winked broadly at Rich. It was all their private joke. A man could go far with a wife like this, thought Captain Richard MacRae.

Lieutenant Duval was having his own troubles. His attention to the colonel's wife was boomeranging. Mrs. Spaulding was by now quite tight. Already she had confided to him that her husband didn't understand her, that he was practically impotent, and that she liked young men very much. Duval was in a panic. *God!* he thought, *why didn't I leave this brass alone?*

"Let's go home," she kept saying, hanging on his arm. "It's

time to go to bed." He knew that Lieutenant Rusnick had over-heard her. He wanted to walk off and leave her, have a good stiff drink and joke with the boys, but he didn't dare risk her wanton anger. *After all,* he thought, *this is the bag who made such a commotion at her own daughter's wedding.* The battalion was still talking about it, and Lieutenant Duval didn't want adverse publicity now when he was bucking so hard for a promotion. *God!* he thought, *why didn't I go after the daughter instead?*

Lieutenant Cutler was dancing with Alice. He thought that the pink of her dress was the most delicate thing he had seen in months. It reminded him of other parties and of Helen. If he could just shut out the army now, it would be like a college dance. He tried to imagine it without realizing that he was staring at the colonel's daughter. Alice looked away over his shoulder at the other dancers, but when she glanced back he was still staring at her in that strange way. He held her closer and she was quite breathless. He really wasn't like the other lieutenants, she told herself.

Colonel Spaulding watched Alice and Lieutenant Cutler. Nice young man, not army, but good education, lots to learn, but acceptable he concluded. *Ah, to be young again,* he thought wryly.

He looked back at his wife and Lieutenant Duval. *She'll get what she's looking for if she acts like that,* he thought. He supposed he ought to take her home.

The music stopped and Alice was at his elbow, breathless and flushed.

"Daddy," she said, "this was a wonderful dance!" The colonel looked hard at her. Suddenly he realized that he didn't trust any of these young shavetails further than he could see them. He didn't want any playing around with Alice. He'd break the man that tried it.

As the dance ended, Lieutenant Cutler stepped through the screen doors onto the club veranda, restlessly searching through his pockets for matches. When he found them, he lit a cigarette and slowly inhaled, blowing the smoke out again into the night. He thought of Helen and of their engagement party when he had been at home on leave in the spring. He wished that Helen could seem real out here in this land of endless plains. She seemed very far away.

The quick spring had come months before, lush, green, gentle, filled with promise, unfolding tiny leaves on the low bushes and cottonwood trees and sprouting tender grasses and little flowers. But now, in September, the land had settled into exhaustion.

Tonight the hot winds, which had blown almost continuously for weeks, had finally quieted leaving an air of cool reprieve. It had been a hot, windy summer, parching throats and tempers. There had been days when men had dropped on the parade ground and, under military discipline, lain in the dust at the feet of their fellows until ranks were broken and they were picked up. This was no world for weaklings.

As Lieutenant Cutler walked slowly back to his quarters, he could see the shadowy barracks and the mess halls luminous in the moonlight. The sound of his footsteps seemed to echo from the barracks' walls as he passed. Sleeping here were men whom Cutler knew well, men of all types and descriptions, men from all parts of the country, men of many beliefs and persuasions brought to this common experience by war. Already he thought of them as his men, men he would be responsible for in combat, and he knew that they were the basic importance of an army. Sleeping here were the men who would go out on patrol, knock out the enemy sentries, take the next hill. They rested now, but in the morning they would come to life again with new-grown beards and need for food and endless banter.

It was easy for Cutler to identify himself with them since such a short time ago, in a different division, he had himself been an enlisted man. When his old division had sailed west, he had been enroute to Georgia for officers' training. At Fort Benning there had been concentrated work—three months to do the job for which West Point allowed four years. He had worked hard at it, felt a responsibility to know his job, to live down the old army scorn of the young lieutenants known as "ninety-day wonders." When he thought of his old division and of friends already fighting, he had felt an obligation to justify being left behind. He had been assigned to Camp Carver to help the cadre form the new division.

Already it was a long job with no end in sight, an endless

round of obstacle courses, target practice, motor pools, getting ready to go overseas for the "big push" somewhere in a future both desired and feared. The initial novelty of a war was over, the surprise of Pearl Harbor, the excitement of talking about it, the firsts were behind. The headlines continued but their effect was not quite so jarring. People began to know what to expect. And yet, there was an undefined awareness, a feeling for which there was no real explanation. The indignation and effort of the country, instead of escaping in many directions, was slowly and firmly being brought into focus like the sundog of a burning glass to ignite, one by one, carefully selected targets.

Cutler wondered where the training would lead him—Europe? Philippines? Japan? He hoped that it would be east, not west, but there was no way of knowing. He hoped that he would stand up under fire. He hoped that he would live through it and get back to his real life; but he wasn't sure of that either, for here, on the dusty plain, General Steed was building an infantry division, fourteen thousand strong, a tough fighting force, a division which would determine a difference in the outcome of the war.

II

Colonel Spaulding, in his shirt sleeves, sat over breakfast reading news of Allied landings in North Africa and the announcement that beachheads were being established. His mind was fully employed as he pictured the terrain and action. Some of his friends were there. He wished that he was there too, as his mind deployed regiments to the right and left and he cut off enemy supply with supporting air power. His mind's war was completely satisfactory to him; a bold sweep here, another there, cutting through petty detail and culminating in victory.

Opposite him across the cluttered table sat Violet Spaulding in a long magenta housecoat with her initials brazenly embellished on one breast. She looked wrinkled and weary without full make-up, but as she sipped a lukewarm cup of coffee, she left lipstick on the rim. She was slowly reading the social notes.

"Well, well," said Mrs. Spaulding, "Margaret Steed is in Washington again. What kind of apple polishing does a general's wife need to do?"

"Maybe you'd better find out," said Spaulding irritated by the interruption.

"Daddy," said Alice, "do you think you'll ever be a general?"

"Why not?" said Spaulding.

"You'd make a wonderful general," said Alice. "You look so distinguished in a uniform." She said it as though she meant it. The colonel beamed at her and put down the paper.

"Good Lord," said Mrs. Spaulding, "save all that flattery for the club. You don't need to practice at home."

Alice buttered her toast.

"I'm glad someone around here thinks so," said Spaulding, ignoring his wife. "You know," he said to Alice, "these African landings mean action. Plenty of fighting ahead. Plenty of chance for promotions in an expanding army. I'd transfer out of here if I weren't so sure that the division is headed over soon. And when

11

we get there, I'll show them! I'll shunt my battalion around aggressively. When I get my regiment, it's going to be known as first rate, outstanding on the line."

"If you get very aggressive," said Alice, "won't a lot of men get killed?"

"Sure they'll get killed," said Spaulding. "That's what war is. The infantry buys ground with men. Always has. It's a calculated risk. The quicker you pay the price for the advance, the sooner the war is over. It's going to cost a certain number of men to win the war, and it can cost a lot more if you're too slow about it."

"What a strategist you are," said Mrs. Spaulding sarcastically. "I'm glad I'm not in your battalion."

"So am I," said Spaulding emphatically.

"Daddy," said Alice thoughtfully, ignoring the quarrel, "is it true that lieutenants are considered expendable?"

Spaulding took a long drink of coffee and looked at her over the cup.

"Nobody's expendable, honey," he said, "unless something happens which creates special circumstances; but in combat sometimes that happens and if it does, anybody is expendable. Rank doesn't determine it. It may be a lieutenant is expendable. We have lots of them, but privates and colonels are expendable too. Proportionally it's about the same risk. There is only one colonel for eight or nine hundred enlisted men. So, statistically, a colonel should get killed every time eight hundred fifty enlisted men get killed."

"Does that mean it's safer to be a colonel?" asked Alice.

"Why no, honey," said Spaulding. "More enlisted men get killed because there are just more of them."

"But, Daddy," said Alice, "won't you be back of the front lines at a command post and the privates out in front in foxholes?"

"I'm a front-line colonel," said Spaulding. "It's the only way to lead the men. My command post will be up where I can know what is going on."

"Don't be so gruesome," said Mrs. Spaulding. "You'll give the girl bad dreams."

"Listen, Violet," said Spaulding, "you don't have to sit there if you don't want to; but if Alice asks me and wants to know, I think I ought to explain it."

"Go right ahead," she said. "Who's stopping you?"

"You are," he said, "with that superficial attitude of yours. The work this division has ahead of it is important. The papers are full of news of Africa this morning, and the only thing that you notice is that the general's wife has gone to Washington."

"Yes, dear," she said with mock humility, rising from the table and elaborately wrapping the robe around herself.

"Well, you'd better think about it," said Spaulding gruffly.

She came up behind his chair. "I do think about it," she said putting one manicured hand on his shoulder. "All the time I think about the fine young men that you'll order into hell to be killed and maimed and. . . ."

"Stop it!" he said standing up suddenly and banging the table with his fist. She turned and left the room. Spaulding sat down again uneasily.

"What a breakfast," he said trying to smile at Alice. "It's enough to give me ulcers."

"She doesn't mean it," said Alice. "She cries a lot."

"Well, it makes a hell of a life," said Spaulding. "I can't wait to get overseas."

"You'll go soon enough," said Alice, "and then what do I do for the duration?"

"You live with her I guess," said Spaulding. "You can stay here or go back to Missouri or even to San Antonio if you like it better."

"I bet Mother chooses San Antone," said Alice. "She likes to party."

"She sure does," said Spaulding frowning.

"Daddy," said Alice after a pause, "do you like Lieutenant Cutler?"

"Sure, why not?" said the colonel.

"He's really quite an unusual man," said Alice.

"They all are," said the colonel wryly, "so don't settle on one till you've looked them all over. The sharp one in that company is Lieutenant Duval."

"He's not nearly so interesting," said Alice.

"What's the matter with old faithful?" asked Spaulding. "Why look at civilians when you can have a regular army major?"

13

"Major Van Tuyl is thirty years old," said Alice as though that settled it.

"That makes him old enough to know what he wants," said Spaulding.

"Really, Daddy," said Alice, "I bet you encourage him to stick around."

"He's a damn fine army man," said Spaulding, "and maybe when you get over these schoolgirl crushes, you'll realize it."

"The way I feel about Lieutenant Cutler isn't a crush," said Alice.

"Oh, I see," said Spaulding. "What does your mother say about it?"

Alice giggled. "She says if I want him, to go and get him."

"That must have been a fascinating conversation," said Spaulding. "Did she tell you how to go about it?"

"Why, Daddy," said Alice playfully, "what a suspicious man you are."

"Look," said Spaulding, bitterly "there are lots of things I don't know, but I'll tell you one thing and it is that if you're thinking about marriage, you've got to realize there's more to it than a flirtation."

"Of course, Daddy," said Alice, her eyes wide and innocent.

First Sergeant Pulska had the men of Company C lined up for inspection. He had been particularly fussy this morning in his big open-mouthed way, walking up and down the line making remarks which the men found humorous. Sergeant Pulska bullied the men for their own good and they knew it. To a recruit, he looked and sounded like a bulldog; but it was mostly bluster, and he put it on because he felt it was expected of him. He lacked the streak of power sadism often associated with sergeants and put on a good show out of a personal apprehension that the men would get the better of him if they really knew him. It was a game he played with them. Often at the end of the day, he would grin to himself as he thought, *Fooled 'em again today.*

" 'Tention!" roared Sergeant Pulska throwing out his chest until it looked as though he would split the zipper on his field jacket. "Right face! Forward march! Hut, two, tree, foa," he said as the men marched off. Private Millen in the front row was out of step. Sergeant Pulska spotted him immediately.

"Company, halt!" He waited for complete quiet. "Lover-boy is out of step this morning," he said sarcastically. "Let's help him to get started again." There were chuckles in the ranks and a loud guffaw from Private Benard.

"Shut up, Benard!" said Pulska. "You want to swallow your false teeth before breakfast?"

The men grinned, but silently this time.

" 'Tention! Forward march! Hut, two, tree," said the sergeant as they started off again. Pulska put them through the routine bringing them back to halt where they had started. The company stopped rigidly in place.

"Left face! At ease!"

"Now," said Pulska beaming at them, "a little matter has come to my attention which I am sure will interest all of you." He paused letting his eyes run over the men in ranks. "We all spend time in that dayroom," he continued. "We have magazines and a radio, but everyone knows that it could be better. Now I want to talk to you this morning about making the dayroom better. The dayroom," he said with just an edge of the old sarcasm in his voice, "is our home away from home. It should be a center to which we gladly return. We have lots of talent in this company," he went on more seriously, "but we have no piano. Now if we had a piano, we could have singing. It would seem like a party every night. It just happens that we have heard of a piano for sale, a really sturdy piano in mahogany which would really dress up our home away from home. But there is the problem," he let his face droop mournfully as he said this, "there is the sad problem of financing."

The men looked straight ahead in ranks. They had seen the stinger.

"Financing is always a problem," said the sergeant.

"Yea man," said a private in the front row under his breath.

"We don't want anyone to feel that he has to help out if he doesn't want to," said the sergeant benignly. "This is to be a strictly volunteer contribution of fifty cents from each man who wants to enjoy some singing and music in the dayroom. If anyone is against music and guys singing together, he can refuse to contribute. We don't want any sourpuss to feel that he's been taken.

15

The rest of us want a piano; and if one or two of you don't want to be good guys and help out, nobody is forcing you. The way it is set up is that the company will just save out fifty cents from each man next payday. Nothing to chip in now. This is painless financing."

The men waited quietly.

"Now," said the sergeant, "I'm giving any man that's against music and singing a chance to refuse to chip in. Will any skinflint who's too stingy to give fifty cents so his buddies can have a piano step forward?"

No one stepped forward.

"Well, good!" said the sergeant happily. "I'll tell Captain MacRae."

III

In the small, dark barracks room Donald Cutler lay sleepless on his cot listening to the drag of the wind outside. He could see the outline of the door where cracks of light from the hall beyond defined its shape, and he could just barely see the faint white spot which was the ceiling light bulb against the black shadows of stringers which held up the roof. Somewhere down the hall he heard a door shut and then, through the wall to the next room, he heard Lieutenant Jensen begin to snore. The snores, faint at first, slobbered in and out. He thought of banging on the flimsy wooden partition which separated the cots, but he knew that it would be useless. The snores repelled and fascinated him. Jensen snored magnificently and, in his oblivion, was deaf to any outer disturbance.

Cutler rolled over wondering whether he had been right to agree with Helen on the telephone. He had called her, as he often did, and she had said, "If we're going to be married, let's get married now before they send you overseas." It had been easy to agree with the warm intimacy of her voice in his ear, but now as he lay here he realized that he had not yet made up his mind whether the fact that he might not come back from the war was a reason for rushing or waiting. He hadn't even been to Peru yet. Everything was being hurried.

He thought back over the years he had known Helen remembering the school where he had watched for her in the corridors and first confided to her his interest in history. He remembered telling her of Schliemann, who discovered the site of ancient Troy by reading literally the epics of Homer and then searching along the shores of Asia Minor for a site to fit the descriptions. He had told her of Breasted's work in Egypt, of the wonderful archaeological discoveries in Mesopotamia, of the Mayas and the Incas.

She had listened, interested in his stories, convinced that

17

their teller would be a great man. Her belief in him had helped him to see himself. Serious and reserved, locked much of the time within himself, he had known then the beginnings of his desire and need to find in ancient patterns the answers to modern riddles.

What is it all about, he wondered, why am I here? "We're here to dance," Alice Spaulding had told him. He wished that he could find it that simple.

His mind turned to the progress of the war. He wondered what the next year would bring. He wished that it could be peace, but his reason told him that that was more than a year away. He felt that his life was being funneled down to a great trial from which he might not emerge. He wondered now about his future. It was bitter to think of losing it before it had begun. Let the old die, he thought. They have had their chance. Why should the possibility of this heavy demand hang over the life of a young man full of plans. War is grim business, he thought, bringing a man against the most basic reality, existence itself. He wondered how many regrets died with a man, how many things undone, places unseen, loves unloved. He wanted to know.

Slowly he tasted the possibilities. They would go overseas— he was sure of that. There would be the enemy to fight, the great impersonal enemy against whom they had endlessly trained. There would be ground to be taken, but what of him personally?

He could understand now why ancient men consulted oracles and sibyls to be foretold their fate. It was basic for a man threatened to seek assurance.

Suddenly and clearly he saw himself in the mud, wounded, bloody, alone. He felt that his life was over before it had started. There is nothing I want so much as to live, he thought desperately, and the intensity of his longing for a future welled up in him. The pity of it made him yearn for Helen. He felt that she could save him, give him back the days and years for which he now mourned. He wanted to marry her before he went. Perhaps she might give him a son who could stay behind as a hostage against the future while he went into the unknown of war. It is decided, he thought, and as he fell asleep he pictured to himself a sibyl in a cave chanting indistinctly the words of his fate while he strained in vain against the sound of Jensen's snoring for a recognizable word.

When Don went to Colonel Spaulding to ask for leave to go east to be married, Colonel Spaulding had barked out a flat "NO." He hadn't meant to be so abrupt, but he was furious. Family pride was involved. Alice had liked this young whippersnapper. She had been chasing him whenever he turned up at the club, had made a fool of herself over him. Colonel Spaulding knew battalion gossip had been betting on Alice in spite of Cutler's New England reticence; and when it turned out that Cutler planned to marry somebody else, the colonel took it as a personal affront.

"No," he bellowed, "this is wartime. I can't have all my lieutenants scattered around the country at highfalutin weddings. If you've got to get married, get married here."

"I haven't got to get married," said Cutler steadily, pale and furious himself by now.

"Well, that's fine," said the colonel.

Cutler boiled as he left headquarters. No colonel was going to run his life. He'd get married if he had to ask Helen to come out here. Just because the colonel was stuck with a tramp was no reason to be against marriage. He wondered how Helen would like to be married at the post and decided to go to see Chaplain Rutherford.

It was impossible to think of Chaplain Rutherford without being aware of good fellowship. This was his prime quality, and he hid the rest of his personality behind this façade. It was actually about the only avenue left open to him in his present job. He had arrived with other young officers of the battalion when the cadre was formed but, lacking their common background of training, had felt and been an outsider. Being somehow above war, above carrying arms, he was suspect. Being a chaplain, he was not invited to drink or play poker with them; and having chosen religion as a vocation, he was somehow expected to have solved all the personal problems of his own life at an age when other men felt no obligation to be complete. Personal inadequacy on his part would always be considered an inadequacy of his religion. It was a difficult role and forced him, without his wanting it, into the role of an observer. He was a mediocre chaplain, nei-

19

ther the best nor the worst of his group. He lacked the rigid intolerance of strict orthodoxy, but he also lacked the understanding compassion of a great chaplain. He was essentially an arranger, an organizer. Buoyant good fellowship seemed to him the only answer to his present dilemma.

When Lieutenant Cutler came to see him, Chaplain Rutherford was sitting at his desk thumbing through a magazine. He rose with exaggerated heartiness to greet Don.

"Hello, hello," he said stuffing the magazine into the top drawer and trying to shake hands across the desk at the same time. "Sit down," he said, "glad to see you."

Don sat on the folding chair opposite the desk.

"How have you been?" asked Chaplain Rutherford lacing his hands together on the desk and pulling against the knuckles.

"Fine thanks," said Don.

"I saw Company C going through the obstacle course the other day," said Rutherford. "Looks like a great outfit."

"That's right," said Don. "Captain MacRae is a great leader. He has the men right behind him all the way."

"Splendid," said Chaplain Rutherford.

There was a short pause.

"I'd like to get married here a week from Friday," said Don.

"Why that's fine," said the chaplain. He leaned back in his swivel chair. "Is the bride a local girl?"

"Oh, no," said Don startled at the idea. "She comes from Hartford, Connecticut, just outside of Hartford that is."

"Well," said the chaplain, "that's a long trip. Has she ever been out here before?"

"No," said Don, "New Englanders seem to stick close to home."

"Will she like it out here?" asked Chaplain Rutherford.

"Well, I hope so," said Don. "I'm going to try to find a little apartment in town."

"Don't count on it," said the chaplain. "You'll be lucky to find a room with kitchen privileges."

"How long does it take to be married?" asked Don.

"Why about ten minutes," beamed the chaplain, "but it lasts a lot longer." He laughed genially.

"Sure," said Don. "What about giving her the ring and everything. Do we have a rehearsal?"

"Oh, no," said Rutherford, "we run these things very informally. I'll tell you when it's time to put on the ring. You just bring the bride and we'll tie the knot for you." He glanced at his appointment book.

"You said a week from Friday?" asked the chaplain.

"That's right," said Don.

"You come to Chapel Number Four at three thirty," said Chaplain Rutherford. "I've got several weddings that day. One at three, another at four; but we can fit you in very well at three thirty. Just don't come before three fifteen or you'll run into the other wedding. Now, you'll need a license and a ring. Have to get the license in town at the courthouse in person. The army can't handle that for you," he grinned genially.

Don was bewildered by the idea that anyone else was being married that afternoon. Perhaps it was less of an ordeal than he had thought.

"Now, any questions?" asked Rutherford.

"Well, I guess not," said Cutler hesitating.

"Fine," said the chaplain.

Cutler walked back to his quarters preoccupied. Now that he had set a date with the chaplain, he was practically a married man. He thought back to what Captain MacRae had said in answer to his questions the day before.

"Sure you should get married now," Rich had said. "Have a child too before you go overseas. I don't suppose Diana is any more remarkable than lots of kids but to me she is. I want a son too," he had said confidentially. "All this talk about postponing marriage and children is overdramatizing. If our ancestors had waited for the perfect time to get married, we probably wouldn't be here."

Don had laughed. "I suppose you are right," he had said flipping rapidly through the index of history in his mind searching for a time lacking war, crisis, famine, pestilence, or depression.

"Yes," said Rich MacRae more thoughtfully, "a son would be good for Fran too; give her more focus in her life. She needs to settle down more. This life is hard on women."

"That's what I'm afraid of," Don had said.

"Hells bells," said MacRae, "don't overthink the situation.

Get married and be happy and meet future problems as they come up. You're a responsible adult with good intentions, and it's my observation that fate tends to favor your type. If there's any way we can help, let me know. Fran can show your wife around town and perhaps help with an apartment. If there's one available, she'll know where."

"Thanks," said Cutler. It suddenly occurred to him that with a wife he would be in a different social position and the idea rather appealed to him. He felt that MacRae, whom he had long admired as his captain, now was his friend as well.

He was thinking of all this as he walked along wondering what made the difference in men, why men like MacRae were able to win the respect and confidence which made them natural leaders. He was glad that he had been assigned to Company C. Working with MacRae had steadied him, he knew, when he had come, a green shavetail, from officer training. Captain MacRae had a natural regard for the best in any man. If orders had to be taken, thought Cutler, he would rather take them from MacRae than from any man he knew.

As he came down the road, he could see several cars parked in front of the barracks waiting for the men to come off duty. He had never been particularly aware of them before, but now he realized that they came at the end of each afternoon and that the married officers who were off duty went home in them as though they held ordinary jobs.

"Hey! Lieutenant Cutler! Hello!" It was Fran MacRae sitting in the MacRaes' coupe in front of quarters. She was waiting for Rich to get off duty. Little Diana was crawling around the small back seat with a toy duck on wheels in one hand. She was black-haired like her father, sturdy and preoccupied. Cutler walked over to the car.

"When's the wedding?" asked Fran.

Cutler told her.

"Well," said Fran, "I'll be there if I'm invited."

"Why sure," said Cutler, "of course you and Captain MacRae are invited!"

"Need any help?" asked Fran.

"Well, I don't know," said Cutler.

"Got a list of guests?"

"Well, no, not yet, but I will have."

"Ordered the flowers?"

"What flowers?" said Cutler feeling that this conversation was going too rapidly.

"Bridal bouquet," said Fran. "You just leave that to me. I'll order them and you can have them delivered wherever you want later."

"Well, thanks," said Cutler.

"Got a best man?"

"Well, not yet," said Cutler, "but I'm going to ask Rusnick."

"Fine," said Fran. "Who's going to be matron of honor?"

"Do we have to have one?" asked Cutler.

"Of course you do," said Fran. "Tell you what. I'm your captain's wife. I'll be the matron of honor if you don't have one."

"Well, sure," said Cutler wondering what Helen would say. "I guess that would be fine."

"Who's going to give her away?" asked Fran.

"Her father's coming," said Cutler feeling on solid ground for the first time in this conversation.

"Too bad," said Fran. "It would have been fun to ask Colonel Spaulding." She looked at him sideways.

Good Lord, thought Cutler. He wished that he and Helen could just take the license to Chaplain Rutherford and get married without anyone else having to be there. He did want Rusnick, of course. They had been to officers' training together, and Helen's father certainly had a right to see the thing through, but he didn't want the whole regiment there. This wasn't a part of his army life. This was a part of his other life which he was going back to someday, he hoped; and he had a feeling that he wanted to keep his two lives separate.

IV

Helen, in a neat traveling suit, followed by her father, stepped off the train in Cowan on the bright afternoon of a late November day. She was somewhat individual with her dark hair and eyes, pretty enough without being outstanding, quietly serious but with a sense of humor.

After two days on the train, it was sunny and pleasant on the busy platform. Express wagons were piled high with luggage, boxes, crates, and haversacks. Each day the trains left more people on the platform. The stationmaster often wondered where they all went, but still the town continued to absorb them. There were businessmen carrying brief cases or sample boxes, women with small children, middle-aged parents come to see a son, wives, and girls. They came from all parts of the country with different accents, different attitudes, different standards, different purposes.

Helen saw the confusion through the short veil on her little hat. To her, the trip was a great adventure. She had come almost 2,000 miles to marry Don. Here on the platform were soldiers coming and going on leave or transfer in long drab overcoats carrying bulging barracks bags on their shoulders, redcaps struggling with matched suitcases, two officers arguing with a Railway Express man. Then the conductor was shouting, "All Aboard!" and the train slowly glided off, gathering speed as it slid down the track to the west. This was merely a stop on the line, a busy stop; but, by leaving, the train seemed to declare that further down the track was the important destination, the terminal to which the railroad had been built.

Back up the straight track to the northeast, Helen could see between the walls of buildings back out to the open plain. For all its self-sufficiency, Cowan was only a dot on that rolling map of dust and brown grasses, a dot where the dust was hidden under pavement and the grass had made way for buildings. Even so, in the parking lot behind the Stevens Hotel, there was grass growing through cracks in the macadam.

As the nearest town to Camp Carver, Cowan had grown in a year from a relaxed county seat to a busy little city. Civic pride had never been higher. The local businessmen were growing up with their opportunities. Even today, the street was busy; and on any Saturday afternoon, the sidewalks were thronged with slowly-moving masses of soldiers with money to spend. Standing in line to be waited on, they bought popcorn, hamburgers, shaving lotion, ash trays, jewelry, satin pillow covers, clothing, sodas, writing paper. Long lines extended down the sidewalk from the two movie houses and formed at the restaurants.

The Stevens Hotel was the largest building in Cowan. Its brick walls with pretentious marble window frames rose eight stories from the main street. Originally it had been used for cattlemen's conventions and later, when oil was discovered, by the promoters. Always it was headquarters for those with business at the courthouse. For years its dining room with the high-arched windows had been the only restaurant in town where you could sit down to a white-clothed table with proper glass and silver and real flowers in a vase, but now the new Steak Palace had been built and was competing.

The Stevens Hotel was still, in point of service, the best Cowan had to offer. Its hospitality was more southern than western. There was still an air of genteel restraint, but now thirty years of tradition was threatened by the army. A hint of the old leisureliness still haunted the place, but as the grizzled old elevator operator remarked often and proudly, "This place is just like New York now!"

Helen's father checked the reservations at the desk, and they went up to their rooms on the sixth floor overlooking the main street.

Driving into town in a little green Chevy he had borrowed from Lieutenant Duval, Don Cutler was nervous and keyed up. He had cut himself shaving, his uniform didn't seem to fit properly. He wondered about taking some flowers, but the stores were all closed.

Brother! he thought to himself. *Of all the places to marry*

Helen. It's almost too late to be sensible. Maybe we should wait until after the war. But I may not be around then.

He swung the car onto Main Street in Cowan, crossed the railroad tracks and three blocks farther along found the hotel parking lot.

The dining room was crowded again tonight. There were the usual hotel guests—parents, several businessmen, two middle-aged women, tables of officers—but the atmosphere was quiet and subdued. As he came in with Helen and her father, Don Cutler had seen First Lieutenant Chivington, executive officer of C Company, at a corner table with Lieutenant Walker. He wished that just this once he could have had a meal without anyone from the company. Not that Chivington would pay much attention; Chivington had a salt and pepper and several rolls spread out on the white cloth and was carefully explaining some maneuvers to Walker, who chewed heartily while he listened.

A colored waiter brought large folded menus and filled the glasses with water floating with crushed ice.

"Let me recommend the Southern fried chicken," said Don. "They really know how to handle it here. We never see anything like it at home."

"Sounds fine," said Helen's father and Helen nodded her agreement.

"Three fried chicken," said Don to the waiter, "soup, peas, mashed potatoes, salad, plenty of rolls and some of that special relish."

"Yes, Sa," said the waiter collecting the menus with a flourish.

They finished the steaming soup and the fried chicken, crisp and golden, ate their way through the salads and French rolls, ordered pecan pie and sat talking over coffee.

Helen sat between her father and Don. She kept watching Don for some indication of what he was thinking behind the conversation. He asked about the trip, talked about camp and of the men and maneuvers and night problems. Helen's father started in on when he was at Plattsburg in 1917 and, between them, the two men had all the conversation. She glanced around her. Two middle-aged women were beaming at her. The officers in the corner looked her over and then turned back to

26

their table maneuvers.

After dinner they said good night to Helen's father, and Don helped Helen into the green Chevy. He wished very much that it were his own car instead of Lieutenant Duval's.

As they turned out of the hotel parking lot onto Main Street, neon lights shone in every direction. They advertised Foot Long Hot Dogs, Quick Shine, Laundry, Barber, Drugs, Theatre, Milk Shake, Cheeseburger, Penny Arcade, Fitts Department Store, Souvenirs—music blared from a loud-speaker in front of a record store. The town had an almost carnival mood. They passed the big drug store, with its windows lit from inside, plastered with paper signs. They passed the penny arcade and shooting gallery where GIs lounged showing off to local girls; they went by the Steak Palace with its spiked plants in the window. Don drove silently choosing the highway west, away from Cowan and the post. Gradually the lights and congestion were left behind. The motor hummed evenly carrying them away from the glitter and bustle of the overcrowded town. As the buildings thinned out, Don slipped his arm around her. The town was left behind and they were on the dark plain. The sky edges seemed to come in close to the car enclosing them under a perforated dome. This was their world now. There was something nice about having Helen close beside him on the front seat. There was a wholeness to life again. Helen watched him as he drove, his profile outlined against the night. The buttons and bars glinted on his uniform as she watched, wondering at this man, half stranger to her. Don slowed the car, running it carefully off the macadam onto the dry grass at the side of the road.

His kiss was hard, deliberate, demanding; the kiss of a man who has been patient a very long time. It was a hungry kiss letting her know his need of her. She pressed against him feeling the protection of the strength of this man who would be her husband. She loved him. Deeply and sincerely she knew she did.

"Helen," he said softly, "is it true? Do you really love me enough?"

"I really do," she said.

"It won't be easy," he said. "You know that don't you?"

"I know," she said looking at his face trying to stain the image deeply in her mind against the uncertain future.

27

"I want you to be happy," he said, "always happy."

"Happiness isn't everything," she said. "We won't always be happy."

He kissed her again and again. Her lips were soft and smooth.

"I just don't want you to ever regret coming out here," he said.

"Don," she said earnestly, "the only thing I would ever regret is if I hadn't come."

"Well, here you are," he said smiling at her. She smiled back.

Enclosed in his arms, she felt safe, protected. Let the future take care of itself.

V

On the day of her wedding, Helen woke in the hotel with the instant awareness that this was a special day. She lay quietly in the big bed thinking of Don.

"Until tomorrow," he had said when he had kissed her good night.

And now it was tomorrow. Her excitement grew. When she could lie still no longer, she jumped up and went to the window. She felt that today was a day when the bells should be ringing, the whistles tooting, the people singing. Today was her wedding day.

She pulled on the window shade and when she released it, it went flapping up to the top of the window revealing a sunny day with deep blue sky.

From the sixth floor window she could look out over the whole of Cowan on the roofs and chimneys, over the tops of trees to where the rows of buildings gave way to grassy plots each with a house upon it and where the white alley fences wove back and forth tying the town together.

Cowan was opening up for another day. Almost directly below her window on the corner she could see the news dealer swapping folded newspapers for change which he dropped in a pocketed apron. His bald head shone in the brisk morning. Customers stopped briefly to talk, and a small boy kept busy with a quick-shine kit. People hurried along the sidewalk on their way to work. A man unlocked the drug store across the street and went in. The bank was still closed, but a porter was polishing the brass sign which said Cowan Trust Company. A yellow taxi was waiting at the hotel entrance while suitcases were put in; and as Helen watched from above, two women walked out under their hats, one black with white feathers, one pink with a brim, and got in the taxi which pulled off. A truckload of spring water in crystal bottles went by and the sun sparkled on the shifting waters. Three blocks down a train slid to a stop at the station, halting street traffic until it moved on and the double crossing gates were elevated again. There was good-natured banter in the street below, people greeting one another with small-town good nature. *It's a happy day,* thought Helen. Today she would be Mrs. Donald Cutler.

She turned back to the room and slipped out of her nightgown. As she turned, she saw herself in the mirror and studied her firm young body, running her hand over one rounded breast and down the curved line of her hip. Her skin was smooth and cool. The excitement in her was too much. She evaded it, forced it back by dressing quickly, picking up last night's newspaper. GUADALCANAL POUNDED said the large black headlines, but Helen didn't see them as she folded the sheets into themselves and placed them in the wastebasket.

Out at Camp Carver the officers of the battalion were having breakfast. The mess boy was enjoying himself this morning. The officers were giving Lieutenant Cutler a real razzle-dazzle.

"Imagine," said Lieutenant Duval, "he's doing this of his own free will!"

"Must have hit his head going over the obstacle course," said Jensen.

"Well," said Chivington, "I've seen the girl. You never can tell. She might be worth it."

Cutler grinned. "Oh," he said, "you're all envious because you don't know any girls that would come 2,000 miles just to marry you."

"Well," said Jensen, "I know a girl I had to come 1,500 miles to get away from."

They piled Cutler's plate high with bacon and muffins. "Eat up, man, eat up. You need strength. Never can tell when you'll get another good breakfast."

Cutler laughed with them, but this wasn't his mood this morning. He was harassed. He checked it all over in his mind. He had the license, he had the ring, Fran MacRae had ordered the flowers, Lieutenant Rusnick was going to be best man, Chaplain Rutherford was fitting them in at three thirty, Helen's father had a train ticket home at seven o'clock.

He hoped Fran MacRae knew what she was doing. She had organized the whole thing. Helen said she didn't care who was maid of honor. The only thing that bothered her was that there was no rehearsal. She seemed to think that you should at least see a copy of the service. He tried to tell her that Chaplain Rutherford would tell her what to say, but he wasn't very reassured himself. The sooner they got this over the better.

As they finished breakfast, Lieutenant Duval came over from the adjoining table. He was a wiry man, dark, almost swarthy, with good coordination. He was known through the battalion as the "eager beaver"; but since he had a generous streak in him and his desires for promotion took the form of transparent apple polishing rather than political knifing, he was considered a stimulant rather than a menace. He kept the standards of C Company high by just being there "bucking." He went up to Don with the keys of his green car in his hand.

"Here you are," he said giving them to Don. "Like I told you, I always lend the Chevy for honeymoons. That car has a lot of personality. It's just lucky it can't tell all it knows. Treat her nice. The Chevy, I mean," he added. There was general merriment.

"Thanks, Duval," said Don. "I'll have her back here for you early Monday morning." He grinned. "The Chevy, I mean."

Fran and Rich MacRae were getting ready for the wedding. The little house was in a clutter. It was small to start with—a little bungalow with a fenced yard—but with Fran's odd hat boxes and tissue paper and Diana's toys spread all over the combination living and dining room, Rich found barely space to turn around.

Through all the confusion, Diana tottered happily in blue corduroy overalls trying to drape a chiffon scarf over her head. She was less than three.

"My God," said Rich, "hurry up or we'll be late. We've still got to drive out to the post."

"Rich," said Fran, who was working on her eyebrows, "what about Alice Spaulding?"

"What do you mean, 'What about Alice Spaulding'?"

"You know she is crazy about him," said Fran.

"Listen," said Rich, "that kid will chase any lieutenant on

31

this post. She's just a mixed-up schoolgirl, and that mother of hers doesn't help."

"Do you think Spaulding is mad at Cutler?"

"Maybe he is but there's no real reason for it," said Rich.

"Cutler's not very smart if he gets the colonel down on him," said Fran.

"Look," said Rich, "I'll keep Don clear of the colonel. It will blow over after a couple of weeks."

"Alice ought to marry Major Van Tuyl," said Fran.

"Well, maybe she will when she grows up," said Rich.

Fran started to blend in her eye shadow. "What do you think of Helen?"

"Oh, nice girl, I guess," said Rich.

" 'Nice girl!' What does that mean?"

"It means she'll make him a good wife, have some kids, probably stick with him."

"Do you think she'll be any good in bed?" asked Fran.

"My God, Fran, what do you want me to do, find out?"

Fran giggled. "She doesn't look like she knows anything about it."

"Well, maybe she doesn't, but she'll learn," said Rich.

"Don't you think I ought to tell her the facts of life?" asked Fran.

"Look, honey, you just get dressed and let Don take care of that department."

"He looks pretty dumb to me too," said Fran. "Why don't you give him one of those French books for a wedding present?" She was peering into the mirror inspecting the job she had done on her face and watching Rich reflected behind her.

"Come on, Fran," pleaded Rich. "If the matron of honor doesn't get there in time, they may not even have a wedding."

Fran combed her hair again, dropped the comb into her bag and stood up on spike heels.

"How do I look?" she asked posing like a model.

"You look swell," said Rich. "Now get in the car."

"Do I look chic?" asked Fran.

"Sure, you look chic."

"Do I look sexy?"

"You always look sexy to me," said Rich.

"OK," said Fran satisfied. "You bring Diana. We'll drop her at Anna's."

"At Anna's?" said Rich. "Isn't Anna coming here?"

"Not today," said Fran.

"But, Fran," said Rich, "I don't want Diana playing down there. The place doesn't even look clean. The yard's full of rusty old cars."

"Oh, don't be a fuss," said Fran. "What's the difference whether Anna comes here or Diana goes there?"

"There's a lot of difference," said Rich.

"Oh, come on," said Fran. "Now you're the one that's making us late."

"But I don't want Diana down there," said Rich.

"OK, Daddy dear, you just bring her along to the wedding in her overalls."

"But, Fran,——"

"Rich, come ON!"

Rich came. He picked up Diana. She rested her head over his shoulder against his cheek. As he carried her down the steps, he felt a smoldering anger. Diana shouldn't be left just anywhere, anytime. She should have a schedule with meals on time and regular naps and be tucked into her own crib, clean and comfortable every night at the same time. The war was making a mess of the things which mattered most. The sooner they got it over with the better.

When Helen went down the aisle of Chapel Number Four on her father's arm, she was aware of all the empty pews. It was strange to have all those empty seats. They represented all the friends who weren't here, all the relatives, all the well-wishers who would have come if the wedding had been at home. There should have been flowers tied to the ends of some of the pews and a white velvet dress and lace veil and Don's friends as ushers to help guests to their seats. There should have been a reception at home afterwards, and she should have stood with Don in front of the fireplace proud and happy and later cut a cake and thrown her bouquet to the bridesmaids from the stairway. This was so different from the way she had pictured.

In the front row were a few officers including Captain

MacRae and Lieutenant Duval. Beside Don stood Lieutenant Rusnick, his long immobile face reminding one vaguely of a faithful hound dog. He and Don had met at officers' training six months before, and Don had quickly appreciated the droll, straight-faced humor of the man. Fran stood pertly on her spike heels on the other side, and in the middle stood Chaplain Rutherford with an open book in his hand, waiting.

Don watched her come. She carried the bouquet for a formal wedding. Fran had seen to that. It was white with snapdragons crisply set among roses and softened with tiny little white blossoms. Streamers of white satin trailed almost to the floor. The afternoon sun slanted into the little chapel from the parade ground.

"Dearly beloved, we are gathered together in the sight of God. . . ."

She looked at Don. He was pale and tense, terribly serious and earnest. She wondered whether she really knew what she was doing, but she was letting it happen. She was getting married.

"Do you, Donald, take this Helen. . . ." He looked at her finally. She hoped that he didn't want to get out of it now.

"I do," he said firmly. Suddenly it was all right.

"Do you, Helen, take this Donald . . . in sickness and in health till death do you part?" *Till death do us part,* she thought, looking at him in his uniform with a gold-colored bar of a second lieutenant on each shoulder. *How long would that be?*

"I do," she said watching the candles gleam quietly behind the chaplain. The chapel was very still as Chaplain Rutherford's voice went on.

"I now pronounce you man and wife."

Don looked at her. He could hardly believe it. Wife! He kissed her quickly. Now they could just run away from everyone. How simple it was! He took her elbow unceremoniously and almost ran her down the aisle.

Diana was having a lovely time. She was throwing little stones in a puddle and watching the splash. The sun glinted on the little pool and sparkled the splash. She did it over and over, and Rosalie helped her. Rosalie was five years old and Anna's daughter. Her eyes gleamed out of her dark face with pleasure, and the little pigtails wagged on the top of her head. She was taking care of Diana. Anna had promised her peanut brittle if she did, and Rosalie liked peanut brittle.

Diana walked to the edge of the puddle and, leaning over, tested it with one finger.

"Look out you, baby," said Rosalie. "Mammy don't want for you to get messed up."

A big goose waddled through the corner of the yard. He was molting and kept thrusting his neck in and out like a nervous snake.

"You see that goose?" said Rosalie. "That goose name Santa. Goin' to eat him when the Christmas comes. Soldier boy brought him for Mammy."

Diana chased the goose. Tottering along unsteadily, she followed it around the shack and cornered it between a pile of old lumber and the alley fence. The goose lifted his head menacingly and hissed at Diana.

"Lawsy, he look mad!" said Rosalie with interest. "Poke him with a stick!" When Diana didn't understand, Rosalie picked up a stained strip of wood with an old nail in the end and waved it at the goose. The goose continued to hiss in a most satisfactory way with his head weaving back and forth. Rosalie put the stick in Diana's hand.

"Hit him, gal! Hit him!" said Rosalie waving her arms to encourage Diana. But Diana didn't understand. The stick was heavy and clumsy in her hands. Finally, with Rosalie's help, she banged it on the ground in front of the goose.

"That's the gal!" said Rosalie encouragingly. "Hit it! Hit it!" Diana lifted the stick and dropped the end again nearer the goose.

"Yea man," said Rosalie dancing around her. "That's a gal. Do it again, do it again!" Diana finally understood. She waved the stick at the goose. The goose dropped his head low, hissing hard. Then suddenly in a flurry of feathers, he came straight at Diana. Rosalie streaked around the lumber pile and turned to see what was happening. Diana was on the ground. Her face was scratched and she was covered with dirt. The goose circled her, head in, hissing and weaving. Diana shrieked.

"Hush you, child," said Rosalie alarmed. Diana rolled over and onto her knees. As she started to get up, the goose came at her again, wings out. This time she fell on her face and just lay there screaming. The goose was circling nervously again when the screen door of the shack slammed and Anna appeared. She chased the goose off and picked up Diana.

"Look at you," she said crossly. "What you mammy goin' to say to me? Why can't you be little lady and leave that Santa goose be?"

Diana shrieked and shrieked.

"You be quiet, you hear," said Anna sharply. "Old goose ain't goin' to get you. Anna's got you now."

Diana arched her back and threw herself back trying to bellow out the terror of that hissing head and the fierce, fierce beating of the wings.

Anna carried her into the shack and seated her on the old carpet in front of the sink while she pumped a pan full of water. Diana turned over on her stomach and clutched at the floor while she screamed. Anna put the pan and a cloth on the table and picked her up, more gently this time.

"Poor little gal," she said, "musta been a real fright. Here," she said, "let Anna wash your face."

"Honeybee," she crooned, "old goose not goin' to get Diana. Anna goin' to eat up that old goose." Diana sobbed, snatching great breaths of air and resting between them against Anna. Rosalie watched silently.

"She just a baby," said Anna. "Don't know no better'n to chase a goose. Maybe she like a drink of coke. You go get one," she said to Rosalie. Rosalie found the bottle and Anna popped off the cap and held out the bottle to Diana. Diana batted it away.

"Now, honey," said Anna, "that ain't no way to act. Rosy'll show you how to drink. Rosalie tipped up the bottle and drank in great draughts.

"Hey, gal!" said Anna, "that's enough. Try her now." They put the bottle against Diana's lips, but she still refused it.

"That ain't no way to act," said Anna. "Here, look at me." She took a drink while Diana watched, still sobbing silently every few moments.

"Now you have some," said Anna forcing the bottle end into

her mouth. Diana looked at her wide-eyed, thrusting her head back as far as she could. She tasted the warm syrupy liquid but still struggled against it. She turned her face in against Anna and shut her eyes trying to block everything out. She was exhausted.

"She goin' to sleep?" asked Rosalie.

"Maybe," said Anna rocking quietly. "That would sure be a good thing. Get her all rested 'fore her mama come for her."

Back in Cowan the festivities were soon underway. Around a reserved table in a corner of the Steak Palace, Helen's father had gathered Helen and Don, Lieutenant Rusnick, and the MacRaes. It was early. At five thirty the dining room was almost empty, but within an hour the rush would start as the men came off duty at the post.

The Steak Palace was large and ornate. The tables were surrounded with red-backed chairs. There was floral carpeting on the floor and mirrors and murals on the walls. The place had a subdued glitter which looked expensive. There was a piano on a little raised platform, and a row of spiky-leaved plants separated the diners from the direct gaze of curious idlers on the sidewalk. The hostess was sleek and blond, the food was good—steaks juicy and brown, French fries crisp, salad strong with onion. It was no wonder that the Steak Palace succeeded.

Fran was very vivacious. She liked parties. She opened her menu and settled down to enjoy herself smiling across the table at Rich. Rusnick was thinking how strange it was to see the Steak Palace half empty, but they had to eat early to get the host on the seven o'clock train. Helen and Don sat side by side. They both seemed a little dazed.

"Well," said Helen's father, "I'd like to order six steak dinners but if anyone can't face it this early, let me know now. How about it?"

"That would be perfect," said Fran thinking with glee that for this meat she wasn't losing any red points. They all agreed and the waiter disappeared.

"Sorry I can't offer you champagne," said Helen's father, "but these two would get married in a dry state."

They all laughed. The conversation was general. The waiter

37

filled the glasses with ice water and brought crackers and cottage cheese with chives. He put salads at their elbows. When the steaks arrived, Fran really warmed to the situation. She told how she had eloped with Rich and how they had lost her suitcase.

"Why don't you get married too?" said Fran to Lieutenant Rusnick.

"Well," said Rusnick, "first I've got to find a wife."

"Naughty boy," said Fran shaking her finger at him, "don't look for a wife. Look for one that's not married."

Rusnick started to explain, but they all laughed.

"Well, you know," said Rusnick gallantly, "it's hard to find a nice girl these days."

"That's not the way they talk at college," said Helen smiling at him. "Back there, they say it's hard to find a good man."

"That's the trouble," said Rusnick. "This war has everyone all tied up."

They finished dessert but could not linger. The room was full now, and the train was due two blocks away in fifteen minutes.

"I hate to break up this party," said Helen's father, but they all rose. As they filed out the door saying good-bye, they passed the line on the sidewalk waiting to get in.

"Another weekend," said Rich nodding to an officer he knew. The MacRaes and Rusnick went off together and Don and Helen and Helen's father turned toward the railroad station.

Don and Helen drove off in Duval's green Chevy, hardly believing that they were married. Miles from Cowan they found the motel where Don had made a reservation. They tried to be casual so that no one would know they were just married. Helen wished that her bags didn't look new. She felt as though the gold ring on her finger shone like a neon light.

Don was afraid that someone he knew would turn up at the motel. He parked the green Chevy almost in back of the cabin in his attempt to keep it from being recognized, and then he grinned to himself when he realized that no one would identify him with Duval's car. He took in the bags and looked around.

The cabin was painted pale pink and had wall to wall carpet. The big bed filled up most of the room, but to one side were two covered chairs and a small table with a metal ash tray on it. Against the far wall was a small glass-topped desk with a rack of motel stationery and post cards.

He looked at Helen. "Come here," he said.

"You're getting awfully bossy," she said, but she came. He put his arms around her holding her till he could hear the singing in his chest.

"Are you glad you're here?" he asked softly.

"Yes," she said.

"No regrets?"

"No regrets."

"Helen," he said, "I want you to be happy. I've told you that," he said feeling that he was repeating himself. "You know that, don't you?"

"I am happy," she said.

"Yes," he said, "maybe you are, but I mean next year and ten years from now and when you're old."

"Let's not worry about that yet," she said. "I don't feel very old right now."

He kissed her, gently at first, and then fiercely as her hands went down his back pulling him closer to her, and he felt her lips yielding. Each marveled silently at the uniqueness of the other. He, coming from a world of men, found her unbelievably soft, small-boned, yielding. She, from her feminine world, found him huge, tough, powerful, overwhelming, and his clumsy gentleness with her from all his strength touched her deeply. Love, when it is not a plaything, is not outgrown. They had from their love, as do all people, the total of what they brought to it.

VI

All four second lieutenants of Company C, Duval, Jensen, Cutler, and Rusnick, lingered near Chivington's desk at company headquarters. They had just turned in platoon reports and now, tired and dusty at the end of the day, were in no hurry to get back to the barracks.

Chivington sat behind the desk. His silver bars of a first lieutenant looked freshly polished. He pulled out a white linen handkerchief displaying his monogram to clean his glasses. The gesture was not lost on any of the other four, who privately called him "Old Mother Hubbard." He was good at organization, a natural for an executive officer. He felt quite strongly that there was a right way to do anything. He ran his part of the army by the book and his personal life with as much comfort and refinement as possible.

"Well, men," said Lieutenant Chivington cordially, "what the officers of this company need is a good party."

"That's an idea," said Rusnick, but his long droll face showed no enthusiasm.

"Wine, women, and song?" asked Jensen with interest. He was the largest of the men gathered around the desk, a man of appetite and direct predictable reaction.

"Why not?" said Duval looking around at the others.

"Duval can bring the colonel's lady," said Rusnick soberly.

"Sure," said Jensen quickly. "Now give us the low-down, Duval. Is she really like Judy O'Grady?"

"Oh, shut up!" said Duval.

"Why worry about women until you've got some liquor?" asked Chivington.

"How are you going to get liquor in this dry hole without going over the state line?" asked Cutler.

"That's a hell of a law about liquor," said Jensen. "No wonder the natives dry up like prunes with the temperance societies running the towns."

"Why not have a big time in Townstake?" asked Duval.

"Oh, no," said Rusnick with mock horror. "Can't have Duval taking the colonel's lady over a state line. We've got to bring the liquor here." This time Duval just grinned.

"I don't like that old bag enough to share liquor with her," he said. "Let's have a stag party, every man have his own bottle, drink it fast or slow."

"Hey, men," said Cutler, "why not make it a battalion party? We could get an accordion."

"Hear! Hear!" said Chivington. "That's the way to have a real party."

"How about the liquor?" asked Jensen.

"Hell," said Duval, "it's as easy to get a case as a bottle."

"Now you're talking," said Jensen, "and it's as easy to get five cases as one case. Make every guy pitch in."

"I'll drive over to Townstake in the Chevy," said Duval enthusiastically, "and we'll load her up!"

"If you're going all the way to the state line for liquor," said Chivington, "why not collect ten dollars from each officer and have enough for another party later?"

"That's the way to do it," said Rusnick. "Think big."

And so it was arranged. During the next week, Duval and Jensen quietly circulated among the officers of the battalion. The plan assumed the aspects of a stock company; and when the collection was complete, shares were owned by officers throughout the regiment. Lieutenant Duval swaggered about. Everyone knew him now—the man with the car who had all the initiative.

When Duval and Jensen could finally arrange a day's leave together, they piled into Duval's green Chevy loaded down with cash and lists. Officers lingered enviously about with last minute suggestions concerning bourbon, scotch, and brand names. There was a great deal of banter, but finally Duval revved up the motor and, steadying his thumb on the horn, took off in a grinding of gravel for the main gate and the state line.

The Chevy was Lieutenant Duval's pride and joy. He kept it polished and all but talked to it. The car kept him from feeling trapped by the army. It was his escape hatch. Even though there was no special place to go, as long as he had the car at the post, he knew that he could get away from the monotony and boredom of the training. And when he did have leave, he could take off for Louisiana to see his family and his girl and be there hours before the railroad could have delivered him.

Sitting on the front seat together, the two men presented an odd contrast. Duval was the smaller of the two—dark, rather intense. His Louisiana family had originally been French, and he had inherited their pointed features and quick reactions. Jensen, on the other hand, was big boned, hearty, red-faced, a mountain man from Montana with squint lines about his eyes which came from looking across long distances in sunlight. He was easygoing, liked his food, seemed to live with a minimum of effort.

It was a fine sunny day, crisp and clear. In the air hundreds of birds circled in flocks as though reluctant to admit that spring was coming and they were on their way north again. Duval and Jensen went over the macadam strip through the rolling grasslands under a bright January sky with the radio blaring out the rollicking song about sitting under the apple tree. Jensen started to sing with the radio.

"My God," said Duval, "save that for the showers. Where's the money now?"

"It's in the glove compartment," said Jensen. He opened the compartment briefly to show Duval the manila envelope. They felt completely carefree, like boys playing hooky. A day like this didn't come often to them, and they intended to make the most of it.

"That's a lot of money," said Jensen. "Bet it's more than you ever had in this car before."

"It sure is," said Duval. "It's damn near what the car cost me. You know," he added, "I'll never forget the day I bought this Chevy down in Baton Rouge." He smiled to himself.

"What about it?" asked Jensen.

"Well," said Duval, "my dad's got a lumber business down there, you know, and he said I had to start out where the trees grow. It's tough work but I liked it—and when I finally had enough money of my own saved I went into Baton Rouge and found the Chevy. It's a sweet little car now that I've got it all tuned up. And the places I've been in it. Went to Pennsylvania once," he said, "and down to Mexico last time I had a vacation. Man, you ought to see that country."

"Like to see that," said Jensen, "but you better see Montana too. That's God's country. I swear the air up there is purer and better than any air you ever breathed. I miss the mountains."

"Ever seen the ocean?" asked Duval.

"I guess we're going to," said Jensen.

"It won't be any pleasure cruise."

"Where do you figure we're going?"

"You guess," said Duval. "I bet right now even the brass in Washington doesn't know."

"Oh, sure they do," said Jensen. "They've got to issue supplies. We can't go to the South Seas or Alaska in the same uniforms!"

"Maybe we'll go to England," said Duval. "That would be swell. Everybody talks the same language and all."

"Don't count on it, friend," said Jensen.

"There will be promotions coming along," said Duval. He had given the subject a great deal of thought. "Chivington ought to move up and then who do you figure will get exec. officer?"

"You will," said Jensen. "Cutler would have been runner up; but since this deal with Alice, I figure the colonel's put him down on the end of the list."

"What exactly happened with Alice?" asked Duval.

"Damned if I know," said Jensen. "That army brat sure went after him tooth and nail. She was all but drooling, but he held her off."

"What would you do if that happened to you?" asked Duval.

"Are you kidding?" said Jensen. They both roared.

"Aren't you afraid of the colonel?" asked Duval.

"Not any more than you are, friend," said Jensen grinning at him.

They watched the land slip by. Far off to one side a column of smoke hung above the plain, but it was only the sludge pit of an oil well being cleaned out and was so far away that they saw it on the horizon for a long time.

"You know what I'm going to do?" said Duval.

"What?" asked Jensen.

"I'm damned if I'm going to polish these brass bars any more. I'm going to let them corrode on my uniform until I get silver ones."

43

"Sure," said Jensen, "just let them turn green. Some day when Colonel Spaulding sees them, you explain it all to him and he'll give you a parade-ground promotion."

"No kidding," said Duval. "I'm never going to polish them again. You wait and see."

"I'll wait to see," said Jensen. "You must be pretty sure of that promotion if you think you'll get it before that brass tarnishes."

The green Chevy came into Townstake about three o'clock in the afternoon and parked in front of the liquor store with its fly-specked cardboard horses and roses in the window behind bottles which gleamed brown and amber and clear.

"There she is!" said Duval. "Shall we buy them out now or later?"

"Later," said Jensen. "Let's not leave the car full of liquor while we wander around. Let's see what this burg has to offer."

The doors popped open on each side of the Chevy, and Duval and Jensen came together on the sidewalk.

The town was like many others—buildings bunched together in defiance of empty space. Except for the liquor store, there was no way to tell that they had crossed a state line. The whole store block was dilapidated, paint beaded and peeling, textured with the slant of the sun. The street was paved now but you had to step high to climb onto the covered sidewalk; and in the glare of the afternoon, it was difficult to see into the dusty store windows. There was a dry goods store with children's sneakers and lengths of printed yard goods, a restaurant called the Black Hawk with a stuffed bird sitting inside next to the cashier, a hardware store with a bold yellow front, a barber shop, a drug store, and stairs to a law office. Across the street, a small brick bank, almost square with a mansard roof, loomed respectably. A man in a large hat and a stubble of whiskers was leaning against the brick wall with his thumbs stuck through his suspenders, resting. He watched the two young officers.

"Well, it isn't New York," said Jensen grinning.

"Seems too quiet," said Duval. "Almost makes me miss the army."

"You must be stir crazy," said Jensen.

They were in no hurry to do their errand. They wandered

into the drug store. Duval bought a paper. The headlines read—
FIERCE FIGHTING ON GUADALCANAL. They sat down in one of the
two booths, and Jensen ordered a quart of vanilla ice cream and
a spoon.

"My God," said Duval, "you and your appetite! We have to
eat supper and get started back in an hour or two. How're you
going to eat a steak later?"

"That's right," said Jensen. "Make it a pint of vanilla and a
spoon."

"Chocolate soda for me," said Duval.

A man in a checkered shirt watched them from a stool at the
counter as they finished.

"You boys far from home," he said. It was either a question or
a comment, whichever they wanted.

"Over from Carver," said Jensen from the depths of his ice
cream.

"That's a big camp," said the man. "I carpentered over there
last summer. Jesus, was it ever hot on those roofs. We had to get
the roofs on 'cus the new guys was comin' in. An' you know how
we done it? We nailed on them boards no matter what length
they was, left the ends stickin' out over the end of the building.
Then, when the whole roof was done, one guy took a buzz saw
and just went down the edge of the roof cutting all the boards off
even. The wind tossed them board ends all over the place some
days."

"You don't say," said Duval.

"Yea," said the man, "don't know how we done it so quick."

"Well, so long, Pop," said Jensen before the man could get
started again. "Been nice knowing you."

Out on the sidewalk again they stood against the plate glass
window and looked out from the shelter of the sidewalk. There
was some traffic but almost all of it went right on through town.
Townstake was not a place you stopped without a reason. House-
wives were shopping at the grocery, some pushing strollers, stopping to talk with each other.

"Slim pickings," said Jensen grinning.

"They keep the beautiful girls locked up," said Duval. "Must
have heard we were coming."

They wandered down the main street. The lawns were

45

browned out to the consistency of steel wool in front of piazzaed houses set back from the street. The concrete sidewalk was cracked and broken and weeds grew between it and the street. They passed a church, yellow brick with pigeons nesting under the eaves and on the end a stained glass window. The colors glowed dully. Along the base, letters were worked into the design, but from the outside they were in reverse and undecipherable.

When they came to the yellow brick library, they hesitated but then went up the steps and through the double door. Ahead of them at a horseshoe-shaped desk sat a gray-haired lady with a pencil stuck through the bun of hair on the back of her head. They turned into the reading room like boys playing Indians with footsteps exaggerated in order to proceed as quietly as possible. Sunlight slanted through the high windows warming the shelves of books until they gave off that slightly musty odor of old paper and glue and printing. The librarian watched them from the desk as they leafed through magazines. The quiet was so oppressive that they could hear a fly buzzing against the window high in the eaves of the oak-beamed room.

When they got up to leave, they felt rather detached.

"It gives me the creeps," said Duval in whispers as they went down the steps to the sidewalk. "If I had to live here, I'd go crazy."

"It's not a friendly-feeling town," said Jensen. "I get the idea everybody's watching us."

"Strangers stick out in a little town," said Duval. "My God, the money! Is it still in the car?" They looked at each other appalled.

"I thought you had it," said Jensen lamely.

"You knew damn well I didn't," said Duval. "You put it in the car compartment yourself!"

Jensen started to run.

"Slow down!" said Duval. "No sense in running now."

As they strode down the cracked sidewalk, Duval wondered what would happen to his promotion if the money was gone, how he would ever face the battalion again. He almost wished he hadn't exploited his part in the scheme. If the money was gone, so were his chances for advancement. He would look irresponsible. As they hurried along, he could feel eyes on them, from the

46

curtained windows of homes, from the group of loiterers in front of the drug store, from a man on the loading platform of the feed store. When they reached the Chevy, Jensen slid quickly into the front seat and opened the glove compartment. His hands were shaking. Duval leaned over him tensely.

"It's here," said Jensen with vast relief hauling out the manila envelope.

"Count it," said Duval hoarsely.

Jensen thumbed through the bills.

"All here," he said at last. They looked at each other and grinned foolishly. Duval mopped his forehead.

"Give it to me!" said Duval. Jensen handed it over. Duval unbuttoned his blouse and then his shirt and, leaning over, slipped the brown envelope inside his shirt. He buttoned the shirt again securely and then buttoned the blouse tightly over it and drew the brass buckle tight.

"Why, Grandma," said Jensen laughing, "How fat you are getting!"

Duval laughed back at him, playfully poking him on the shoulder.

"Look who's talking," he said.

"Time for chow," said Jensen, "and then we'll get this show on the road."

The Black Hawk Restaurant boasted five tables and a counter. It was painted green with black trim and above the molding were giant red flowers repeated and repeated around the sides of the room.

"Regular greenhouse," said Jensen as they sat down still full of the gregariousness of nervous relief. "Guess I'll get a steak. What's for you?"

Duval thought a moment. "If we were in Louisiana," he said, "I'd have some shrimp baked in butter and batter and crumbs till it's golden brown, but here I'll settle for a steak too."

"You want the steak plate or the steak dinner?" asked the waitress standing with her weight on one hip. She was young but with a no-nonsense air about her. Wisps of curly hair stuck out from under her cap.

"Well," said Jensen eyeing her, "we'll take the best steaks you've got, two of them rare, with all the fixings, french fried

47

onions, whatever you got, and bring us some coffee with it and rolls and butter, relish—the works!" he ended expansively.

She flipped back the order form and dropped it in the pocket of her apron.

"Cute kid," said Jensen when she went back for the orders.

"Sure," said Duval still thinking of Louisiana shrimp.

"Bet I could get a date with her," said Jensen.

"Bet you couldn't," said Duval.

"Five bucks?" asked Jensen.

"You're on," said Duval.

When the girl came back with the order, Jensen smiled his big Montana grin.

"Honey," he said, "that's the best looking steak I've seen since I left home. Did you fix that steak yourself?"

"Sure," she said, placing the dishes on the table.

"You know," he said, "you remind me of my sister. She's a good cook too. Makes me lonesome for home," he added as wistfully as he knew how.

"Where's home?" she asked.

"Montana," he said, "God's country. You ever been there?"

"Not yet," she said.

"I'd sure like to tell you about it."

"Sure," she said, but she went back to the counter leaving them with their meal.

"End of round one," said Jensen. "You know," he said, "she's not half bad looking."

"Just your type," said Duval. "The way to a man's heart is through his stomach. You better look out or she'll get you."

"Brother," said Jensen solemnly. "No woman catches me; I catch them."

"Quit bragging," said Duval, "and show me how it's done."

"Five dollars a lesson," said Jensen tackling his steak with relish.

It was quiet while they ate. Occasionally from where he sat, Jensen smiled at the waitress. Finally he beckoned to her, and she came over to the table.

"My pal and I," he said, "would like to settle an argument. He says you're from Louisiana, but I say that you've lived in this town all your life. Now, who's right?"

The girl grinned. "You are," she said, "born and raised right here. Do you want more coffee?" she asked.

"Sure," said Jensen, "that's a fine idea, and some pie and ice cream with it. You too?" he asked Duval.

"You bet," said Duval grinning.

She went off again.

"That's real progress," said Duval, "but you'd better hurry. We're at dessert already."

When the pie came, Jensen was ready. "Listen," he said to the girl, "you got a movie or a bowling alley or something around town where two lonely officers can find something to do tonight?"

"Nothing like that around here," she said. "There's Joe's place down the road about ten miles. They sell drinks, got a nickelodeon and slot machines."

"Well," said Jensen, "how about getting a friend and showing it to us?"

"Can't do that," she said.

"Ah, come on," said Jensen. "We have such a dull life. Just want some fun once in a while."

"No, can't do it," she said. "I've already got a date."

"Listen," said Jensen thinking of the bet. "If you didn't have a date tonight, you'd show us the place, wouldn't you?"

"Sure," said the girl and walked off.

"Give me five dollars," said Duval grinning.

"Now wait," said Jensen. "She liked me fine. She just happened to have another date; but if she hadn't, she'd have won that bet for me. That's a technical win."

Duval was grinning. "Come on," he said, "I won and you know it."

"Did you stop to think" said Jensen, "what would have happened if I had won. We don't have time to go on a date and get back to camp before midnight."

"I'll let you off easy," said Duval grinning. "You can pay for my dinner."

"OK," said Jensen, "but next time remind me to show you how we really operate in Montana."

"This I've got to see," said Duval.

They left the table and while Jensen paid the bill, Duval looked over the mangy stuffed hawk on the counter.

"No place to order chicken," he said to Jensen and then added with mock hospitality, "Have a toothpick on me." Jensen took two and left with a toothpick bristling from each side of his mouth.

They walked back toward the car, Duval clutching at his middle to reassure himself that the money was still there.

"Haul out the list," said Jensen as they came to the liquor store.

Duval went up to the counter and was confronted by a little man with big shoulders and dark eyes in a deeply-lined face.

"Yes, sir," he said putting the palms of both his hands on the counter and leaning forward. "What will it be?"

"Well," said Duval holding the list in his hands, "we want three cases of scotch and four cases of bourbon and. . . . " He read off the rest of the list as the man assembled the order on the counter. The last item on the list was three bottles of port for Chivington. When the man went out back to look for it, Duval said, "Why in hell can't 'Old Mother Hubbard' drink ordinary liquor like everybody else?"

"He just hasn't got the guts for it," said Jensen.

They loaded the cases into the trunk of the Chevy, but the loose packages wrapped in brown paper they arranged carefully on the back seat and covered with a blanket. When it was all done, Jensen came around the car with a fifth of whiskey in his fist and climbed into the front passenger seat.

"Home, James," he said. Duval backed out into Townstake's main street and headed back toward the state line.

Rusnick and Chivington were playing checkers in Chivington's quarters. The game progressed slowly, partly because they were both excellent players and partly because there were so many interruptions. Officers kept dropping in to find out whether Duval and Jensen were back.

"Thirsty bunch," said Rusnick.

"Most of them have no real taste for liquor," said Chivington. "They don't know one brand from another. Just as soon swill down raw whiskey as an aged variety."

"Get the same result," said Rusnick.

"Well, no, you don't," said Chivington. "With raw whiskey

50

you just get drunk, stinking drunk; but with the real thing that's been aged in fragrant old vats, you get mellow. You get happiness out of whiskey that's been handled properly, coaxed along. I'd rather not drink than have that bathtub stuff."

"Quality counts," said Rusnick.

"It's the same with women," said Chivington. "So many men don't realize that. It's important. It's a question of taste, of doing things nicely."

"You know what Ben Franklin said," said Rusnick. "He said that they're all the same with a basket over their heads."

"I don't agree with Ben Franklin," said Chivington. "There is a big difference. Now you look at that girl Cutler's married. You don't see many like that out here. Living out here may confuse her or make her unhappy, but she won't change much."

"Those two have sure got it bad," said Rusnick.

"Yes," said Chivington moving a checker. "You know," he added, "sometimes I think a girl has to be a little stupid to fall for a man as hard as that. The smart ones can see through us and look out for themselves."

"Well, save a stupid one for me," said Rusnick.

"Perhaps it isn't stupidity as much as emotion overruling judgment," said Chivington thoughtfully. "Maybe the best kind would be smart but emotional."

"Do you think a woman can understand a man and still love him?" asked Rusnick.

"Oh, I suppose so," said Chivington. "As a matter of fact my mother's been proving that for years."

"Where do you find these ladies you admire so much?" asked Rusnick.

"Well, the one I've got my eye on is home in South Carolina. They know how to raise ladies over there."

"Well," said Rusnick, "why don't you marry her?"

"And bring her here!" asked Chivington.

"It isn't so bad," said Rusnick, "Cutler did."

"No, it wouldn't work," said Chivington. "When I get married, it's going to be done right. Have a home to take her to; plenty of silver, linen, furniture."

"You're being pretty material about it, aren't you?" asked Rusnick.

51

"That's the way my family has always done it," said Chivington, "and so far it's worked out pretty well."

"Well, have it your own way," said Rusnick, "but I'm sick of kicking around. If I knew a gal who wanted me, I'd marry her tomorrow."

Lieutenant Walker from cannon company stuck his head in the door. "Where's Duval?" he asked.

"Not back yet," said Chivington.

"Good Lord," said Walker. "What are they doing with the stuff, having a private party? It's eleven already. I was counting on a nightcap before I turned in."

"Maybe they had a flat?" said Rusnick. "Duval was complaining that all he could get were retreads."

"Say," said Chivington, "how much money did those two finally collect?"

"You guess," said Walker, "but everybody's in on the deal."

"Party's tomorrow night," said Chivington. "This old barracks is going to bulge. You're bringing the accordion, aren't you?" he asked.

"Sure," said Walker, "all tuned up and rarin' to go."

"Well, skip your nightcap and save it for tomorrow," said Rusnick.

"Guess I'll have to," said Walker. "I'm scheduled for target range in the morning and Colonel Spaulding is coming to watch."

"Well, luck to you, man," said Chivington. "He's hard to please. Say, you know that camera case he carries around his neck all the time?"

"Yea," said Walker. "What about it?"

"Ever see him take a picture?"

"No, don't think I have."

"Well, I got this straight from the horse's mouth," said Chivington confidentially. "Lieutenant I know at headquarters says there's no camera in that case. What he's really got in there is a little flask. Do you believe that?"

"No, I don't," said Walker.

"Pretty neat," said Rusnick. "Do you suppose he thought that up all by himself?"

"Don't sell the old guy short," said Walker. "He's got a lot on the ball still even if he is beginning to look like a walrus. Did you know he went hunting kodiak bears in Alaska on his last leave?"

"Probably rather fight bears than that wife of his," said Rusnick dryly.

They all laughed. Walker hung around for a while still hoping for a drink but finally went off. Chivington and Rusnick finished the game, but even at midnight Duval and Jensen had not reappeared.

VII

Helen drove up to the MacRae's bungalow in a taxi. As she paid the driver, she could see Diana sitting on the bottom step pushing a wheeled toy along the splintery board. She was jabbering to herself; but when she saw Helen get out of the taxi, she crawled up the steps and pounded on the door. Fran opened it, and Diana tumbled in and watched from behind her mother while Helen came up the walk.

"Hi!" said Fran, "so you found us."

As the door shut behind her, Helen glanced around. She saw the gas log burning in the corner. It was the first one she had ever seen; it was gorgeously ornate with scrolls and chrome grill work before the glowing flame. Shiny finials like twin spires guarded either side, and the legs were squat and sprung like a Queen Anne teapot. Along one wall was a lumpy studio couch covered with flowered cretonne and the curtains matched with yellow and green tulips climbing upward. There was a small table against one wall with a green pottery lamp shaped like a funereal urn and the shade was appliquéd with more tulips cut from the material. On the floor was a faded fiber rug. Opening off the living room were two bedrooms and a kitchen.

"Welcome to our rented home," said Fran taking her coat. "We're not responsible for the décor. We're lucky to have the privilege of trying to pay for it. Have you found a place yet?"

"I've tried," said Helen, "but we're still at the hotel."

"Best thing for you to do is to get a furnished room with kitchen privileges," said Fran. "You're lucky. It's a lot easier to find something without a child."

"She's very sweet," said Helen looking at Diana. "How old is she?"

"She's two," said Fran, "and will I be glad to get her out of diapers."

"How did you find a house for rent?" asked Helen.

54

"Well," said Fran, "we came out here with the first of the cadre almost a year ago. Rich was hauled out of the Second Division. You should have seen this place then. Sleepy little town. Rich got the house from an ad in the paper then, but you can't do it that way now. Just got to know someone who's moving out, and not many will be going before the whole division moves."

"When will that be?" asked Helen.

"Who knows," said Fran, "six months at the most, but they could move out sooner and finish training somewhere else. They've probably got two or three months of maneuvers. Rich says that he hopes they have because they need it."

"Well," said Helen relieved, "they won't send them until they're really trained."

"Don't be too sure of that, honey," said Fran. "Have you read the papers lately?"

"Sure," said Helen. "I guess they are needed all right." They sat down in the living room. Diana climbed on the couch with her mother and solemnly watched.

"Now, let's see," said Fran. "We haven't seen you since the wedding."

"Thanks again," said Helen, "for the things you did to organize it. We both appreciated it."

"It was sort of fun," said Fran. "We don't have many weddings in the company."

"You wouldn't have had this one if Don could have had leave to come home," said Helen.

"Have you met the Spauldings yet?" asked Fran.

"Oh, yes," said Helen. "They seem very formal."

"Do you really think so?" asked Fran smoothly. "It never seemed to me that Alice Spaulding was particularly formal."

"Alice?" said Helen. "Is that Mrs. Spaulding?"

"Oh, no," said Fran. "Alice is the daughter."

"I don't think I've met her," said Helen.

"How stupid of me," said Fran. "She went to New York on a visit just about the time you got here. Of course you haven't met her. She used to be around the club on Saturday nights. You'll probably meet her later. Get Don to tell you about her."

She watched Helen carefully but there was no response to

the bait. Diana slid down off the couch and took her toy duck over to show Helen.

"Listen," said Fran abruptly changing the subject, "do you know that a lot of these men are going to be killed in this next year?"

Helen stared at her, unsure that she had heard correctly.

"Sure they are," said Fran leaning forward and looking right at her intently. "Don't kid yourself about it. It's a game I play. I look at them at the club and wonder which ones it's going to be."

"That's an awful game," said Helen.

"Well, that's not the worst," said Fran. "Some of them will be horribly wounded and live. Do you ever think of that?"

"I don't want to," said Helen. "There's nothing to be gained by talking like this." She felt a little knot of sick fear welling up in her, but Fran went on almost obsessed.

"I've figured it all out," said Fran. "I'd rather have Rich killed than come back paralyzed or mutilated or something." Helen wondered how she could stop this conversation. It wasn't right to stir up these areas of dread.

"I just want Don back alive," she said. They were both quiet a moment. Fran stood up.

"Well," said Fran cheerfully, "come on out in the kitchen. I've got a couple of things to do before Rich and Don get here. Why don't you feed Diana?"

"Sure," said Helen quickly, "if she'll let me." She was wishing that she had waited to come later with Don. Fran's words went echoing back and forth in her head.

"She better let you," said Fran grimacing as she popped the lid off a can of baby food. "If she objects, just force it down."

Diana sat in her high chair staring suspiciously at Helen. When Helen smiled at her and held out the spoon, she let out a little sigh and opened her mouth. Helen was relieved to have something to do. Fran busied herself making a salad. She sliced green peppers and wedges of tomatoes into the lettuce in the bowl.

"Tell me," said Fran, "is it true that Don went to Harvard?"

"Why, yes," said Helen.

"You know," said Fran, "I've always wondered about those ivy league boys. They just must get some polish coming from all those snobby old families and all."

Helen was amused. "Well," she finally said, "the boys I knew there didn't seem particularly influenced by the age of their families. They were just nice boys trying to figure things out."

"Well," said Fran, "before I'm through I'm going to see something of that side of life. We won't find it in the army, but after this war Rich and I are going to move to Philadelphia or Virginia or somewhere with some class. I'm sick of cow towns."

Diana had finished eating and was squirming in the high chair eager to get down. "What happens to her now?" asked Helen.

"We slam her in bed and hope that she won't yell," said Fran.

"Would you like me to put her to bed?" Helen asked.

"Tell you what," said Fran. "That's a swell idea. You just put her to bed while I finish up here. Everything is in her room. Help yourself."

Helen carried the baby across the little living room. The child felt relaxed and heavy in her arms. She wondered whether she would have a child of her own to hold. She washed Diana's hands and face and had her in her night things when the MacRaes' coupe drove into the side yard and Don and Captain MacRae came noisily in the back door, uniformed and hearty.

"We're starved," said Rich. "What's for supper?"

"Leftover baby food," said Fran. "Helen's putting Diana to bed," she said to Don. "I think I'll invite you two every night." Don moved into the living room. Helen was standing in the bedroom doorway with Diana on her shoulder. He had never seen her holding a baby. Rich came striding in.

"Where's my princess," bellowed Rich, "come to Daddy, baby doll!"

Diana wriggled all over with excitement and recognition and held out her arms to Rich, who thrust her high in the air and down again. Diana chortled with delight.

"Oh, Rich, for God's sake," said Fran, "let's get her settled and have dinner like civilized people." She took Diana from him. "Get Don a drink. He probably needs one after watching you fool around with this baby." Diana was carried protestingly to the bedroom.

"I thought this was a dry state," said Helen as the drinks were poured.

"It is," said Rich. "If you get stuck though, you can usually get a bottle of pretty good stuff from the elevator operator at the hotel."

"Is he a real bootlegger?" asked Helen with interest.

"Sure he is," said Rich. "Didn't you know any real bootleggers in Hartford?"

"That's not a dry state," said Don quickly. "Say, do you know who came to the post today?"

"Franklin D. Roosevelt," said Fran from the door of Diana's room, straightening her hair with her free hand.

"No," said Don with a grin. "Chivington told me they brought in three hundred German prisoners from Africa. They're going to bring more. This is just the start. They've got a compound all built for a couple of thousand with double fences and watchtowers down off the southeast sector."

"Can we see them?" asked Fran with interest.

"You can't, baby," said Rich, "but I hope I can and I want my lieutenants to see them. If we go east, that's what we'll be up against."

"Do you think North Africa will be finished before you go?" asked Fran.

"North Africa!" exclaimed Rich. "What makes you think the division isn't going to land on some hot hell hole in the Pacific?"

"Are you going to have Jap prisoners here too?" asked Helen.

"Who knows," said Rich, "not many Japs give up alive."

"They won't put Japs in with Afrika Korps," said Don.

"You know," said Rich, "those battles on the desert could have been run by the navy. They deployed the tanks like battleships in formation, and it was all maneuvering for position and strategic advantage."

"There was infantry in there too," said Don.

"Sure, the infantry was there," said Rich, "lots of it. We're the backbone of the army. All the air corps can do is soften things up. The engineers just facilitate things and the navy carries the infantry. Sort of a chauffering job." He grinned.

"Don't you let the navy hear you say that," said Don.

"Well, it's true," said Rich. This was one of his favorite conversations, and he had a new audience. "Wars are fought, won or lost, by infantry. Squads, companies, battalions, or di-

58

visions, whatever the unit, it must be trained so that every unit does its own job well, and so that the sum of the jobs means an efficient fighting force." He waved his hand in the air for emphasis.

"You know," said Don, frowning thoughtfully, "the position of the foot soldier is an interesting thing to trace historically. At first, he was a sort of local vigilante protecting himself or his family. Then as things became more organized he was hired or drafted to meet a crisis. Gradually soldiering became a vocation. There are interesting differences in motivation. At times men have fought just for money or goods, but at other times men have fought for ideals."

"What do you think we'll be fighting for?" asked Rich.

"Well, it certainly isn't for money and goods," said Don, "but compared to the idealism of World War I, it isn't for ideals. It lies somewhat short of idealism. This seems to me a protective war. We're fighting to prevent losing what we have already gained. In a sense, it's a war of justice. We feel it's unfair for Hitler to over-run Europe or the Japs to attack us. We want to stop them. We want to give conquered people back what they have lost. In that sense it's an idealistic war, but we are not fanatics about it. It's not a holy crusade, it's just a dirty job. We fight this war out of a sense of obligation, because we couldn't live with ourselves as men if we didn't go."

"Well," said Rich, "what do you say to the men to get them to fight well and risk everything if this is just a holding action?"

"It isn't just a holding action," said Don. "It's a test of a system. Civilizations rise and fall in relation to their response to these crises. When the response is weak, the civilization goes down and the challenger takes over. When the response is adequate, the civilization is maintained for a time; but when the response is overwhelming, the way of life surges ahead." Fran looked around the room. She was obviously bored.

"What do you think of the response we're making now?" asked Rich.

"It's too soon to tell," said Don, "and we're too close to it, but its got to be overwhelming. This country is too young and has too many resources, both material and human, to start downward now."

"What's the average life of a civilization as you historians figure it?" asked Rich.

"There's no average life," said Don, "it just depends on each crisis being met as it comes along. When the resilience is gone, the decline sets in."

"Well, let's not have that," said Helen. "Do you think that this applies to people as individuals too?"

"Well, I suppose it could," said Don.

"Sure," said Fran, "when you see a decline setting in, you should shake up your life, do something about it."

"Action isn't always progress," said Don. "You've got to know what you are doing."

"OK," said Rich to Don, "you seem to have it figured out for yourself, but what do I tell the men when I'm supposed to give them morale-building talks?"

"Well," said Don, "I don't think talking is what builds morale. Maybe a good talk helps, like a coach between halves; but even in that case the morale is something that is a long time building. It's based mainly on knowing what you can depend on. We can't test the men in every possible situation; but after a while, an officer, if he's any good, should have the respect and trust of his men. He should also know what he can depend on them to do. The better the officer, the better the platoon or company. And if he's in combat, he wants to be pretty darn sure that they'll follow him. His life depends on it."

"Does that mean," asked Helen, "that the army is based on personal loyalty to leaders?"

"Not loyalty to one man but loyalty to the group and system," said Don. "The army has to have a code of law which demands that each man obey orders given to him. This applies to colonels as well as privates even though the privates don't realize it. If a man disobeys orders, he is subject to court-martial, but I maintain that a man can't do his best job unless he understands why he has been asked to do something."

"Now you're back to morale talks," said Rich.

"This is a citizens' army, you know," said Don. "We have no authoritarian background. The Germans have evolved from the Prussian military tradition; the Japs believe the highest glory and salvation comes to those who die in battle. Those two traditions give our opponents a fanaticism which we are attacking from a sense of injury."

"Perhaps the attacker always has to make it a holy war in order to find backing at home," said Helen.

"Aggression seems to grow from frustration," said Don. "In Germany's case, it is the frustration of Pan-Germanism and the need for markets and what they call 'Lebensraum'—living space. The German people are capable. There are between seventy and eighty-five million of them, depending on whether you choose to include Austria and Czechoslovakia. That works out to the densest population of any country in Europe today. Simply stated, the bitterness of defeat in the First World War coupled with the original impetus to expansion have created the present fanatical aggression. There must be some sort of natural law about it, a formula which would prove that the greater the frustration, the larger the aggression." Fran moved restlessly in her chair drumming her fingers on the wicker arm.

"That wouldn't always be true," said Helen. "Under too much frustration, people are defeated to the point of inaction."

"Perhaps," said Don, "but a civilization isn't like a person. It's always losing frustrated people off the top and adding new people at the bottom; and when enough new blood has been added to neutralize part of the frustration, the group lashes out again."

"Are you saying," asked Rich, "that once the system is in operation, aggression at certain stages is inevitable?"

"That's the possibility," said Don, "but I like to think that the chain could be broken by enough people understanding what was going on and doing something about it."

"You're an idealist," said Fran disgustedly. "People aren't like that. Everybody in this world is out for himself. I know."

"You may be right," said Don, "but I hope not.

"Aren't you out for yourself?" asked Fran.

"Only to a certain extent," said Don thoughtfully. "If that makes me an idealist, then I guess I am one."

"Is this a holy war for you?" asked Fran. "Are you fighting to save the world for democracy or for a League of Nations or something?"

"Not exactly," said Don, "but sometimes I wish that we did

have a certain amount of fanaticism about it. It would be easier to go, easier to get the men to follow. If I'm fighting for anything, it's to restore decency and fair play, the right of a people to determine their own form of government."

"There's just one thing," said Helen. "If you fight now and win, does that just lead to more frustration and then more aggression?"

"Listen, honey," said Rich impatiently, "don't you worry your pretty little head over that. This time when we lick them, they're going to know they're licked. All this talk isn't proving much. All we've got to do is get out there and annihilate them. None of this theorizing is going to win the war."

Don looked at him closely.

"Frankly," said Fran seeing a chance to end the conversation, "I think it would have been much simpler to have lived in the time of the cave men. Then Rich would have dragged me home by the hair, and we wouldn't have worried about saving civilization."

"Let's eat," said Rich, "I'm starved."

VIII

Colonel Spaulding was going over the morning report. Even with Major Van Tuyl's help it took several hours each day just to keep the paperwork straight. When the telephone rang, Van Tuyl picked it up.

"Battalion headquarters, Major Van Tuyl speaking."

"This is the Provost's Office. Do you have lieutenants named Duval and Jensen in your C Company?"

"Yes, sir."

"We just had a call from the State Police in Sildon. They're under arrest, being held for release to the military police. We're sending a car over for them now."

"What's the charge?" asked Van Tuyl.

"Bootlegging, possession of liquor, driving under the influence."

"My God!" said Van Tuyl, "what's the penalty?"

"Confiscation of car used for illegal transport, fine and/or jail sentence. The car is already confiscated. The fine will be determined by the courts later. Duval and Jensen are to be returned to the army for discipline."

"Thanks," said Major Van Tuyl. "Send over the official report and bring them to battalion headquarters when they're back."

Van Tuyl relayed the information to the colonel.

"Damn messy," said Spaulding. "Call in Captain MacRae."

Captain MacRae had been expecting the call. Two officers can't be AWOL for long without repercussions.

"MacRae," said Spaulding, "where are Lieutenant Duval and Lieutenant Jensen?"

"I do not know, sir," said Rich.

"Is Cutler here?" asked the colonel glowering.

"Yes, sir."

"Where do you think we could find Duval and Jensen?" asked Colonel Spaulding.

"Well," said MacRae, "they were going to Townstake yesterday, and they haven't come back. They may have had an accident."

"Damn tootin' they had an accident," said Spaulding. "What did they go to Townstake for?"

"They had a day off," said MacRae.

"Could they possibly have had in mind to buy a little liquor?" asked Spaulding sarcastically.

"Usually anyone going that far brings back some liquor," said MacRae.

"Did you know they were going for liquor?" asked Spaulding.

"Yes, sir."

"Did you do anything to stop them?" asked Spaulding.

"Why, no, sir," said MacRae, worried by the colonel's sudden moral tone.

"As their commanding officer, wasn't it your duty to remind them of the law concerning liquor in this state?"

"Why, sir," said MacRae, "every bit of liquor on this post comes from Townstake. It has for almost a year."

"That's not the point," said Spaulding. "The point is that the State Troopers picked up two officers of your company and arrested them for bootlegging. It's a disgrace to the battalion. I hold you personally responsible, and I want the names of anyone they bought liquor for."

"Sir," said MacRae, "they bought liquor for almost the whole regiment."

"Don't be ridiculous," said Spaulding. "They didn't go over there in a truck."

"But, sir, it's true. They collected from almost every officer in the regiment."

"In my battalion?" yelled Spaulding.

"Yes, sir."

"Who is involved in this thing?" demanded Spaulding.

"Almost everyone," said MacRae.

"Who isn't involved?" asked Spaulding.

"To tell you the truth, sir, the only one I can think of is Chaplain Rutherford."

"This is preposterous," said Spaulding. "I can't punish all the officers in the whole battalion. Did you put in money yourself?"

"Yes, sir."

"Van Tuyl," roared the colonel, "are you in this thing?"

"Yes, sir."

"My God," said Spaulding. "How can we keep this quiet?"

Duval mourned the Chevy. He and Jensen were confined to the post for one month. Duval was a changed man. Without the opportunity of leaving the army, he became morose, sorry for himself. Without a car, he was just one more second lieutenant. He knew that the promotion he had worked so hard for was now further away than ever.

Jensen took a "what the hell" attitude, but Jensen had not lost a car. And, in spite of Spaulding's precautions, word of the calamity filtered out of the Provost's Office and, by the usual rumor channels, found its way to the men.

"Can you beat that," said Benard to Covalos, the radio man, "the poor guy goes all the way to Townstake to get booze for his buddies and then loses his car and gets confined to post."

"Lousy trick," said Covalos. "What those officers should do is take up a collection and buy him a new car."

"Fat chance," said Millen.

"Boy," said Benard, "I'd a liked to see old Spaulding's face when he heard the news! Some day that crusty old bastard is going to have apoplexy. Do you know what he said to Captain MacRae the other morning on rifle range?" Benard twisted his face to resemble Colonel Spaulding until deep lines ran from the corners of his nose down to the base of his cheeks. "He said, 'MacRae, why aren't these men trained to hit the target?' My God, we was doing pretty good that morning."

"Oh, they're never satisfied," said Millen. "You sweat like a pig and blister your feet and they're still bitching about why ain't you perfect."

"Don't know why they should have their liquor when it's so hard for us to get it," said Benard, clicking his false teeth back into the roof of his mouth with his tongue.

"Christ," said Millen, "they get most of the women too."

"Listen to who's talking," said Benard. "How many you got on the string now besides the wife in New Jersey?"

"Wouldn't you like to know?" said Millen beaming at them.

"Well, lover boy," said Benard, "I'll be glad to take over any you can't handle any Saturday night. Just let me know."

"All you need is initiative," said Millen grinning broadly. "It's like Lieutenant Cutler said, 'You got to take initiative to get ahead in this army.'"

"Sure," said Benard, "look where initiative got Lieutenant Duval."

IX

"Well," said Jensen to Rusnick and Duval the following Saturday afternoon, "coming to the club tonight?"

"What for?" said Duval, struggling through a head cold. He pulled out a khaki-colored handkerchief and wiped his nose.

"Well," said Rusnick dryly, "why not give that lousy cold of yours to Mrs. Spaulding?"

"The hell with her," said Duval.

"Listen," said Jensen, "it's not going to do you any good to sulk around. You come with us."

"There's not a guy there I want to see," said Duval, "and that goes double for the women."

"Come on, Duval," said Jensen, "Alice Spaulding's back from New York. She's sort of pretty and she'll be lonesome now without Cutler to chase. You come and be nice to her and maybe she'll chase you."

"Steer clear of colonels' daughters," said Duval. "If you dance with them, papa thinks you ought to marry them."

"You don't have to marry her," said Jensen. "Just come on down and have a good time."

"She's too sweet for me," said Duval morosely. "Just like a booby trap. You never know with these little blond gals. First they seem so helpless and feminine but later out come the claws and you better look out. Probably turn out just like her mother."

"God forbid," said Rusnick rolling his eyes.

"Well, what are you going to do?" asked Jensen.

"I can't leave the post," said Duval, "so I'm just going to hack around and eat my supper and then hack around some more."

"Listen, we could go down and see the German prisoners. That's on the post. How about it?" said Rusnick.

"That's a swell idea," said Jensen. They waited to see whether Duval would agree.

67

"OK," said Duval finally. "Let's go see what we're going to fight. I wish we were overseas right now."

Out on Roosevelt Avenue they flagged down a jeep.

"We want to go down to the prison camp," said Rusnick to the sergeant who was driving. "Can you run us down there?"

"Hop in," said the sergeant. "I got time to run you down, but you'll have to get yourselves back. This jeep is due for the major in twenty minutes."

"OK," said Rusnick.

They all climbed in. The seats were high and hard, and with no side curtains it was a windy ride.

"You seen the Kraut prisoners?" Jensen asked the sergeant.

"Yes, sir," said the driver. "They're rugged-looking characters. All come from Hitler's Afrika Korps they say."

"That was a crack army," said Jensen, "supposed to be the cream of the crop. Surprises me that so many surrendered."

"I don't know how they rounded them up," said the sergeant, "but they sure are rugged looking. Hate to meet any of them out in the open with a gun."

"Well," said Rusnick, "you better get ready to."

The jeep scooted over the ridge and before them was the prison compound. High barbed wire fences defined the area. The sergeant stopped the jeep by a small guardhouse and the three lieutenants got out.

"Thanks," said Rusnick.

"Sure," said the sergeant and drove back over the ridge.

A first lieutenant sauntered out of the guardhouse. It was late afternoon. He was bored and had been wishing for a diversion.

"What can we do for you?" he asked.

"Just came down to look around," said Rusnick.

"Just tourists?" asked the lieutenant.

"I guess so," said Jensen.

"How many prisoners have you got in there?" asked Duval showing some interest for the first time.

"About fifteen hundred now," said the lieutenant. "More coming in next week. We'll have several thousand before we're through."

"What do they look like?" asked Duval.

"See for yourself," said the lieutenant and led them over to the outside fence.

As they looked through, they could see the space between the inner and outer fences and, beyond in the compound, hundreds of sullen men. Some were in German uniform, some in coveralls, but they stiffened as they saw the lieutenants by the outer fence. Silently they gathered by the inside fence staring out.

Duval was struck by the blondness of their hair. There was scarcely a dark-headed man amongst them. The four on the outside could feel pride and hatred in the area between the fences. There was something ominous about these caged men and their arrogance as they held the eyes of the Americans in sullen silence.

"Jesus," whispered Jensen softly to the others, "they're still tough." He felt shaken. "Hitler's young Aryan gods."

Involuntarily Rusnick glanced again at the two fences checking them for safety. For a moment, it had seemed to him that he was vulnerable, that this combat-hardened troop would surge forward and annihilate them.

"We've got to be tough," said Duval, "if this is what we're training for." They were silent again, just letting the quality of these caged men find its place in their consciousness.

Then one of the Germans spat through the fence and made some sort of derisive remark in his own language. The others took it up. They jeered, they spat through the fence too and laughed together.

The four Americans kept their places. They felt like animals in the zoo with the crowd outside looking in at them. It was a moment they would never forget.

Finally the guardhouse lieutenant turned abruptly on his heel and led the way back across the field.

"Boy," said Jensen nervously, "those fences better be strong."

"They're electrified," said the lieutenant.

"Are the Krauts always like that?" asked Rusnick.

"Pretty much," said the lieutenant. "Sometimes they sing German songs though and then they seem almost human."

"Human!" said Duval. "They'd have murdered us with their hands if those fences hadn't been there."

"Those men have been in combat," said the lieutenant.

69

"There's a war going on even though people here don't seem to know it yet."

"Lord," said Duval, "we better find it out pretty quick. Did you feel how they hate us?"

"It's funny," said Rusnick, "I don't think I ever really hated a man. Some I like better than others, but I've never really hated another person. Makes you feel funny to have someone else hate you."

"Look," said the guardhouse lieutenant, "I see these guys every day. Sometimes I think I'm the only one on this post that realizes that we may not win this war. There are plenty more where those came from. They're tough and disciplined and they hate us. It's been trained into them. All the time we were going to school and fooling around with jalopies or girls and trying to scrape up money to go to the movies or something, those Germans were learning to goose step and being told they were oppressed and that the Fatherland needed them. Those men were dedicated to our destruction and still are. You ought to see them march. Every man in step. Nothing sloppy about them even now. They mend their uniforms and keep them clean. Some of them even seem a little crazy. There was a work detail out on Roosevelt Avenue one day cutting the lawn in front of the Officers' Club and they were working their heads off. Finally I said to them that it was hot and we didn't expect them to kill themselves working and it was all right to let up a little. And you know what happened? One man looked me right in the eye and said he wasn't fixing it up for us, but he wanted the place to look nice when *der Führer* got here. Makes you stop and think. I don't think Hitler's coming to Camp Carver, and neither do you, but plenty of those men do."

"Do you speak German?" asked Jensen.

"*Ja wohl,*" said the lieutenant. "That's why I got this crummy job."

"Do any of them ever get out?" asked Duval.

"Not yet," said the lieutenant, "but they are bound to try it. A lot of them speak some English and will think it worth a try. They probably don't have a very clear idea of where they are, but we figure any that get loose will try to head south to Mexico. If any of them could get 20 miles from here safely, they might make it all the way. So few people have any idea we have German prisoners in this country."

"How do you figure they might make a break?" asked Rusnick.

"Well," said the lieutenant, "tunneling is the first thing you think of, but that's the adventure-story way. They might also try to foul the electric circuits and get through the fences or somehow impersonate an American or be carted out with the garbage or pretend to be sick and try to escape from the post hospital or force a break through the gates. It's hard to outguess them, but we think we're ready for anything they can think up."

"Well," said Jensen with a grin, "take good care of them. I sure don't want to meet those boys until I've had a little more training."

Jensen, Duval, and Rusnick started walking back up the road to camp. At the roll of the ridge, they paused and turned, looking back and down on the prison encampment. The Germans had left the fence and were once more tramping at random within the enclosure, wearing out their shoes on endless circles trying to erode time away.

"Funny to see people in cages," said Rusnick thoughtfully. "Seems sort of wasteful—all their energy against all our energy. Why couldn't they be sensible and see that Hitler is wrong. This way we have to prove it to them."

Duval said, "Starting tomorrow, I'm really going to work. Those men in my platoon won't know what hit them. It's the only way. We're headed into the home stretch now, and we've got to be better prepared."

Jensen said, "Captain MacRae has got to see this." They walked on in silence.

"What do you figure the odds are?" asked Rusnick.

"You mean on getting through this alive?" asked Jensen.

"Yea," said Rusnick softly. It was a subject which was rarely discussed and only brought up now because they were on the lonely road and had shared the experience at the prison fence.

"Second lieutenants are expendable," said Duval. "The chances are in combat, we'll never all three get through."

"If one of us pulls through, he'll be lucky," said Jensen.

They walked on in silence, each with his own thoughts.

"Tell me," said Duval, "how does it all add up? What's the sense to it?"

"Who knows," said Rusnick. "Sometimes I think the only answer is to find a good wife and settle down to raise a family without worrying about answers to what it's all about. Let someone else figure it out."

"You know," said Lieutenant Duval, "I'm not going to miss that car so much now I know what we've got to be ready for. I'm going to train that platoon. They'll hate me for it, but later when they're overseas they'll understand."

There wasn't much more to say. The sun was setting over the low hills, and they watched it dip down ahead of them, fiery red in a washed-out sky leaving a halo on the hill. The plains around them deepened in color. Here and there a bird circled and wheeled high in the free air. The clouds, bunched low on the horizon, changed color from moment to moment, defining space with exultation and defiance. The three men walked along, each complete in himself but feeling a kinship to the others, like three silent ships on a sea of grass. From far off, the sounds of the main post, which they were approaching, became more distinct; but for a little while they had escaped into a different reality, seen further, stretched in understanding.

X

Helen Cutler and Fran MacRae, pushing Diana in a stroller, came down the sidewalk and turned into the big drug store opposite the Stevens Hotel. It was an unofficial meeting place for Cowan and, at most hours of the day and night, was crowded with soldiers and civilians. There was a chrome-glittering soda fountain down one whole side with red leatherette stools lined up opposite booths. The two telephones in the back corner caused congestion by the prescription counter because people almost always had to wait in line to phone. The druggist, in his white coat, looked harassed, as though he felt somehow professionally out of place in all the turmoil of milk shakes, sun glasses, tooth brushes, magazines, cigarettes, shower caps, toys, and hamburgers.

Fran lifted Diana from the stroller and held her on her arm almost breathing down the necks of a group of privates in a booth as they finished their ice cream. She waited impatiently.

"OK, it's all yours," said one of them as they got up to leave.

"Thanks, handsome," said Fran smiling at him as she plopped Diana down on one of the benches and slid in beside her. Helen took the opposite bench and watched the soldiers leave. They were kidding the one Fran had called handsome. He turned back and waved as he went through the door.

"Aren't you afraid they'll try to pick you up when you talk like that?" said Helen.

"Why, honey," said Fran, "your background is showing. It doesn't mean anything. They're just good guys."

They ordered hamburgers and milk shakes and a dish of ice cream for Diana.

"This way," said Fran, "I won't have to bother making lunch. I'll just toss her in for her nap. How's the apartment hunting?" asked Fran.

"Nothing yet," said Helen. "I'm looking for a room with

kitchen privileges now. It's got to be near the bus line so Don can get back and forth. I've got a lead on one over on Dow Street to look at this afternoon."

"You better take it," said Fran. "You won't find an apartment now."

They ate in silence for a few minutes. Diana was completely happy with her ice cream.

"Bet you can't guess what I'm going to do this afternoon," said Fran grinning.

"What?" asked Helen.

"Well," said Fran, "first I'm going over to talk with that nice druggist. Going to get him to sell me some little pills."

Helen was puzzled. "What do you mean?" she asked.

Fran laughed at her. "I think I'm pregnant," she said. "Going to do something about it. Can you imagine me with two babies and Rich overseas? One mistake was enough."

Helen didn't know what to say. "Don't you want Rich's baby?" she asked.

"Listen, honey," said Fran, "you've got a lot to learn. Anyone who'd start in with diapers and bottles on purpose is crazy. I suppose you're crazy?"

"I'd like a baby before Don goes overseas," said Helen.

"You are crazy," said Fran. "What would you do with it if you end up a widow?"

"Does Rich know that you're going to try to do this?" asked Helen.

"Rich wants a son," said Fran. "I'd be a nut to tell him."

"Maybe you'll be a nut if you don't have this baby," said Helen.

"Listen," said Fran, "it's as simple as this. The division will be leaving soon, and I don't want to be left big as a cow. Men will take advantage of you if you don't look out. Rich would like me pregnant because then I'm more dependent on him. Men have a joke about it—keep them barefoot and pregnant and then you know where they are."

"If that's the way you feel about it," said Helen, "why did you ever get married?"

"You better go back to New England," said Fran. "Here, hold Diana while I go see the druggist."

74

Diana came happily to Helen. These two had made friends since Helen had come to Cowan. Helen rather pitied the child, felt that she was dragged around too much, that her meals were at Fran's convenience, that she often was up too late. Helen played quietly with her, and Diana responded with smiles and babblings and at times with real glee. She stood now in Helen's lap with her arms around her neck playing peek-a-boo. Helen watched Fran lean confidentially over the counter to talk with the druggist. After a time, he drew back and shook his head. Fran talked with him again, but still he shook his head. Fran came back to the table.

"No luck," she said, "but I'll try some place else; and if pills won't do it, I've got a line on some doc that's making a business of it. Remember what Don said the other night? Response to crisis and all that? Well, I'm responding to crisis, but I'll bet it would shock him to know how."

Helen could think of nothing to say. Her sensitivities were outraged. She just wanted to get away from Fran. This whole town seemed so very far from home. People were different, food was different, landscape was different, values were different. Don was her only connection with her past life, but he was also part of this life here and of her future. She was wearied by the confusion of it all. The noisy drug store seemed to personify the vulgarity of this life out of context. She only wanted to see Don, to have the reassurance he gave her, to forget about Fran and Cowan and armies and war and shut it all out in his arms with the darkness around them and the sound of his breathing beside her.

XI

On a cool February afternoon Lieutenant Donald Cutler was preparing to run his infantry platoon through the obstacle course at Camp Carver. He had the men lined up four abreast at ease in ranks. Dry winds swept over the plain picking up dust from among the stubbles of brown grass and depositing it indiscriminately in the folds of the men's uniforms, in their hair and ears, even against their teeth. They could taste the grit of it as they waited, shaded from the receding sun by their helmets.

Lieutenant Cutler walked down the line of waiting men, and at the far end of the course Sergeant Pulska stood with a clip board and stopwatch to record the finish.

At the signal, four men sprang off, sprinting like rangy jack rabbits down the first stretch of the course, to dive into parallel brush tunnels. Almost simultaneously they popped out on hands and knees at the far end and picking up speed, rose to running positions. They scaled ladders, up and down like khaki apes, arms and feet flying, ran the stretch to the wall, leapt at it, clinging with tense fingers to haul themselves up and over. Then they thudded down on the far side and ran, staggering, at ropes suspended over the ditch near the finish line.

Behind came the second group and then the third, released on signal until the whole course was swarming with men. One soldier fell on the near side of the wall, one was sprawled in the muddy ditch, but the others ran by in uneven waves, shouting at the end. Lieutenant Cutler watched knowing that mastery of an obstacle course develops in a soldier a sense of competence. As a man learns to scale a wall or swing high over a ditch, he masters hesitations born of self-doubt and smallness. Muscles harden, nerve stiffens, until he gains the ability to commit himself to action. This is largely an act of faith. He saw that the men were hardening, the job was beginning to be done, but that the task still lay before them.

The atmosphere at the post was changing. It filtered down from division to regiment and battalion headquarters and spread like a contagion through the companies. The pressure was on. For the first time, the men sensed somewhere in the near future a definite time limit to their training. The night problems were stepped up. GIs spend days each week on forced marches or bivouac. In the very early spring they slept out on ground still cold from winter, rolled in single blankets over their uniforms. They were called at all hours of the day and night to march muddy miles, they munched C-rations, dug fox holes, and made river crossings. Between times, they slept or waited. It was a process of "hurry up and wait." They were roused in the middle of the night, assembled in their battle gear, feeling that the march was ready to leave only to sit breakfastless till ordered out in mid-morning. It was a system that makes little sense to the GI— "Hurry up and wait." It was practice in the coordination of units, in timing, in maneuverability.

Gradually the division began to emerge as an entity. General Steed strode through the field with his binoculars, hawk-eyed, followed by his headquarters command. He asked endless questions, gave endless orders, giving the impression of having his hand in everything. He turned up in so many places and so unexpectedly that the men began to call him Eleanor.

"Better duck, there comes Eleanor," said Private Benard to Private Millen when they were sitting under a little cottonwood tree sharing pieces of a comic book which Millen had brought out from the post for dull moments.

"My God, here comes Eleanor," said Lieutenant Chivington to Cutler at C Company Headquarters which, at that moment, consisted of a folding table covered with papers and Chivington on a camp stool. The general came up to them. Cutler observed him closely.

General Steed was a short, stocky man. He seemed to bristle with importance and competence, and his eyes were everywhere. His uniform was immaculate and his field boots shone.

"Where is your captain?" he demanded.

"He's gone to battalion for a meeting, sir," said Chivington on his feet and saluting.

"When did these men eat last?" General Steed asked Cutler.

"At 1700 hours, sir," said Cutler.

"Any difficulties?" asked General Steed.

"None, sir," said Chivington wondering how big a difficulty should be to be brought directly to the general by a first lieutenant.

"Splendid," said General Steed. "Carry on. Now where is this battalion headquarters?"

"About one-quarter mile along the ridge," said Chivington pointing out the way.

When the general and his staff disappeared in the brush, Cutler grinned. "Think we should warn them by radio?" he asked.

"Let's," said Chivington, "it should be worth a promotion in any army."

Cutler rang Major Van Tuyl on the field phone. "Green rabbit to sky-blue fox." He waited for the reply. "General Steed and party headed for battalion headquarters," he said.

"My God!" said Van Tuyl. "We'll take care of it. How did you make out?"

"I guess we passed all right," said Cutler.

"Maybe we will too," said Van Tuyl. "Thanks, Cutler. Over and out."

Jimmy had been left in charge of cleanup. The mess sergeant had long ago learned how to extend his own free time and Jimmy, now promoted to corporal, was one of the keys to his freedom. The pots and kettles had been washed, the equipment was lined up ready to be packed, and the field kitchen was almost ready to move on to the next location. There remained only a large can of garbage around which lazy flies were already beginning to swarm. It was at this moment that a runner from battalion came racing down the hill into the area.

"General Steed's coming with a whole gang of officers," he said breathlessly and continued on down the slope disappearing among the brush in the erosions of the gully below.

Jimmy looked around quickly and suddenly the presence of the can of garbage put him in a panic. "We've got to get rid of it," he said struggling to lift it by the handle. A private on K.P. grabbed the handle with him and together they half ran, half staggered with it down the slope toward the gully. Jimmy knew that there was not time to bury it. They would have to hide it, and the brush seemed sparse and thin as he looked about for a hiding place. In the back of his mind all he could think of was the fact that a general was coming; and since he was in charge, he was sure to catch it.

As they looked about, he found a small overhang on the bank and tried to thrust the garbage can under it. He saw a shelter-half which he quickly appropriated and threw over the can.

"Hey, you leave that shelter-half be," yelled a soldier.

Jimmy turned quickly. "The general's coming," he announced with a wild look in his eye. "We got to have it."

"Holy cow," said the soldier. "Let's get out of here."

Jimmy dragged some dry brush and threw it over the shelter half before he turned and tried to run back up the hill. He reached the mess area flushed and out of breath just as the general and his party arrived.

"Who's in charge here?" bellowed the general.

"I am, sir," said Jimmy weakly.

"What are you doing at present?" barked the general.

"We're just finishing cleaning up from chow," said Jimmy feeling as though his knees would buckle under him. He could not tell whether it was the run up the hill or the presence of the general which made him feel this way.

"Where is the garbage?" asked the general.

"No garbage here," said Jimmy breathlessly.

"No garbage," said the general sarcastically, turning to a colonel who followed with a clipboard taking notes.

Jimmy could see a puzzled look on the face of Captain MacRae, who followed the group.

"Has the garbage been buried?" asked the general throwing out the question like a dart which wings gracefully in the air but stings as it reaches its mark and stands quivering.

"No, sir," said Jimmy, "no garbage." He felt a great confusion descending over him as he stood there surrounded by high-ranking officers feeling trapped by his own panic.

"Did you tell me," shouted the general, "that this company ate a whole meal and there is no garbage!"

"Yes, sir," stammered Jimmy.

The general turned abruptly on his heel. "Find the garbage!"

he said to the officers with him.

There was a momentary pause. Then, as the general waited with Jimmy standing before him, the officers of the entourage fanned out in a half-hearted search of the area. They lifted the covers off pots, looked under the parked jeeps, poked into the supplies, roamed the area with their eyes on the ground.

"Damn it, men," yelled the general, "step it up, step it up."

The colonel with the clipboard finally reported back to the general. "No sign of it, sir," he said.

"Well, look further out," barked the general. The circle widened until several of the officers were out of sight. Jimmy wondered how far down the hill they had gone and whether any of them had entered the gully, but he dared not turn around to look. Suddenly it occurred to him that he ought to have left the garbage where it had been and explained to the general that they were about to bury it. That was the usual procedure and could have called down no more than an order to hurry up about it. He thought of the large pail as he had left it under the shelter half. It was not really hidden. Even the brush he had dragged across it had not helped much. He could be court-martialed for this. He had lied to a general.

To Jimmy, the time which he waited facing the impatient general seemed interminable. The general paced, looking at his wrist watch, scowling at Jimmy, watching the progress of the men he had sent searching. Finally they wandered back. The general sent one more black scowl at Jimmy and, without a word, turned abruptly and started back toward the ridge above. The other officers moved quickly in behind him matching his pace.

Jimmy stood with his mouth open, hardly daring to believe in his escape. Captain MacRae turned back as the others left. He put his hand on Jimmy's shoulder.

"Just one thing to remember," he said.

"Yes, sir," said Jimmy knowing that Captain MacRae could feel him shaking.

"In the future," said Captain MacRae kindly, "our company has garbage."

"Yes, sir," said Jimmy.

MacRae turned again and, grinning to himself, followed the others.

"Lieutenant, sir," said Millen to Cutler as the company broke ranks after retreat one night and headed for the mess hall. "Could I talk to you a minute?"

"Sure, Millen," said Cutler. "What's on your mind?"

"Well," said Millen looking around to see whether anyone could overhear, "I don't know just where to start. I wouldn't want any of this to get around. That's why I thought I should talk to you, Lieutenant."

"Sure," said Cutler, "what is it?"

"Well," said Millen, "it's about the allotment for my wife. I don't know just how to make out the papers."

"Well," said Cutler, "that isn't too difficult. I've got a wife now myself, you know," he added genially. "I made out allotment papers last week."

"Well," said Millen, "it's all sort of mixed up."

"Do you know how much you want sent to her while you're overseas?" asked Cutler.

"That's part of the trouble, sir," said Millen shifting uneasily back and forth from one foot to the other and avoiding Cutler's eye.

"Well," said Cutler, "I'll help you make out the papers, but I can't do much until you know how much you want sent to her each month. My guess is that if you have children, she'll need everything you can spare; but if she's alone and working, she won't need as much. Do you have any children?"

"Got a girl," said Millen, "three years old and a boy that's a little over a year and," he added unsteadily, "got one on the way."

"Well, that's fine," said Cutler wondering how they could get along on a private's pay. "Congratulations."

"Well, sir," began Millen again, "it's all sort of mixed up."

"Looks to me," said Cutler, "as though they'd need all you can spare. Now you won't need much spending money where we're going. Save out enough for cigarettes and beer and then send the rest along to your wife. I'll help you fill out the papers."

"Lieutenant," said Millen looking straight at him for the

81

first time, "I know how to fill in the blanks. It's just that I don't know what to do."

Cutler was tired. He wanted to get into town, but he tried to be patient.

"What's the whole problem, Millen?" he asked.

"Well," said Millen, "it's this way. I don't know how I got into it, but the trouble is that I've got two of them. It's the wife in New Jersey's got the two kids and it's the one in Cowan that's expecting. It's just a mess," he said sheepishly. "I don't know what to do."

"You've got two wives!" asked Cutler.

"Well, yes," said Millen reluctantly.

"Don't you know that's bigamy?" asked Cutler.

"Sure, Lieutenant, that's why I wanted to talk to you. You won't tell on me, will you?" he added anxiously. "I just figured you'd know how to fix it up so everything will be all right."

"How did you happen to marry the local girl," asked Cutler, "when you knew you had a wife already?"

"Well," said Millen, "you know how it is." He started weaving back and forth again. "The Mrs. was way back in New Jersey. Didn't know when I'd see her again. Guess I got sort of lonesome. That kid in Cowan is kinda cute. The next thing I know she's telling me she's knocked up and I gotta marry her or she'll tell Captain MacRae, so I figured best way to fix everything up was to just get hitched. It don't mean much. Just a lotta words and it made her happy. But now I gotta fill in the papers about allotment and insurance and next of kin and all that stuff, and I don't know what to do."

"Well," said Cutler, "I don't know much about the legal end of all this. Which one do you want to be married to?"

"Gee, Lieutenant," said Millen, "honest, I don't know. The kid out here is cute, but I kinda figured on going back to the kids and the Mrs. in New Jersey. I guess they're both sort of crazy about me," he added with a grin.

"Look," said Cutler, "you better go and see the chaplain about this. I'll fix it up so you can get a leave to go to New Jersey, but before you go you ought to know what you want to do. If you're going to divorce the wife in New Jersey, you'll have to get things all signed while you are there."

"Gee," said Millen, "I don't want to tell the chaplain about it. I thought just me and you could fix it up."

"Listen," said Cutler, "he can help you a lot more than I can. All I can do is get the leave for you, but he can help you decide which one you're going to be married to."

"OK," said Millen reluctantly. "Does the captain have to know why I get the leave?"

"How's this?" asked Cutler. "If anyone asks, I'll say it's for family reasons; and if they ask any more, I'll say it's a question of a divorce."

"You won't tell them any more than that?"

"No," said Cutler, "you have my word on that."

"Thanks, Lieutenant," said Millen. "It's like they say. You're a right guy. You just let me know when I can do somethin' for you."

"Sure," said Cutler thinking of the fable of the lion and the mouse.

XII

It was Wednesday night again. All afternoon Don Cutler, in the back of his mind, had been looking forward to getting into town to see Helen. Now that the schedule was tightened up, the officers were free only on Wednesday nights and weekends, and then only when they were not on bivouac or had not caught a turn at O.D. duty. As he headed into Cowan, he felt content, just like an old married man, he thought, going home to his wife. It was a role which still amused him because the novelty had not yet worn off.

Helen had finally found a room with kitchen privileges in the home of a widow on Dow Street, a tidy place and quiet. Their room was comfortably furnished with ruffled curtains and a couple of chairs and a desk where Helen could keep busy. She was studying archaeology, she told him, so that they could talk it over together. He grinned to himself. When they were together, the last thing either of them thought of was archaeology, but it was a nice idea he thought, and there must be lots of lonely hours while he was busy at the post.

She's made a pretty good adjustment, he thought to himself. She seems happy, says she's happy, maybe she is. It pleased him. I'm getting used to being married, he thought. It's going to be hard to leave. But tonight he didn't have to leave her.

She was watching at the window as he came up the walk. She smiled and waved to him, and he found that tight feeling in his chest catching at him again. What was she to do this to him so often? He hurried up the steps and she met him at their door. He put his arms around her and as he backed her into the room, closed the door with his foot. He gave her a long kiss, and they sat down on the blue bedspread. He couldn't take his eyes off her. There she was—she belonged to him and they both knew it.

"Look," she said, "I did it again!" She turned her arm over showing him a fresh scratch on the inside above the elbow. There were several old scratches near it. She had done it on the corner of his lieutenant's bar as she put her arms around his neck.

"That's silly," he said. "You'll have to learn to do that without getting wounded. What if I were a captain?"

"There's too much hardware on uniforms," she said. "Those brass buttons feel like acorns."

"I'll tell the general that you don't like them," he said.

He lay back on the soft chenille of the familiar spread and looked at her. It was moments like this when he could shut out the army and feel that life was worth living. She leaned down over him, and he shut his eyes feeling as though he were floating into some sort of completely satisfying existence. Her hair tickled. She put her lips down and gave him a warm clinging kiss. He sampled it carefully until he seemed to himself to be slipping away from her. He opened his eyes abruptly to stop the drift.

She was still there. "I've missed you," she said.

"Good!" he said emphatically. "I don't like to sleep out on the ground in a blanket any more. When this war is over, I'm never going camping again."

"What about Peru?" she asked.

"I don't know, Helen," he said thoughtfully. "Maybe I won't ever get there, but somehow it doesn't seem to matter so much any more. It's funny. I used to think it was so important. All that seems a long time ago."

"You'll still go," she said.

He pulled her down to him rumpling her hair and biting playfully at the earring on the tip of her ear.

"You're all dressed up tonight," he said.

"It's a special occasion," she said.

"It's always special when they let me come to town to see you," he said.

"Don," she said, "I've got supper ready for us."

"Who wants supper," said Don.

"It will burn on the stove," she said.

"Who cares," said Don.

She sat up, leaning over him running her fingers across his forehead and through his hair.

"Come on," she said.

"You're a slave driver," he said sitting up.

The widow's kitchen was immaculate. The widow judged character by housekeeping ability and never left herself vulnerable to criticism. Everything was in order, in dying condition, in case she should suddenly go. She wouldn't care who came in to go through her things. Above the sink on the window sill were the widow's geraniums, pots and pots of them and slips which she was growing to give away. A fresh roller towel hung on the back of the door. Don never used it for fear she would hurry in and change it immediately. In the middle of the kitchen, the oilcloth-covered table was set for two. Helen had put down their own place mats and silver but the flowery dishes belonged to the widow.

"Where is she?" Don whispered.

"Out," said Helen. "You can relax."

"Good," said Don coming up behind her at the stove and putting his cheek against her hair. She had tied an apron around her waist. He thought she looked very domestic getting her husband's supper.

"Look out," said Helen, "you'll make me spill it!"

They sat at the little table.

"Did you ever hear the story of the lion and the mouse?" asked Don as they ate.

"Tell me about it," said Helen.

"Well," said Don, "once there was a very fierce lion who lived in the jungle and hunted. One day he caught a little mouse. The mouse begged the lion to let him go and the lion, being a noble beast, turned him loose. But there came a day when the lion was stuck in a great hunter's net and who turned up to help but the little mouse, who gnawed the ropes and set the lion free."

"Well," said Helen, "that sounds just like Aesop."

"That story has a moral," said Don. "It means that when a lion can ruin a mouse, he had better think twice."

"What are you going to do," asked Helen, "rewrite Aesop?"

"Nope, just apply philosophy," said Don.

"What are you talking about?" asked Helen.

"I just told you a little story to amuse you," said Don, "now you tell me one."

"I'll tell you a story later," she said, "all about us; but not here in the kitchen."

They finished eating. The house was very quiet. They washed the flowered dishes and put them back in the cupboard. Helen took off her apron and they went back to their room.

"Now," he said as he shut the door, "we're not going out again tonight."

"Yes, sir," she said saluting.

"That's a sloppy salute, private," he said. "Try it again!"

She giggled but complied.

"You'd be no good in the army," he said. "You better stick with me."

"Oh," she said teasing, "I wasn't thinking of the army. I think I'll be a WAVE!"

"Oh, no you don't," he said, "you're married to me."

"There you go being bossy again," she said. "Would you rather have me join the WACS?"

"I don't want Mrs. Donald Cutler in uniform," he said vehemently, and she could see that it had gone beyond a joke.

"Well," she said a little timidly, "you don't really have to worry because I couldn't get in now."

She looked up at him waiting to see whether he understood.

"We're going to have a baby," she said.

He put his arms around her. He wanted to swing her off her feet, but he was afraid of hurting her. This somehow released some nagging anxiety within him. Now he was both completely tied and completely free.

"Do you like the idea?" she asked.

"You know I do," he said. "It's what I've been hoping for."

"You've been doing more than hoping," she said mischievously.

"Well, I guess you might say I have," he said grinning. "We're quite a combination. Helen," he said suddenly earnest, "you're going to have a lot of responsibility."

"I know," she said, "but it will give me something to do for you while you are gone. Perhaps it won't be so lonesome that way."

"I'm going to miss you a lot," he said.

"Don," she said suddenly and rather desperately, "let's not talk about when you're gone. Let's just pretend it's going on like this till we get old."

"Sure," said Don. "On second thought," he added trying to regain the air of light teasing, "perhaps I don't feel so strongly about you in uniform. Why don't you join the Waves?" he said. "They're a real trim little outfit."

As she started to cry, he put his arms around her silently. "I can't help it," she said. "It's just that I'll miss you so very much."

XIII

Day after day the bugle blew reveille at the post echoing out into the hills in the early mornings of another spring. Day by day the men lined up by platoons for report while the green flush of new grass spread from the small protected spots to cover all the rolling plain as far as the eye could see. Each day the sun sailed higher and dropped a little later, and relentlessly time went by.

Stocks were checked, new clothing issued, broken parts replaced, depleted equipment brought up to count. In shifts the men were given leaves to go home; and at the station in Cowan, a bottleneck of confusion developed. Sometimes there were a hundred soldiers waiting to get on a train which was already almost full. When a train stopped to leave mail or collect freight, if the crowd was overwhelming, the conductor would not open the doors to the passenger cars but call down to the platform that the next train would have more room. Often a soldier met trains all day before finally finding one headed in the right direction which would open its doors and let him aboard.

Once aboard, the men sat on their duffel bags in the aisles or in the men's room or on the platforms. When a man with a seat left it even briefly, he lent it to a man in the aisle who gratefully sank into body-fitting comfort to ease weary muscles and often played possum when the other returned. There was a constant restlessness aboard these wartime trains. Even in the middle of the night there were people roaming the aisles, people eating, people talking, people reading, people trying to sleep on their feet, people on the edge of despair from weariness.

The men had their leaves. They went home to parents, wives, friends, relatives, even to familiar places for one last look around. Some, deciding that the time had finally come, moved wives and families home from Cowan to get the job done while they had leave. For the first time, one heard of apartments for rent in Cowan; but most of them would stay vacant until the post was cleared and a new cadre arrived to start the long process of building a division all over again. Cowan's future, as long as the war might last, was to stand by while every eighteen months Camp Carver spewed forth from a colossal labor a new division.

Fran telephoned Rich at the post. She had become a little desperate. She had had no idea he would take it all so seriously. He's a moody man underneath, she had thought, but he'll get over it. In several weeks he had not. She wasn't sure whether he was staying at Camp Carver because he wanted to or because they were so busy getting the company ready to leave that he couldn't get into town.

"Rich," she said brightly when he finally came to the phone, "when are you coming in again?"

"I don't know," he said guardedly. "We're pretty busy here. How's Diana?"

"She's fine," said Fran. "She keeps asking for her daddy."

"Well," said Rich, "I'll be in after a while."

"But when, Rich?" asked Fran.

"How the hell do I know," said Rich.

"But if I know which night you're coming, I'll have a nice meal ready," said Fran.

"Never mind the meal," said Rich. "When I come it's to see Diana, not to eat."

"Rich," said Fran, "are you still mad at me?"

"Well, what do you think?" said Rich.

"I didn't know it was so important to you," said Fran.

"You knew darn well it was important to me," said Rich, "so what more is there to say."

"Rich," she said, "we've got to get along. You should think of Diana."

"I've been thinking about her a great deal," said Rich emphatically.

"Rich," she said, "when you come in, let's pretend it never happened. You'll be going off so soon. Let's not part fighting over nothing."

"It wasn't nothing," said Rich quietly. "It might have been my son."

"Well," she said, "I don't want a fight, especially now. If you

90

go off without making it up, it's your own fault. Nobody can say I wasn't willing to forget the whole thing."

"Thanks for being so magnanimous," he said wryly.

"Rich," she said, "I'll tell Diana you are coming tonight. If you don't come, she will be unhappy."

There was a long pause.

"Okay," said Rich wearily, "I'll be there."

"Will you make it up?"

"I'll try," he said.

"Now that's the way to see it," she said. "I'll have a nice supper ready."

As the day of departure approached, Colonel Spaulding mellowed. All the battalion noted it. He had a new spring in his step, a new purposefulness. He cracked a few jokes at company commanders' meetings. He was glad to be going and prepared for adventure. He even danced with his wife at the club one Saturday night.

The Officers' Club became much livelier. There was a recklessness about these last weeks. The atmosphere, with the orchestra whining in the background, became almost frenzied. To everyone's amazement, Alice Spaulding eloped with Major Van Tuyl. The colonel was relieved as well as pleased. He liked Van Tuyl, but Mrs. Spaulding was less than delighted. She had planned to spend the duration in San Antonio, and it had suited her plans much better to have an unmarried daughter. But she had to admit to herself that, even in San Antone, Alice might not have landed a major from the Point.

Don Cutler was concerned about Helen. They had agreed that she should go home to have the baby and to wait out the war. Don, for his own peace of mind, would have liked to have personally seen her settled there; but at her bitter protest, he had listened to his own yearnings as well as hers, and they had decided that she would stay in Cowan until the division moved out. He had some misgivings about it. There was the baby to think of now, but neither of them wanted to cut short their time together.

However, there came an alternate impulse which neither one admitted, urging time on to its inevitable conclusion to save them from despair and the agony of having something dear which must be given up. It was anguish to have the process drawn out. They wanted to delay the parting and also to get it over. The inevitable good-bye hung over them, coloring their relationship.

XIV

When the sun came up on that March morning, it found the total resources of General Steed's division lined up on the streets of Camp Carver. Jeeps and trucks were lined bumper to bumper, crowded with men, thousands of them. Command cars ran briskly up and down the long line on Roosevelt Avenue churning up clouds of dust which blew in billows and then slowly dispersed.

The men were exuberant with excitement. They wore full battle equipment as though they expected to meet the enemy. The griping was gone. Everywhere was a great genial feeling of cooperation and well-being. They were on the way but still too far away to contemplate the true nature of their adventure. Here and there a truckload of men burst into song and then others took it up and carried it along in a sweeping chorus. Men talked in excited voices; enterprising soldiers were making pools on the possibility of heading east or west; junior officers were hurrying in and out of buildings checking off their assigned responsibilities.

"What we waiting for?" said Benard clicking his false teeth cheerfully.

"General Steed can't find his razor," said Millen.

"Well, let's go," said Benard. "I'll lend him mine."

But still they waited while details were covered, reports turned in, position in convoy checked and rechecked.

Lieutenant Donald Cutler stood in the front of a jeep and looked out over the trucks full of men he knew. Beside him in the driver's seat was Sergeant Pulska and in the back, Covalos, his radio man, with the field radio beside him.

When the order to start finally came, the men in the rear knew it long before their trucks moved because of the low roaring cheer which came from the head of the column like a ground swell until they were all cheering at leaving Camp Carver. In a few minutes the cheer was gone, and the men were craning their necks for a last look at their barracks, at their mess halls, at the parade ground with the flag high and clean on the slim white pole. They were on the way.

"Jeez," said Pulska to Cutler, "I sure wish we could bring that piano."

At the gate the convoy turned toward Cowan, sweeping along the military road which had been built from the town, spaced and traveling slowly. Bright unit flags identified the vehicles as they went on in order. Cutler's jeep was about mid-distance in the convoy; and as far as he could see, the trucks full of men spread out in each direction.

It was a stirring thing to be part of it all. This morning the division was invincible. Strength and confidence soared from these units in an invisible cloud. It was a spiritual reality. The men rolled forward as though to some great victory from which each man would return a hero.

But on this morning, there would be no opportunity for courage, no demands made on this strength, no combat with an enemy. That was all to come later. As they rode by the prisoner of war camp, the Germans stood sullenly by the fences watching them pass.

When the convoy approached Cowan, it began to pass little groups of people gathered beside mail boxes at the ends of lanes, gathered at a crossroad or in front of an isolated gas station. They were silent people for the most part, withdrawn in rural dignity. Many had friends leaving with the division, others had just come to see them off. The trucks passed one by one in a sort of hypnotic rhythm—a whir of motors coming to a crescendo and then receding to be repeated endlessly.

At first the men were excited, waving wildly to the little groups; but as they went on, they were sobered by the repetition of so many serious watchers until they talked quietly among themselves in the trucks and waved almost sheepishly only to those they had known personally. The sadness in the town broke the spirit of the morning. Here on the sidewalks and lawns were hundreds of women, children, and older men—the left-behinds. They stood in little groups talking quietly or alone endlessly watching the convoy. For the most part, there was great silence.

Helen stood at the end of Dow Street searching through the thousands of men in uniform for Don. She was afraid that she might miss him, there were so many and they looked so much alike as they came on endlessly. The minutes went by like the truck and jeeps never to come that way again. She had had no idea how large a division was. There seemed to be enough men here to win any war. Her throat was tight with emotion, but she didn't want Don to see her crying this last time. When she began to see the faces of officers she knew, she redoubled her searching efforts in a panic lest Don slip by her without being seen. Colonel Spaulding went by in a command car. He looked very stiff and military. She saw Captain MacRae and Lieutenant Chivington ride by under a C Company pennant followed by men in trucks and then, finally coming up the street, she saw Don in the front of the jeep. He was searching the crowd for her. She waved frantically, and he saw her and smiled and held her eyes for that brief, brief interval before he was relentlessly carried out of her blurring sight. She turned and stumbled up Dow Street seeking sanctuary in their room where he was still familiar.

When Helen packed to go home it didn't take much time. Her clothes all fit into the suitcases she had brought out with her, and the radio and silver and linen were easily packed in two cartons which the widow found in the back entry. The biggest problem was a train reservation. The doctor insisted that she sleep in a berth at night, and so she waited three weeks in Cowan to get the proper tickets.

She was lonely. She felt torn in two, as though part of her was here and another more important part had gone off with Don. She consoled herself with the thought of the baby and busied herself as best she could. She read long hours, took her daily walk. She hardly knew anyone in town except Fran MacRae; and now that Don and Rich were gone, there seemed little reason to look her up. Finally she did try to telephone, but Fran was out, so in the end she stopped trying. She expected that Fran would call her; but when she didn't, Helen was rather relieved.

The widow was pleasant. They sat together in the evening now listening to the radio or sewing or reading, each seeming to feel a little less alone because the other was there; and the days went by slowly. Helen felt a little numb. A great inertia bound her. It was partly physical, but it was also that she somehow wanted to shut off everything until Don could be back. She wrote to him often wondering where and whether he would receive the letters. She remembered hearing about a soldier who had not received any mail in three months and then had forty letters all at once. She wondered whether this could happen to Don. The mail was such a tenuous contact but it was better than nothing. She wondered how many of her letters would be lost.

When the date stamped on her ticket arrived, she said good-bye to the widow, went down to the station, and headed home.

For Helen the bottom had dropped out of her world. The longing, the tenderness which she felt for Donald Cutler found no relief in her routine days. She ached for him and in her mind went back over the little incidents of their life together, relived the fragments, holding them close to her, extracting from each the stark comforts of reminiscence. She wept silently for him at night, hoping him safe. Gradually the life of his child stirred within her. She roused herself from her deep lethargy for his child's sake, planning, purchasing, making ready the necessary things; but there was no sharing in this experience. There was the desire to show Don what she had done. In this, their great experience, she was alone, fumbling, without focus, merely waiting out the days.

She wrote to him, long letters, less emotional than she felt, always with the necessity of not worrying him. She hid her aching for him in cheerful paragraphs, in little descriptions and anecdotes dredged out of the day's happenings. She searched for him in his letters, but always the presence of the censor with his black pencil and scissors came between them, and the fact that their letters were read even routinely by anyone else seemed to muffle any written contact between them.

When the little microfilmed letters arrived, folded into themselves, she felt that an impassable barrier was being built between them, that it grew taller and thicker with each week until what they might have said in a whisper to each other would have to be shouted to be heard. She despaired at times of ever having him back. She felt that the substance of her life had gone with him and that this shell she lived in had no significance except as protection for the child. She lived in a constant apprehension for the safety of Don's life which was to her so valuable and unique. She felt that by caring enough it might be possible to keep him alive by the force of her need of him, and so she never relaxed her mental vigil. When the mail arrived, she looked at the date on his letter and knew that he had been safe and well ten days ago, or a week ago, but at no given moment could she say to herself, "Now he is alive."

Each parting is a little death and over a parting in wartime hangs the dread finality of the great death. A man sets out with purpose to a strange, distorted land, even as Aeneas, hoping to return, found his way into Hades. As dangers increase, such a traveler—committed to his task—withdraws like a threatened turtle into the far corners of his scarred shell seeking to protect identity and existence; and even if favored by the gods, it is long before he emerges to take up his normal life again.

And how is one to welcome a shelled exile from this return, never the same but recognizable to love?

XV

Fran MacRae sat in a booth of the big Cowan drug store methodically feeding ice cream to Diana. Now that the division had left, the town was strangely quiet. It reminded Fran of their first days in Cowan when the town had still been a leisurely county seat. To Fran, it was depressing.

She found the little house empty with only Diana at home. There seemed little reason to get up on time, to bother with meals, to make any effort. She felt doomed, trapped, as though caught in the vacuum left by the departing division. She had no particular plans. She didn't want to take Diana to her mother's. She had married partly to get away from that situation. There wasn't anywhere else to go except to Rich's family. Rich's sister had written suggesting that she bring Diana and take a small apartment near them, but the thought appalled her. She didn't want Rich's family criticizing the way she took care of Diana. They are fussy people, she thought. I'd be a dope to get involved there. She looked ahead and saw nothing but endless months tied to Diana wherever she went. She felt cheated, as though Rich had tricked her into this situation. It made her sullen and resentful. She wondered about boarding Diana somewhere and getting a job.

When she pictured Rich with the division, she thought of him as free and carefree surrounded by Wacs and Red Cross girls. It's not fair, she thought. Men are all alike. Can't trust them further than you can see them. She built up a whole fantasy about Rich. She almost convinced herself that he had never loved her, but somehow even now she knew he had. She wondered whether he still loved her.

He had come into town that night quiet and patient and played with Diana, but somehow he was frozen in a reserve toward her. It frightened her. He had sat down at the dinette table after Diana was asleep and told her about his will and the army allotment and insurance. He had given her the bill of sale and registration of the car. She had tried to joke about it, but he had only smiled politely at her from behind his reserve. She had never seen him like this, so unemotional and correct. He gave her everything and at the same time nothing. She had felt vaguely insulted but she couldn't reach him. She listened carefully—life insurance, the car, a monthly allotment coming in regularly. She realized that she was financially better off now than she had ever been, but she did wish he wouldn't be so wooden about it.

When Rich had explained all the arrangements, he walked into Diana's room, picked up the sleeping child in his arms, kissed her gently, returned her to the crib, and then left the house without a word.

After he left, the days were long. Diana tottered around asking, "Where's Daddy? Daddy come?"

"No," Fran said finally in exasperation, "Daddy bad boy. Stay at camp."

Diana was baffled. "Daddy bad boy?" she asked over and over with a little frown wrinkling her forehead.

"Oh, shut up," said Fran.

They stayed in the little house for days after the division left. Fran telephoned for groceries and magazines and told herself that people were no damn good. But finally the morning came when she couldn't stand it any longer. She wanted to be where there was some activity. She dressed herself up, put Diana in her best coat and pushed her in the stroller to downtown Cowan. After she bought a new dress and hat, she began to feel better. When Diana became restless, she took her into the drugstore for ice cream.

The townspeople seemed once more in possession. There were only a few soldiers anywhere in town. Fran wondered whether these were the last of the old division or the first of the new cadre until she saw the patch of a new division. It reminded her of the movies. This was where she came in.

"Daddy bad boy," mumbled Diana as Fran seated her on the bench beside her.

"Diana," said Fran, "you want ice cream?"

"Ice cream?" said Diana. "Where's ice cream?"

Fran ordered and watched the other customers. There was a

group of teenagers fooling in the next booth.

When Diana finished, Fran lingered over her coffee, smoking thoughtfully. She was in no hurry to return to the desolate house.

Diana stood up on the bench and looked around the store. Her mouth came just to the top of the back of the bench so she chewed on it.

An officer came through the swinging door and went over to the soda fountain.

"Daddy!" shouted Diana and started to bounce up and down on the bench. Fran looked around quickly and saw a captain with a small black mustache. He looked about thirty and moved with an air of confidence.

"That's not Daddy," said Fran crossly, but Diana continued to bounce. The captain was at the counter ordering a milk shake.

"Der's Daddy," said Diana again loudly. The captain turned around and looked at them.

"Daddy come," shouted Diana happily. The captain grinned.

"That's not your daddy," said Fran somewhat embarrassed.

"I want Daddy," said Diana emphatically, holding out her arms.

The captain picked up his milk shake and came over to the booth.

"Hello," he said to Diana.

Diana took one full look at him and sat down abruptly as close to her mother as possible.

"She saw the uniform," explained Fran. "She's been looking for her daddy ever since the division left."

"Sorry to disappoint her," said the captain.

Diana looked at him open-eyed.

"Let me give her a lollipop," said the captain.

"Well," said Fran hesitating just a little but smiling at him, "that's nice of you."

The captain put his milk shake on the table and was back almost immediately. He slid into the bench opposite Fran and Diana and held out a big red lollipop to Diana.

"Here you are," he said, peeling off the cellophane.

"Where's Daddy?" asked Diana looking at the captain.

"Your daddy told me to give you a lollipop," said the captain.

Diana reached out and took it but still eyed him dubiously.

"Daddy bad boy," mumbled Diana licking the lollipop and frowning.

The captain reached for his milk shake.

"I really shouldn't have barged in," he said genially. "Do you mind if I finish my milk shake here?"

"Why, go right ahead," said Fran with just a touch of coyness as she looked him over critically.

It is hard to gauge a man in uniform, but she could see that he knew his way around. She was immediately interested.

"Where do you come from?" she asked pleasantly.

"Maryland," he said, "outside of Baltimore."

"Oh," said Fran, "I love Maryland. Beautiful houses in Maryland and nice horses too," she said thinking of a magazine article she had seen recently.

"You ride?" asked the captain with interest.

"Well, a little," said Fran thinking of three lessons she had had in a ring the first year after she married Rich.

"That's wonderful," said the captain happily. "We have a lot in common. Wish I could show you the hunter I left behind at home. Some men leave women," he said gaily, "but I left a horse."

Fran laughed. "Is it your own horse?" she asked.

"Sure," said the captain. "My family raises them."

"To sell?" asked Fran probing.

"Sometimes," said the captain, "but the good ones we keep."

"You must have quite a stable," said Fran.

He looked at her closely wondering whether she was capable of a double entendre.

"Well," said the captain casually, "my great-grandfather started it and we've had horses ever since."

Fran's eyes opened a little.

"You must have a large place," she said.

"Well," said the captain, "we're not complaining."

"I just love horses," said Fran.

"You look like a rider," he said while Fran imagined herself on a tall hunter dressed in immaculate riding clothes.

"Now why do you say that?" asked Fran archly. She was beginning to enjoy herself.

"Well," he said looking her up and down with a gleam of

amusement in his eye, "you're quite trim, nice posture, hold your head well. I'd say you were a natural."

"You must have told that to a lot of women," said Fran.

"Oh, come now," he said, "you know I mean it this time."

They both laughed.

He finished his milk shake and offered her a cigarette. After he lit them, he asked, "Isn't there anywhere in this town I can get a drink?"

"Not really," said Fran, "but you might try the elevator man at the Stevens if you want a bottle."

"I'll do that," he said. "I'm staying there."

They smoked in silence for a few moments.

"Tell me about yourself," said the captain. "Where do you come from?"

"New York," said Fran. "I'm thinking of going back there."

"Do you want to?" asked the captain looking thoughtfully at her through their mutual smoke.

"No," said Fran, "but what can I do stuck in this wilderness for the duration?"

"You don't look to me as though you need to be stuck," said the captain. "You must have lots of friends here."

"Oh, sure," said Fran, "but most of them bore me."

"What do you like?" asked the captain.

"Well," said Fran deciding to be honest with him, "I like some life around me—parties, clubs, dances."

"But so do I!" said the captain as though he had made a discovery. "This place is a hole," he added confidentially. "I came in last night, too early to report to camp and you're the first human being I've met in this town. Why don't you let me take you to dinner tonight?"

"Well," said Fran, "I'd really like to but. . . ." She knew that she was going to accept. She could feel interest and enthusiasm returning and felt the wild gaiety of liberation.

"What's the harm?" he said. "I'm lonesome, you're lonesome, so we just have a steak together." He smiled disarmingly, holding his cigarette to one side.

"All right," said Fran suddenly smiling.

Diana still sucked on her lollipop.

"Where's Daddy?" she asked again mechanically.

XVI

Sea gulls circled crying plaintively for food. Their orange bills and silver wings flashed in sunlight against the sky as they swooped low over the harbor wheeling in space. The gulls flew through the pungent air, now lifting, now diving, always on the buoyant grace of clean wings, quickly flexed. They fanned the odor of dank pilings and sunbaked wood, of oil and sea water. They plopped heavily into the water retrieving unknown morsels, quickened the rhythm of wings and rose again mingling their cries with the other sounds—the sounds of whistles and distant shouts, of tools clanging, and bells, and the constant grinding of winches.

In the harbor there was activity everywhere. A dozen cranes were swinging cargo aboard waiting ships. High over the murky dock-side waters swung big nets full of cartons, huge crates, even command cars. The division was loading.

The gulls in their freedom seemed almost to taunt the men of Colonel Spaulding's battalion as they waited patiently in lines to board the ship *Caieta*. With them stood a detachment of air force maintenance men and a field hospital unit. There was some banter but through it came an underlying tension. Not all of these soldiers would return. There was the desire to linger on the dock, to delay the final ascent up the swaying gangplanks which would separate them so completely from their past lives. But, as the orders came, they marched in olive-drab lines into the gaping opening and down to the unknown hold.

The *Caieta* was an old ship. In her gray paint, she was stolid and bedraggled, like an old nurse who had been useful for many years but now has only past performance to recommend her. She had a dependable air but certainly no glamour. She was hardly a ship one would choose in which to cross an ocean.

Lashed to her decks under canvas covers were huge mysterious lumps of construction equipment—the outline of bulldozers, of a cement mixer, a road scraper. They seemed to overweigh the upper deck, to consume most of the free space and yet men flowed in around them adapting the human mass to the angles of the equipment.

By the rail, ship's officers watched as the loading was completed. They looked immaculate in navy uniforms with braid on their hats, waiting to get the ship underway, to carry one more load of the ingredients to war.

In the hold, Benard and Delaney managed to find bunks, one above the other.

"Jesus," said Benard, "is this the way the navy lives?"

"Don't be silly," said Delaney, "this is just for the army. The navy boys sleep upstairs in suites."

"Must be an old slave ship," said Benard looking around at the tiers of canvas lashed on metal frames endlessly repeated in lines as far as he could see.

"Where in hell do we stow our gear?" Millen asked Pulska.

"Take it to bed with you," said Pulska.

"Millen in bed with his battle gear! That's a come down," said Benard.

"Oh, shut up," said Millen.

"Lover boy's touchy these days," said Pulska.

"He probably has a big future when we land," said Delaney. "How about it, Millen," he asked, "you going to find us two nice chickens that can talk English?"

Millen ignored him.

"What I want to know," said Benard, "is are we below the water line down here because if we are, I sure don't want to sleep down here goin' across."

"Tell it to the admiral," said First Sergeant Pulska.

"I'm hungry," said Delaney. "When do we get some chow?"

"Search me," said Pulska shrugging his big shoulders. "Nobody's briefed us yet."

The men milled about gradually finding places for their helmets and packs. Some stretched out on the bunks testing them for length and comfort and trying to imagine what it would be like to sleep here night after night for several weeks. It hardly seemed possible that they were to cross an ocean packed in like this. In spite of the ventilators, it was already hot in the hold.

A sailor appeared searching out Sergeant Pulska. He carried an armful of mimeographed sheets, ships regulations for distribution to the men.

"Get this, men," said Pulska handing them out. The men scrambled for them, playfully jostling each other.

"Gripes," said Benard reading the information, "we only get two meals a day." He was incensed.

"Where does it say that?" asked Delaney looking over his shoulder.

"No smoking on deck," read Millen. "I sure hope we get there soon."

"So do I," said Delaney. "I bet I get seasick as hell on this old tub."

"If you're goin' to be seasick," said Benard, "you give me that upper bunk right now."

"Stow your gear," said Pulska, "and then you can go up on deck to wave good-bye to your Uncle Sam."

As Benard and Millen climbed up the ladderways, they became more aware of the metal monster throbbing with machinery and activity which was the *Caieta*. Everything was painted gray but not freshly. Chips and initials and dates in the paint bore witness of other outfits which had crossed before them. To get from their bunks in the hold to the open deck, they became part of a vast shuffling line of GIs. Now and then they saw a familiar face headed back down toward the hold; but separated now from their company group, they began vaguely to grasp the enormous exodus of which they were a part.

On deck men lined the rails two or three deep. They stood on hatch covers, perched on the lashed cargo and stared around the crowded harbor.

Red Cross girls still stood on the dock below. They had given each man a blue bag as he came aboard. The bags contained paper novels, candy, sewing kits, soap, small games; and now the men were aboard, the girls waited to wave goodby. As the gangplanks were drawn in, men called across the narrow water jovially to the girls who smiled good-naturedly and waved back.

Sailors loosened the lines and the last ties with the mainland were dragged aboard. As the engines backed and water widened between dock and ship, a hush fell on the watching men. The water churned like green oil, sucking flotsam from beneath the docks. Sea gulls screeched apprehension and flew higher. At the end of the dock, a winch man sitting in the cab of a crane saluted silently as the ship slowly dragged by the dock end to pick up speed in the open water beyond. The *Caieta* was once more underway and headed for the open ocean.

Men and guns, bandages, vehicles, fear and hope; all traveled out on this ship. The battalion was entering a new dimension. The world of land was giving way to a world of water.

Watching from the rail, Lieutenant Cutler saw the land fall back, silently slipping, slipping into time past. He thought of Helen and of their child to come and wondered whether he might again see this mainland when the dread of withdrawing was over and a reverse pull of expectancy was bringing him back. He wished desperately for peace. While he watched, the men on the docks became specks and disappeared. Doorways blended into the sides of buildings, buildings merged with others forming a skyline, and gradually the skyline itself faded and receded. The wind became stronger, whipping white edges on the short jagged waves. Men around Cutler found their mess kits and formed long lines, but still he stood and looked back until the land sank slowly into the waves and, with the roll of the sea, he could no longer be sure whether he still glimpsed it or merely imagined it, so ephemeral had it become.

Into his mood gradually the old unreality crept until Helen's existence seemed dubious to him, as though their life together had been an interlude of fragile imagination tentatively remembered and now threatened with oblivion. He tried to think of his child. He was sure that it would be a son, but this strange personality to come was only part of the unreality, and each moment the swirling sea was dragging him farther from assurance.

He wanted to go back now. He didn't want to fight. He wanted to pick up his life again where it had been cut off, but now there was a deep confusion in him. He seemed to have three lives—one was history and books and the archaeology from which he had been so abruptly called; one was the intimate personal life which had been his with Helen; and now there was this

106

relentless predetermined life which was the army. They were all pulling at him on this watery sea, and he realized with irony that no single one of them could satisfy him now.

He forced himself away from the rail and slowly started a tour of the deck. Men were everywhere, coming and going. Their faces revealed little. What were they leaving? His old sense of responsibility stirred him. He glanced about more closely as he slowly walked along, greeting men of the company by name. His job was leadership.

"Benard, Delaney, how's it going?"

"Okay, sir."

"Covalos, did you bring the radio?"

"Sure, Lieutenant."

"Millen, hope things are straightened out at home for you now." Millen grinned back at him.

"Everything's just fine, Lieutenant," said Millen. "All my troubles are behind me." He winked knowingly at Cutler. Cutler grinned.

"That's one way of looking at it," he said.

"Where are we going, Lieutenant?" asked Millen.

"I don't know for sure," said Cutler, "but it looks like Europe anyway."

He walked further around the deck making the turn at the stern where the flag blew briskly. As he rounded the far side, he looked out to sea and was amazed at what he saw. There had been a few ships following them as he had watched the land recede; but here, as he looked outward, the sea was full of ships as far as the eye could reach. Each proceeded grayly toward a rendezvous. His eyes lingered on the large cruisers, on a battleship, on little sub chasers dashing in and out like motorized tin cans; and suddenly he appreciated the fact that the navy was here with them to convoy them safely through. The hazards of the sea were surely minimized by these silent gray ships escorting them through the choppy waves. He found Lieutenant Rusnick by the rail.

"My God!" said Rusnick, "did you ever expect to see anything like this? I didn't know there were so many boats."

"It's a welcome sight," said Cutler. "A convoy is quite a thing."

They stood together silently watching. The wind increased. As the sun slipped down behind the ship, sailors adjusted double blackout curtains at each companionway and soon the men returned to their bunks. On deck only the seamen remained, and the gun crews, alert and ready, waited by their guns in big gray helmets.

The officers of C Company shared a cabin. It had three sets of bunks, upper and lower, and a light bulb in the middle of the ceiling. In one corner was a tiny washbasin. The men piled up their luggage and soon were at home in the little room. There was one porthole, but it was tightly shut and painted over completely with black paint. Captain MacRae, Lieutenant Chivington and Lieutenant Duval drew the lower berths by lot leaving Lieutenant Cutler, Lieutenant Rusnick and Lieutenant Jensen to climb into the uppers. Chivington had come prepared. From his barracks bag he pulled out a rubber air mattress and a little pump. While the others watched in amazement, he inflated it and arranged it in his berth. Cutler winked at Jensen. "Old Mother Hubbard" was living in style again, and it didn't make any of them fonder of him.

Captain MacRae fell into his berth fully clothed and turned his face to the wall. From time to time, he traced a crack in the gray paint with one finger and scraped his boots together restlessly. The others hung out of the berths talking. There was nowhere else in the cabin to sit. Finally Jensen produced a bottle which was met with cheers even though it was half empty. Mess cups were rapidly produced. Rusnick pawed into the piled luggage and came up with a small red cheese. Again there were cheers from the others as Rusnick cut pieces from it. The lieutenants looked questioningly at Captain MacRae and then back and forth among themselves. Cutler raised his eyebrows and when they all nodded, went over to Captain MacRae.

"Come on, MacRae," he said, "have a drink with us."

Captain MacRae rolled over slowly.

"Why not," he said morosely as he sat up. He put his booted feet on the floor and sat with his hands on his knees until Rusnick handed him a cup.

"Cheers," said Chivington gaily waving his cup before he

downed the liquor. He came up sputtering.

"What kind of whiskey is that?" he asked belligerently.

"Do you like it?" asked Jensen. "It's called Elsie's Fancy and it's a real bargain."

"Very unusual," said Chivington reaching rapidly for a slice of cheese.

"You ought to see Elsie," said Jensen passing around the empty bottle so that they could see the label. Elsie was pictured as a voluptuous redhead with her green dress falling off her shoulders.

Duval whistled through his teeth and flashed his dark eyes knowingly.

"We'll make her the cabin mascot," said Jensen. "Soak off the label and paste her to the porthole." He put the bottle in the small basin and turned on the water. It was cold and salty. Elsie showed no inclination to unglue herself so he left the bottle soaking.

Captain MacRae looked once more around the cabin and then swinging his legs into the berth, turned again toward the wall.

"Well," said Rusnick, "guess we better turn in." He took off his boots. Chivington finished arranging his bed, tucking his life preserver carefully in against the wall. He undressed and put on a pair of pajamas with a monogram on the pocket.

"Hey," he said to Jensen, "get Elsie out of the sink so I can brush my teeth."

"My God!" said Duval, "I think I'm going to be seasick tonight."

"It's all in your mind," said Cutler, who himself felt as though perhaps cheese and Elsie's Fancy had not been an ideal combination.

Jensen finally peeled the label off the bottle and carefully smoothed it out against the glassy, blacked-out porthole.

"There," he said happily, "pretty as a mountain girl."

"Come on," said Rusnick, "douse the light."

Jensen dropped his boots and climbed up to his berth. The light was turned off before he was settled up there, and the others could hear him thrashing around trying to fix his blankets. He sat up, bumped his head hard on the ceiling, and swore.

"Quiet," yelled Rusnick and slowly, in the dark, each man relaxed again into his own individuality.

Duval lay still on his back feeling the churning of his stomach as the cabin shifted slightly back and forth, back and forth. He wished that he had skipped the whiskey tonight on this queasy sea where nothing seemed to stand quite still. Whiskey, he thought, was bad luck to him and he ought to remember it by now.

Rusnick concentrated on going to sleep. He was a practical man who did things in the most direct way. He just shut off his thinking and slept.

Cutler thought of the afternoon and their withdrawal from the land while the gulls followed the ship out, and he thought of Helen. He wondered what lay ahead for him as he headed out into the unknown.

Chivington stretched out in comfort. His pajamas were clean and pressed, just as they had come from the laundry, and he couldn't help being pleased with his own foresight. Life was very simple if you just knew what you wanted and planned ahead.

Jensen thought of Elsie, the mountain girl, with peach fresh skin and laughing eyes and sensuously imagined her coming to him in the night.

Captain MacRae lay longest awake. He had dark murderous thoughts which turned inward, twisting in his brain. He loved and hated Fran. If she would not love him, give him a son, he would gladly kill her, he thought fiercely, but he was powerless here on the dark sea.

XVII

At sunrise next morning the whole ship was teeming with men. The silent departure was behind. They were at sea in convoy; and on the clear sunny day, their natural good nature and exuberance returned.

The sea was relatively calm, stretched out around them and filled as far as they could see with gray ships. It was impossible to count them for behind each ship were others. The *Caieta* steamed ahead pushing before its bow one wave which trailed off endlessly on either side.

The men lined up unshaven for breakfast in their life jackets, joking, fooling, banging their mess kits, stretching after the first night in the hold. At the head of the mess lines, army cooks were serving the first hot meal at sea. The food was lumpy, greenish-gray, and flecked with black pepper. It was the consistency of water-logged cardboard. The men had never seen anything like it.

"What in hell is this?" asked Pulska as his mess kit was filled.

"Navy eggs," said the army mess sergeant grinning. "Made out of powdered eggs, powdered milk and salt water."

"Like fun it is," said Pulska.

"It's the powdered eggs," said the mess sergeant. "The cook's never worked with them before, but we'll get the hang of it one of these mornings."

"Well, let's not waste much time," said Pulska. "If I eat this, I'll be seasick and if I don't, I'll starve."

The line moved slowly and as the mess kits were filled, the men gathered in little groups to eat. There was a great deal of griping about the powdered eggs. Sergeant Pulska moved from group to group.

"What's the matter with you?" he asked. "Griping about the food on a cruise to Europe! You never had it so good."

As the men finished, again they formed lines, this time to wash out the mess kits in big barrels of steaming water in readiness for the only other meal of the day many hours away.

All morning men lounged on deck in the sun using life preservers for pillows. They talked, some read, groups broke out cards and soon there were men rolling dice and playing poker surrounded by circles of kibitzers. There were some seasick soldiers at the rail, but mostly there was an air of excitement and novelty on this first brisk morning at sea. Men wandered the decks curiously examining the ship and watching the navy gun crews going through dry runs, with the anti-aircraft guns. The crews worked together like a machine. Their timing and rhythm drew an army audience as, with extra precision this morning, they went through the orders. When they finished, the GIs cheered. Surely they couldn't be attacked here in the middle of a convoy with all those guns on their side.

Each day on board the rumors grew. Some thought that the division was headed for England, some to Africa, some claimed a direct landing in France, a corporal in C Company was taking bets on Norway. A private claimed to have talked with a sailor who knew for a fact that they were going to Algiers. A sergeant claimed a lieutenant told him the ship was going to the Balkans to join the Russians and attack Austria from the rear. Pools were formed, but for the most part men were apathetic. Wherever they went, it was army and fighting ahead. There wasn't much choice.

Up on the officers' deck, Colonel Spaulding was finally happy. He jovially clapped junior officers on the back, lavishly distributed cigars from the private stock which he had brought aboard, and generally enjoyed himself. He made himself a nuisance to the ship's captain with constant questions about the zigzag proceedings of the convoy, about submarines, about torpedoes, about landing procedure. Wearing his life jacket, he looked enormous and more like a walrus than ever. He studied maps and drew his officers into discussions of strategy. He awed them. They had never seen him so active. He quickly knew the officers of the medical unit aboard and held long discussions with them on evacuation of wounded troops. He made suggestions, kindled their interest. He held regular morning meetings with his offi-

112

cers. In short, during those lazy days at sea, he became a human dynamo.

Each day as he went over maneuvers with his officers, from the deck below came the solid plink, plink, of the widening rims of fifty-cent pieces which the men were constantly dropping against the deck, over and over again, while they talked and waited. Slowly, as the ship pushed its wave ahead through the days, the coins widened at the edges, and finally the men cut out the centers and wore the thickened rims as rings.

Some days they sailed through rain and fog, and on these days the cold damp winds blew low over the rolling gray ocean. There were days when the general quarters alarm was sounded, but never anything to see. The voyage was monotonous. Gradually the weather improved. During the third week the weather became warmer, and the convoy left radiant sunsets behind. Men brought out banjos and harmonicas and sang at the end of the day. As they sang, "You Are My Sunshine" or "Lay That Pistol Down, Babe," it was easy to forget that they were on the way to war.

Finally there was the early morning when Donald Cutler came sleepily on deck to see suddenly before him the mass of Gibraltar looming silently in mist. The rising sun glinted through clouds on parts of the massive rock. As they passed through the straits, the light increased; and Cutler saw the rising mists swirl in the upper air and vanish, unveiling the naked rock. To the north lay Europe, to the south, the low coast of Africa. Between the continents Cutler felt strangely awed thinking of the history of this crossroads of land and sea.

He knew that long ago there had been no joining of sea and ocean, and elephants had wandered across the isthmus to leave their bones in Spain. The ancients credited Hercules with having forced the breakthrough which joined the waters of the cold Atlantic with those of the warm Mediterranean Sea, here, where their waters now mingled. Looking back as they passed the Rock, Cutler wondered at the courage of ancient sailors who had dared to venture from these "gates of Hercules" into the waters of the unknown Atlantic. He found himself again longing for peace so that he might be free to follow the history of the lands surrounding this interesting sea.

It was on that day that the booklets about Italy were distributed, and the demands of modern warfare quickly supplanted his musings on the past.

Private Millen and Corporal Delaney sat on the deck trying to learn Italian from the manual. They had recruited the help of Private Corelli, who spoke Italian fluently and was exuberantly headed back to the land from which his parents had come.

"Oh, boy," said Corelli, "the time I'm going to have! Mama Mia! All the beautiful girls I can talk to!" The men gathered round.

"Who wants to talk to them?" asked Millen. "Just tell us how to say 'Let's go to bed, honey.'" The men laughed raucously.

"Sure, Corelli, how do you say that?" asked Benard.

Corelli looked at them shrewdly. "Lessons like that," he said, "cost money."

"Ah, Corelli," said Delaney, "come off it. We're all your pals."

Corelli thought it over. "OK," he said, "as long as I get first pick."

"OK," they chorused.

Corelli went to work. He taught them useful phrases such as—"Where have you been all my life?" "You're a beautiful girl." "I need you, honey." "How about a snuggle." "Hold me tight, baby."

The men learned rapidly. In no time at all they were exceedingly pleased with their progress and the phrases were by-words on board.

The war in Italy had started with landings in Sicily and then spread to the beaches of Salerno. Punching ashore, American troops had gained a beachhead foot by foot against heavy German opposition. The LST's had spewed forth men, tanks, guns, supplies over heavily contested land.

As the Fifth Army forced its way inland, taking Salerno, the Germans had retreated leaving the harbor of Naples in shambles, sunken ships blocking the docks. The advances were hard won. Engineers moved forward clearing mine fields, filling in craters, building temporary bridges but always just ahead of them were more demolitions, more mines, more booby traps. They cleared the worst of the destruction from Naples Harbor and soon Allied ships were struggling to unload at the battered docks. Unloading went on round the clock except when interrupted by air raids. Then everything stopped while Allied planes rose in pursuit and ack-ack crisscrossed the sky.

The water was gray-green, flecked with white caps as the *Caieta,* waiting her turn, pitched on the choppy sea beneath barrage balloons which floated against the lead-gray sky. GIs lined the rails, contrasting the olive drab of their uniforms against the gray of the ship. Before them lay the curve of the Bay of Naples dominated in the background by the slopes of Mount Vesuvius. In every direction the old battered hulks of sunken ships lay tipped and twisted, tortured to submission by bombings and demolition. Allied salvage boats were working with cranes dragging at the tangled metal.

To Donald Cutler, it was exciting to come to Italy. To him, the past and present mingled in this landing. He saw the cluttered bay but, for the moment, his mind eliminated the gray skys and the destruction. Here was the vacation land of emperors—the Isle of Capri, Sorrento, villas of wealthy Romans. Here were the isles and grottoes of the legendary mermaids and ashore still lived old fishermen who claimed to have seen, long ago, when young and full of wine, real mermaids playing in the waves.

To Donald Cutler, this was a land of beauty, of myth, held only temporarily in the grip of one more war. To him, this was a coast explored by Phoenicians, Etruscans, and Greeks. Here men had braved whirlpools and rocks and the anger of their gods. Here, on these shores, many a ship had floundered in wind and storm. Here nearby, Aeneas had been shipwrecked and gone in quest of the sibyl at Cumae.

Cutler's eye traveled down the sloping side of Vesuvius noting the grace of the line. He thought of Pompeii and of that day in 79 AD when this same volcano had buried that city almost intact. He knew that the excavations of that ancient city must lie there now somewhere on the southern base of the mountain. The whole area was of volcanic origin. It was a land of legend. He thought of the old tales of the nearby Lago d'Averno which the ancients had believed to be the entrance to Hades because of the noxious fumes which rose from the ground and destroyed all birds. He had read of it in Virgil and of how Aeneas, after his shipwreck, was shown the way into the underworld by the

Cumaean sibyl. She had been famous for her prophecies. He would like, he thought, to walk into that famous cavern where men had come seeking the sibyl for answers to the riddle of their futures. Perhaps he, like Aeneas, was landing on this coast to be led into hell. He thought of the mythical Charon, dread ferryman guiding souls over the lake of the dead, and he shook himself. Surely such morbid mythology should not dominate his arrival. He remembered with relief that Aeneas had returned from Hades to his destined work, but only because he was specially favored by the gods.

As Cutler looked about, he longed again for peace for it seemed to him that this wrecked harbor lying under the clouded sky was indeed the entrance to a modern hell.

As the *Caieta* went in the harbor, waters lapped gently, deceptively, against the rusting wreckage and inshore seaweed rose and fell on the shifting sea. The buildings clinging to the sides of steep hillsides which sloped abruptly into the sea showed much destruction.

As the ship was secured, crowds of ragged children gathered at dock side. They sang shrilly "Pistol Packin' Mama" and watched eagerly as the soldiers struggled bulkily down the gangplanks with all their gear. There was a great deal of equipment. Each pack contained a blanket, shelter half and pins, pole and rope, raincoat, mess kit with knife, fork and spoon. Over the shoulders of each soldier hung a rifle and a gas mask. Other gear swung from rifle belts. Helmets were on at all angles, some tilted back on the head, some down over the eyes, some rolled to the ground followed quickly by an oath.

The children watched them come off the ship. Soldiers were already familiar to these scavengers of Naples.

"*Caramelle, caramelle,*" they cried, pushing and shoving to be in the front.

It was strange to be on land again after almost a month at sea. The stability beneath their feet was deceptive. It seemed to the soldiers that the land rocked gently, coming up unexpectedly beneath their feet as they walked. They joked about it as they noisily adjusted their gear and assembled by platoons to be loaded into trucks and driven from the docks.

The trucks went slowly through streets of shattered build-

116

ings and broken pavement. Destruction was everywhere. Buildings gaped with open sides or without roofs. Dusty rubble lay where it had been pushed aside. Twisted iron balconies hung from the walls and everywhere sullen, hungry people gathered as the division rolled by, truckload after truckload, on the way north to a bivouac area. The destruction about them, both physical and human, quieted the men. The war which they sought lay ahead of them to the north.

XVIII

Colonel Spaulding's jeep stood under the protecting branches of a large olive tree. On its side the official white numbers gleamed freshly on the rain-washed surface. The driver had carefully put up side flaps to protect the elaborate upholstered seat with deep springs which had been installed beside the driver's place for the colonel's use. It had been Chivington's idea, and it pleased Colonel Spaulding very much.

It still rained, but not as hard as before. Across the muddy roadway from the jeep, a sentry walked up and down before the headquarters tent. Inside the tent, with the front flaps up, sat Colonel Spaulding and Major Van Tuyl facing each other across folding tables which were cluttered with papers spread out between them. In one corner a clerk worked at a typewriter flanked by portable files. The sound of the machine punctuated the slow dripping of the rain on the canvas.

Messengers came and went dragging muddy boots. Company runners waited huddled in raincoats under the gray-green branches of an olive tree.

Major Van Tuyl rose from his chair, stretched his neck and shoulders, and turned to the corporal.

"Send an inquiry to Company C," he said, "to find out if a Private Nolan has checked in as replacement yet."

"Yes, sir," said the corporal inserting a blank in the typewriter.

Van Tuyl went to the tent entrance and looked out. They were surrounded by other tents. Far down the muddy road to the right, a company was being marched out for drill; and through the quiet sound of the typewriter, Van Tuyl could hear the muffled orders—"Hut, two, tree, foa."

As he watched, a jeep came churning up the muddy road. A sergeant with red hair stuck out his head and yelled at a runner who waited under the tree.

118

"Hey, bub," he yelled, "where's the colonel of this outfit hang his hat?"

The tent was pointed out. The jeep churned forward again and stopped in front of the tent. The driver leaned over the wheel while a large man with glasses backed slowly out of the jeep bringing with him a field pack and a very battered portable typewriter. Van Tuyl was puzzled about the man's rank until he spotted the arm band of a war correspondent.

"Here comes the press!" said Van Tuyl quickly to Colonel Spaulding.

Spaulding looked up with annoyance. "Damn it," he said. "Wind it up fast."

The man from the jeep came up to Van Tuyl at the tent entrance. He looked about forty and had lost most of his front hair.

"I'm Hutchins," he said, "—Allied Press Releases, featured column in fifty-four dailies." He held out a plump hand which Van Tuyl shook.

"Glad to know you, Hutchins," said Van Tuyl introducing himself. "What can we do you for?"

"Well," said Hutchins genially, "I'm here to see how the GI lives, doing a feature on the final training for battle, all that kind of stuff," he said.

"I see," said Van Tuyl. "Suppose you talk it over with the colonel." He introduced them.

Colonel Spaulding beamed at the correspondent. "You've come to the right place," said the colonel heartily. "How long have you been in Italy, Hutchins?"

"Three days," said the correspondent.

"We've been here two weeks," said Spaulding, "and this is the best damn battalion in the Fifth Army. Our training is complete right now. We're just waiting for orders. We've got more fighting power, better officers, more guts in this battalion than you'll find anywhere in Italy. You put this in your report— Colonel Spaulding's battalion is ready for action as of now. These men know how to shoot straight and fast, and I'll match them with anything the Wehrmacht has to offer because I know that they are ready."

"Do you mean," asked Hutchins taking out a small notebook,

"that you consider your battalion well ahead of the rest of the division?"

"You're damn tootin' that's what I mean," said Spaulding. "We're one aggressive bunch."

"Well, that's fine," said Hutchins writing in the notebook. "How was this training accomplished?"

"The same way anything's accomplished," said Spaulding. "Hard work, no coddling, plenty of toughening. That's the way to take care of men in a command. And we'll train right up to the time we enter the line, which should be pretty soon," he added.

"What do you think of Germans as fighters?" asked Hutchins.

"I respect them," said Spaulding. "They are well trained, but they're fighting a losing battle and should know it by now. We're going to push them all the way to Berlin and then take on the Japs."

"You mean your battalion is going to do this?" asked the correspondent raising his eyebrows quizzically.

"Why not?" asked Spaulding, staring him down.

"Okay, sir," said Hutchins, shrugging his heavy shoulders.

"The main thing," said Spaulding confidentially, "is to build up morale. Give the outfit confidence. Now you take your position," he said to Hutchins. "You're in a unique position to spread confidence and improve morale. You can write a feature that makes people discouraged or you can write a feature that reflects confidence. People are just waiting to see which it will be and then follow along. You newsmen are pace setters. I wonder whether you realize your importance?"

Spaulding watched Hutchins carefully. Van Tuyl was thinking that to observe the colonel at work was an education in itself.

Hutchins shifted his feet.

"Speaking of morale," he said, "there are three sacks of mail in the back of the jeep."

"That's splendid," said Spaulding. "We'll have it distributed while you are here and you can write about that too."

They got rid of Hutchins by appointing a corporal to show him around. He was to visit each of the companies in turn, and Van Tuyl dispatched runners with this news to the company commanders.

The sky was still gray, but the rain had stopped; and from the front of the tent Colonel Spaulding and Major Van Tuyl could see through the clearing mists as far as the Villa d'Alenzo which perched on the hillside to the north. Below the old villa lay gardens leading down to a columned garden house which sat atop a massive retaining wall. Below the wall lay terraced vineyards which merged with the olive grove. The old trees dripped dampness now as the companies marched through the mud to the mess tents for the noon meal.

As they watched from the tent, reluctant to step into the mud outside, Spaulding and Van Tuyl could see a brightening of sky and land as though some hand were on a giant rheostat and the crescendo of light would be complete and absolute when the hidden sun soon burst forth. They could see the stooped figure of an old man outlined against the colonnade of the villa high up the slope. He also watched the changing light as the mists swirled above the olive grove, and he searched through it for the still hidden mass of Vesuvius far to the south. Then his eyes dropped to the tent city in his olive grove. His curiosity and interest were evident.

"It must be the Count d'Alenzo," said Van Tuyl to Spaulding.

"We're supposed to maintain friendly relations," said Spaulding thoughtfully. "Like to see the Villa?"

"Sure," said Van Tuyl.

"I think," said Spaulding, "that it would be wise for a few of us to call on him officially. I'll take you and Chivington, full dress uniform, 1530 hours.

"Yes, sir," said Van Tuyl, and the two men left the tent to cross the road to the officers' mess.

In the villa, Contessa Lucia d'Alenzo sat brooding at the massive fruitwood table in the dining hall. Maria had cleared the lunch dishes long ago; and now Lucia sat in the dim, damp, room unaware of the passage of time, suspended almost in a state of numbness, unaware of her surroundings. She lived deep in the inexorable despair which possessed her. Her agony showed on her tearless face from which her dark hair was swept back smoothly and caught just above the nape of her neck. She was small boned, almost delicate, with large eyes hollowed now with shadows.

The old count, her father, had left the table more than an hour before, going to his library across the gallery, feeling that helplessness which is particularly pathetic in old men. Because for years he had read after lunch, he continued the old habit finding solace in the mellowed leather of old books and finding a larger world in their pages.

Lucia stared straight before her into the polished grainings of the old table lost in the intricate patternings of her own depression.

When the door to the kitchens opened she did not look up. She knew it was Maria, and she wished Maria would leave her alone. Ever since their trip from Rome, Maria had hovered over her. The concern of the old woman irritated her. She wished to be left alone.

"Have a little wine," said Maria coaxingly.

"Thank you, no," said Lucia formally.

"It will ease you," said Maria setting a glass before her.

"Nothing will ever ease me," said Lucia d'Alenzo.

"You must try," said the old woman bobbing her head back and forth.

Ignoring the wine, Lucia rose from the table and slowly made her way through the gallery with its carved beams to the room where the count sat reading before a small fire. Maria watched her go and taking the wine from the table, carried it back through the kitchen door, mumbling as she went.

As Colonel Spaulding, Major Van Tuyl, and Lieutenant Chivington climbed into the jeep that afternoon the sun was shining brilliantly. The three officers were immaculate—clean shaven, brass and leather gleaming. The driver was Corelli, promoted already to sergeant because of his knowledge of Italian and usefulness to headquarters. He was present now as official interpreter as well as driver. In the jeep was a large box of canned meats and vegetables as a present for the count. Colonel Spaulding inspected the jeep, well pleased as he climbed into his upholstered seat.

They drove slowly up the long cypress-lined drive. The tops of the trees were slashed and broken by artillery, but actually this section was not badly damaged. Through here, the Germans had withdrawn rapidly to consolidate on higher ground some miles north.

As the jeep climbed the hill from the olive grove, the vista widened giving a greater view of the terrain. They could see Mount Vesuvius to the south. Van Tuyl looked back at the rolling hills, thinking he might, from one of the twists in the road, be able to see Naples Harbor, but he was disappointed.

"Listen, men," said Spaulding turning in his seat. "Intelligence briefed me on this count. Seems he came down through the lines from Rome. He turned up in Naples with valuable information, so we're supposed to treat him right and keep him happy."

"What did he tell them?" asked Van Tuyl.

"How do I know," said Spaulding, "but it must have been good to rate him the red carpet treatment."

Chivington sat quietly enjoying the view from the hill and thinking that, if it weren't wartime, he might sometime like to have a villa in Italy.

Surrounded by overgrown lawns scarred here and there by small craters stood the villa. It was a mellow old building somewhat battered now. Several windows were boarded up; and as they approached the weathered door, studded with huge nail heads and ornate iron hinges, an old gray hound which had been sleeping on the steps began to bark. He bared his teeth but at the same time cringed back against the door. Corelli rang the bell rope as Spaulding composed himself on the doorstep with Van Tuyl and Chivington behind him. They waited silently hearing far away the rumble of distant artillery.

At last the door moved on its hinges. As it opened, a little old woman with a white cap on her head peered out, and the timid dog brushed by her skirts and disappeared within.

Sergeant Corelli stepped forward. In Italian he introduced the three officers and explained that they had come to call on the Count d'Alenzo bringing a gift from the United States Army.

The woman hesitated but finally opened the door admitting them to a paneled entrance hall. She mumbled something and disappeared.

"She says to wait here," said Corelli enjoying his linguistic advantage over the officers.

The men waited standing on the marble floor until they

began to feel like small boys waiting to be admitted to a special adult sanctum. Chivington dusted off his bars, Van Tuyl cracked his knuckles, and Spaulding found it necessary continually to clear his throat. Corelli lounged against the door frame nonchalantly.

The woman came back and led them the way she had come. The visitors advanced over old carpets laid on floors tiled in mosaic marble. They passed doorways as they walked down a long hall hung with faded tapestries. With Corelli following and carrying the box, they were led into a huge beamed room.

There in the shadows before a huge gaping fireplace sat a small man in a tall-backed, red velvet chair. As they approached, he put down a leather-bound book on the small inlaid table beside him. He was keen-eyed but frail looking, almost yellowed, and on each side of his shiny bald head grew a grizzled fringe of gray hair. He looked at them with an air of tolerant amusement. It was impossible to guess his age, but Spaulding thought that he must be at least seventy-five, wondering at the same time if he could possibly be a well-preserved ninety.

"Welcome to the Villa d'Alenzo," said the count in English, rising graciously and extending a long slim hand on which a large gold-seal ring glinted in the dim light.

Corelli stepped back realizing that his knowledge of Italian would not be needed.

Stiffly Colonel Spaulding introduced himself and the others.

"We have brought a small gift," said Spaulding indicating the box of canned goods.

"We thank you for your consideration," said the count formally bowing from the waist. With a sweep of his hand he directed their attention to the other side of the fireplace.

There hidden in a huge wing chair sat a dark-eyed woman. Her hair was sleek and caught together at the back. She was watching them intensely. Her eyes seemed completely unguarded, as though by looking into them one could read her thoughts; but in spite of her direct gaze, she remained an enigma. She had an air of lethargy about her, of patience tried to exhaustion, of the resignation which lies beyond bitterness. Her dress, plain except for a delicate lace collar, blended with the upholstery of the chair, leaving the accent of her face and hands

124

against dark drapery like an old portrait.

Spaulding was startled. He had walked into the room without seeing anyone but the count, and now his sudden awareness of this woman had given him the impression that she had magically appeared at the moment in which the count had flung back his hand. Repeating the names of the three officers, the count said, "May I present my daughter, Contessa Lucia d'Alenzo."

She spoke quietly to Colonel Spaulding. "We knew that in time someone would come," she said slowly. Her English was not as facile as the count's, and she spoke with a distortion of accent which added a certain mystery to the simple sentence. It made a strange impression on Spaulding.

Sergeant Corelli still held the box. His confidence had disappeared. The count's English had reduced his importance.

"Maria," said the count to the old woman in Italian, "show the soldier where to put down the box."

Maria and the sergeant went out and the door was shut.

"We regret the necessity of using your grounds," said Spaulding collecting himself. "The men have been directed not to harm the olive trees or to bother you in any way. We trust that you will let us know at once if any difficulties arise while we are here."

"Certainly, Colonel," said the count. "We appreciate your concern. Your troops in the olive grove are a small inconvenience beside what we have already experienced in this war."

"Your services to the forces are much appreciated at Allied Headquarters," said Spaulding, wondering how this frail man had survived his trip from Rome and to what extent he had been motivated by a desire to protect this villa full of antiques.

"My services are small," said the count, "beside the services of your country in liberating Italy."

Chivington glanced about him. The large windows at the near end of the room were boarded over, darkening the room. Part of the terrazzo floor was broken. An ugly crack scarred the wall above the fireplace; but even so, the room was beautiful. At the far end, long glass doors, still intact, opened onto the terrace facing south with a view over rolling hills of vineyards and olive groves to where Mount Vesuvius rose surrounded this afternoon in faint haze.

Maria came back carrying a small tray of wine and glasses, and Chivington sipped slowly savoring the excellence of the count's wine.

"Sir," said Major Van Tuyl, "we are much interested in your trip from the north. Would you care to tell us about it?"

There was an embarrassed pause. The woman gave a little gasp.

"Certainly," said the count gruffly. "It will give you more reason to fight."

Colonel Spaulding, turning toward the woman, saw her stricken face as she rose in confusion.

"Excuse me," she stammered as she rapidly went to the door and hurried off down the long hall.

"Oh," said Van Tuyl about to apologize, but the count silenced him.

"She is a woman," said the count, "and should never have had to make the trip. She cannot yet talk of it."

"I had no idea," stammered Van Tuyl, who dared not meet Colonel Spaulding's eye.

"We were living in Rome," began the count. "My property was confiscated by the Fascists. We were forced to find rooms. They thought I was an old man. They thought an old man could not harm them, but they were wrong. They were wrong," he said again deliberately nodding his head slowly up and down. "I have struck them a blow!" His eyes gleamed. "It has been costly, but I have shown them that the Count d'Alenzo is not defenseless." He stopped talking and stared into the shadows over their heads. They waited for him to resume. The large gilt clock on the carved mantel ticked in the gloom. Spaulding stirred uneasily in his chair.

Suddenly the count turned and looked him full in the face.

"The Huns are in Rome again," said the count quietly, but his face was almost purple. "I work for the free Italy that Garibaldi envisioned in my father's time." He waved his arms. "Camp in our olive groves, blow up the countryside, drive the Huns out; but when you are through, let us have a free Italy."

He talked on. To the officers sitting in the chairs before him, the atmosphere of the room became almost unbearable.

"We came like refugees," said the count, "asking no favors or

126

consideration, only the right to return south; and they killed him, they killed him in front of my daughter, shot him down!" The count stood by the fireplace quietly pounding a clenched fist into his open palm. His eyes were cold, furious. The count's controlled voice was so completely at variance with his appearance and with what he was saying that it reminded Van Tuyl of a steam boiler getting up steam with all the valves shut. *God!* thought Van Tuyl apprehensively, *he'll have a stroke.*

"I tell you this so that you will understand," said the count.

"Surely," said Spaulding embarrassed by the emotion of the old man. "We understand."

"Ah," said the count, "you think you do, but as yet you do not. Wait until you fight your way to Rome. By the time you reach Rome, you will understand. That I can guarantee." There was a long pause.

"But let us speak of something more pleasant," said d'Alenzo resuming his seat by the fire. "Do any of you have an interest in books or antiques?"

"Yes, sir," said Chivington nervously. Spaulding and Van Tuyl were relieved to have him take over the conversation.

"Indeed," said the count graciously. "Perhaps you will be interested in some of my family pieces. The chair you are sitting on is sixteenth century. The carving is unusual, is it not?"

Chivington rose to admire the chair. He knew that Colonel Spaulding was watching him with approval. For a junior officer, this was heady satisfaction. The count pointed out a chest and explained a hanging, as gradually his color returned to normal. Lieutenant Chivington listened with interest asking questions when the count paused.

When the colonel rose to go, the count said, "Perhaps you will call again soon. We have few visitors now and enjoy any opportunity for conversation. We should like to welcome you again."

"Thank you," said Spaulding with military correctness. "Please let me know when it will be convenient."

"I shall send you a note," said the count, "and you must bring back this young man who likes my furniture."

Maria came and led them back through the gallery to the entrance hall. Looking back, Chivington saw the count pick up the leather book from the table.

Sergeant Corelli was waiting in the jeep. He was slumped in the driver's seat with his hat down over his eyes and his feet stuck out over the folded-down windshield. He sat upright quickly as the officers marched stiffly down the shallow steps.

As they drove down the drive, Major Van Tuyl finally relaxed. "God," he said, "fighting is easier than that!"

Colonel Spaulding chuckled, "Don't let it worry you," he said.

"Did you ever expect to call on a count?" asked Lieutenant Chivington.

"Really quite an experience," said Colonel Spaulding. "How formal he was."

"I certainly put my foot in it with the daughter," said Van Tuyl wiping his forehead.

"She speaks English," said Spaulding thoughtfully.

"These Italians have a great sense of family," said Chivington. "That daughter is a real aristocrat."

"Sure," said Van Tuyl, "a sad countess living imprisoned in a villa waiting to be liberated. She looked spiritless to me."

"Some women have too much spirit," said Spaulding thinking of his wife.

"Was it her husband who was killed?" asked Chivington.

Spaulding shrugged his shoulders. "Intelligence doesn't tell me everything," he said.

"The old boy seemed lonesome," said Van Tuyl, "but it could be quite a strain if he expects us to entertain him often."

"I think he's a charming old gentleman," said Chivington, "a real aristocrat. He reminds me of my grandfather."

Spaulding was silent. For some strange reason, Van Tuyl's remark about the woman waiting to be rescued had seemed to him very apt. Perhaps it was because of his surprise in turning and discovering her there in the chair, or what she had said about knowing that they would come; but somehow he couldn't shake the impression she had made on him with her solemn dark eyes. He wanted now to be quiet himself, sampling the kind of resignation and timelessness which he had felt in her before Van Tuyl upset her with his question.

Sergeant Corelli said nothing, but he was wondering what

was so all-fired important about an old man that had managed to inherit a villa and some old furniture. The sergeant's democracy lacked reverence. He considered himself as good as the next man, and it irked him to see deference to this titled old man with his faded velvet and books and antiques. *What the hell,* he thought, *the old bastard couldn't drive a jeep if his life depended on it.*

XIX

The following letters were among the mail brought by Hutchins' jeep to the bivouac area for Company C————
Letter to Colonel Malcolm Spaulding from Alice Spaulding Van Tuyl:

Dear Daddy,

I wonder just where you will be when you get this, and I am writing to let you know that Mother and I found a nice house in San Antonio. It has seven rooms and four bedrooms so Mother says that we will be able to have old friends visit us here if they are passing through. We also have a nice garden in the back with a tree that shades a little patio. Mother says we were very lucky to find it and we never would have if Bea Whiting, you remember Major and Mrs. Whiting—we knew them at Benning—well he is a full colonel now and Bea knew about the house and got it for us through a friend. Mother is very happy about it and so am I except that it does seem very lonesome with you and the battalion gone and nothing to do but shop and go out to meals or movies. Mother and Bea are very busy all the time, and sometimes I go along. We saw a cute skit at the Officers' Club last week about the army and the navy. The army won of course.

I wish that I had something to do with my time. Do you have any ideas of something I can do? Would you mind if I got a job? Mother seems to think that I can't do anything or shouldn't tie myself down. What do you think?

I hope everything is going well with you. If you need anything special, just let me know and I will try to get it and send it to you.

With love,
Alice

Letter to Lieutenant Duval from Mrs. Violet Spaulding:

Duval—you charmer. Have you any idea how much I miss you? Really I am sure you have not or you would have written long before this to reassure a good friend. It was simply devastating to have the battalion go, and I think that of all my friends I miss you most. Do let me know how you are. Do you ever think of me? Do be careful. You must take good care of yourself and not expose yourself to needless danger. You mean a great deal to me you know, and I am lonesome for you. Life is dull, dull, dull.

Affectionately,
V.

P.S. Please burn this note.

Letter to Private Millen from Miss Mary Realey:

Dear Mitch,

This is just to say I miss you, big boy. It's like they say—some men are more important to a girl than others. I hope you'll be back this way before too long and drop in again. Meanwhile how's about writing me a post card now and then?

I tell the girls where I work what a good guy you are, how you took me to the beach your last leave. We really had us a time, didn't we! Brother—I'll never forget it. I trust you are sober again by now. I'll never forget that look on the cop's face when you finally offered him the popcorn all polite and nice. It was a howl, and you got a real sense of humor, and I'm not kidding. I thought them two sailors would die of apoplexy they was so mad when the cop let you off. I got to hand it to you, big boy, you've got a glib tongue in your head to outtalk an Irish cop.

Well—all for now pal. See you around.

Love,
Mary

Letter to Major Van Tuyl from Alice Spaulding Van Tuyl:

Dear Husband—

It seems so strange to call you that even though I should be used to it by now. How are you? Well I hope. It seems as though I have so much to say to you that I don't know where to start. If only

I'd had the sense to marry you sooner, we could have talked about so much by now.

Mother and I have a nice house. It is really bigger than we needed, but Mother liked it so here we are all settled in San Antonio. We have a nice garden and I am going to plant things out there some day soon just the way old Miss Jarvis taught us to in botany last year. It makes me laugh to think of last year now. I never dreamed I'd be married and settled down so soon. It still makes me feel so funny when someone calls me Mrs. Van Tuyl. I went downtown and opened some charge accounts, and I swear I hardly think the stores believed me when I said that I was Mrs. Van Tuyl. Maybe I should start wearing older-looking clothes or something. Honestly, I feel like a character in a play.

Daddy's last letter said that you were doing splendid work. Isn't that nice. He wouldn't say it unless he meant it. I hope that you will watch Daddy and see that he doesn't overdo. Sometimes he goes about things in such a fierce way that I worry about him getting hurt even if Mother thinks it's silly. She says he's tough and thrives on war just the way he likes to hunt those bears in Alaska.

Mother says no man likes his wife to have a job. Do you feel this way about it? I have so much spare time that I have been wondering whether I could do something useful. Will you please let me know whether you agree with Mother.

The postman will be coming soon so I must close.

Your loving wife,
Alice

Letter to Captain Richard MacRae from Fran MacRae:

Dear Rich—

Wherever this reaches you I hope you are well and feeling fine. I don't really know how to start this letter. I ought to prepare you because it may come as a shock to you, but I guess you can take it so here goes.

You know as well as I do that before you left we weren't getting on so well. I think we both gave it a good try but actually if a thing isn't right, it just isn't right and there's not much anybody can do about it, especially with the war on and all. What all this is leading up to is that I want a divorce. I just don't think that we should stay married since we have nothing in common any more. There is

Diana, of course, and I know how you feel about her and because of that I'm perfectly willing to be cooperative about you seeing her whenever you want. I won't make any trouble there although I think that you will agree that at her age the court will probably give her to me. And anyway, how would you ever take care of her now? I won't ask for much alimony which is a break for you, but I do think you ought to give support money for Diana. You realize, don't you, that I could demand a lot of alimony and claim desertion since you stayed away in those last weeks at Carver even though you were free part of the time and could have come home anytime. My lawyer tells me that could be built up as part of the case; but, of course, I don't want trouble and just want to get this over with as soon as possible. As soon as I hear from you, I plan to go to Reno and wind the thing up on grounds of incompatibility. That's exactly what it was. We just didn't get on so well together, and five years from now you will thank me for your freedom even though right now you may not believe it. Let's be sophisticated about this and get it over with quickly. All you have to do is sign some papers which the lawyer will send you. Simple, isn't it?

I don't mean to upset you with this. You must not be sentimental and stupid about it. I am sure that you will be able to find another wife anytime you want to be married again, and Diana can visit you. I'll tell the lawyer to put that in the papers. After all, you are her daddy, and she is fond of you. We'll all be friends if you will just accept this and not fight it because it won't do you any good to delay because I am going to divorce you some way or another.

Fran

Letter to Lieutenant Jensen from his father:

Dear Son—

Your letter came saying you was in Italy. Ma got out the atlas and showed Milly and Buzz where you was at and I must say it seems like you're a long way from home. I'm not one for writing letters, as you know, but I want you to know that we're proud of you and it's men like you that will keep this country decent and strong. We brought you up to be a real mountain man son and I reckon you know what a rattlesnake deserves.

Buzz seems awful anxious to join up too an' I recon he will soon

133

as his birthday comes. Your ma won't even talk about it but she'll be O.K. when it comes time for him to go.

Your Aunt Rachel was up on Sunday. She says Betsey is studying typewriting and aims to be a secretary. Old doc Henshaw fell down stairs and broke his own arm which was a mess because there weren't nobody around could set it for him so they had to take him all the way to the city. Said he was an honery patient—told them how to do everything.

Milly is busy with the 4H. She got a blue ribbon in the meeting last month. Now she has three. That's about all the news there is. We're all fine. We all miss you a lot.

Dad

Letter to Lieutenant Donald Cutler from his wife, Helen:

Dearest Don,

As I sit here tonight thinking of you, everything is quiet and it seems to make me more lonesome than ever for you. I do wish so that I could see you for even just a few minutes in order to know that you are well and how things are going with you. I wonder just where you can be and whether you are fighting yet and hope that this war will be over soon so that we can be together again.

The trip home was uneventful. I am back in my old room with everything sorted out. I have our radio on the desk and your picture in its old place. If we weren't going to have a baby, it would almost seem to me that I had dreamed of going to Cowan and being with you all those weeks which went by so rapidly. Time seems to go slowly now, but three months from now when the baby is here I expect that it will be different.

Meanwhile I keep busy. One morning a week I pack bandages for the Red cross, and it does seem to me that if our output of the other morning was duplicated all over the country, there could never in fifty years be need of all those bandages. I sincerely hope not but will keep at it as long as I can. I am also getting some reading done, especially archaeology because I want to know more about your field. I'll have to admit that it sometimes seems rather dry. It's much more interesting when you tell me about it.

I hope that you will have a little time to explore Italy because I know that in many ways army routine is dull for you.

There is very little news. Fran MacRae has not answered my letter, but she was in Cowan the last I knew.

Your mother dropped in on Friday. She seemed fine and was especially pleased to have heard from you that you had landed safely in Italy. She recalled her trip there, but I suspect things look a bit different now. She feels very badly that the Cassino Abbey was destroyed.

There is so little to say except that I miss you terribly and won't feel whole again until you are back. If only I could be in Italy and see you sometimes. I do love you so much, Don, and hope and pray for your safety through the days which lie ahead. I know that you will do your job well; but I live now, and you must too, for the days of peace which will follow this war when we will finally be able to be together. Sometimes I wonder how we could ever have taken peace for granted.

> *Much love as always,*
> *Helen*

XX

North of Naples the Italian countryside is rolling and spotted with small towns. Through it, in their free time, the GIs of Spaulding's battalion foraged for wine and chickens, or adventure with the renowned farm women of the area who worked the fields and vineyards in the absence of their men. The GIs were amazed at the strength of these women. They could be seen returning from a hillside with bundles balanced on their heads, gracefully finding their way home with a new supply of firewood; or working in the fields with heavy tools preparing the ground for planting and harvest. The only Italian men present were either old, young, or crippled and often took to roadside peddling. They bargained shrewdly with the GIs, exacting the last lira of advantage in each transaction. The relative value of things had changed. A cake of soap was extremely valuable, so were cigarettes and eggs. Jewelry was worth anything a GI would pay. A pair of army boots was worth a great deal on the black market. A chicken was so valuable that soldiers with a yearning for a drumstick usually managed to catch their own. There were many feathers in the bushes near the olive grove.

When the companies gathered at "chow time," they were haunted by the eyes of hungry Italians hovering at the edge of the area, waiting patiently to see whether something would be left over or whether any of the men would make donations from their own rations. The Italian family sent either its oldest or youngest member with a pail. The MPs tried half-heartedly to drive them away, but they always filtered back.

"Jeez," said Benard after a particularly rugged morning of training. Captain MacRae had them climb a small mountain before daylight and circle back to camp on a long march. "I can't eat with them looking at me like that. Makes me want to get drunk."

Over a period of time, certain children seemed to attach

themselves to some of the outfits. The men saved out part of their rations for them. There was something about these bold little ragamuffins that appealed to the GIs. Corelli's platoon regularly fed a wiry boy of about nine who talked long and earnestly with Corelli, supplying him with much information about the area. Corelli knew where to get the best wine, how to contact the black market, where to find women.

Each man knew that it was only a question of time until he was in the line. At night the sound of artillery rumbled to the north, and through the nearby town loaded trucks rolled north and ambulances headed south.

The town nearest the bivouac area was built, like many others, along a ridge making possible only the main street bordered by buildings which were a whole story taller in the rear. The battered buildings were of stone with tile roofs and chimneys at the corners. They reminded Cutler, as he walked up the street, that this was an old country with long memories of many conflicts. The newer scars still showed, but soon they would blend. He saw old Italian women in their black clothes and shawls, each wearing a metal cross and thought that the scene was almost unchanged since the Middle Ages.

From the narrow street, he turned in at a stone doorway. The carving was intricate and ornate, grapes and leaves; and Cutler wondered whether it had led to a winery. But now was his opportunity to take a bath and to get clean clothes.

He stumbled onto the earthen floor of a darkened room. A humid cloud of steam and sweat met him. Water boiled in huge kettles over a flickering fire. Several young soldiers were bathing in halves of large wooden wine barrels darkened with age. Bare skin glistened in the fire-light. The men laughed and joked as they vigorously removed the dirt and grime of days from their muscled bodies.

Cutler was assigned a barrel-half and quickly stripped leaving his clothes in a loose pile on his boots. He climbed into the warm water grinning to himself, soap in hand. Quickly he splashed feeling strangely playful. He washed his face slinging the water up over his head, blowing bubbles in his hands. Slowly he washed himself performing the bathing ritual almost automatically.

He looked about. It was almost a cannibal scene, he decided gleefully, with the men immersed in the steaming barrels and the firelight flickering and the henchmen putting on more water to boil. He tried to rest back against the barrel, but it was far from comfortable. By squatting down, he could immerse himself up to his neck. He wished that he could stay in the warm barrel all afternoon. It was such a pleasure after so many days in the same clothes. A soldier came by and picked up all his old clothes leaving only the boots on the dirt floor.

Reluctantly he climbed out and dressed in clean clothes. Their freshness felt as good to him as the warm water had, emphasized his awareness and aliveness. He handled his old boots gingerly as though somehow they were no longer a part of him. When he went once more into the street, it was with a feeling of being completely whole once again.

As he lingered beside the road watching a line of supply trucks go north, it occurred to him that this town was noted for its Roman ruins, for parts of an old wall and villa; and it seemed to him that his day would be complete if he were to find and explore these old ruins. He could write to Helen about it, he thought.

When the truck convoy had passed, he stepped into the narrow street and ambled along in the direction it had gone. He went down through a narrow alley picking his way carefully over old barbed wire which was rusting now. As he left the shelter of the buildings behind, he could see the old wall way ahead, broken and crumbling. He skirted old shell craters made the winter before; and as he walked down the sloping path, he sensed a great difference in atmosphere. He left the voices and sounds of the town behind. A gun-metal overcast spread out over the sky, and the sound of artillery was muffled in the clouds. There was a hush in this little valley walled in on both sides by ridges.

A feeling came over him of being in a place apart, of emptiness in space, as that of a vacant theatre, but with ghosts in every seat watching.

German equipment lay all about. Four rifles rusted on the ground, their wooden stocks bleached by the sun and weather. The broken wheel of an artillery piece was half buried in the earth. Ammunition lay in deranged piles. Bits of leather, a gas mask, a canteen, a helmet—he looked again. There beneath the German helmet was the face of a man. His body was wrapped in a blanket of earth, one foot protruding. The face was tanned to a dull brown leather, and rain and wind had given it a slight gloss. The shrunken visage with features sharply drawn leered up at him with a hollow sunken eye. He glanced away and saw another foot sticking out of the earth a short distance away. A hand, too, was thrust out and lying on the ground, the same color and texture as the face except for one shadow-filled hole. Erosion was eating the soft earth; corrosion, the steel, and weevils, the flesh. It was like the dried mummies he had seen in museums except that now, for the first time, Cutler realized that even mummies had once been men.

There came an awareness of backbone, a feeling for his hair, a sensation in his skin. He felt the mortal boundaries of his body. The desire to blot out the scene filled him. And yet, the desire to see, to peek, to examine curiously overcame the fears. He glanced over the barren rocks of the ridge to the left, at the torn and shattered trees, at the crumbling Roman wall ahead against the face of the hill. Nothing moved. All was hushed stillness. This place was left to utter desolation and to death. Death seemed here to lie in wait for him. Two dead men were visible, how many more lay nearby? How many ancient deaths had happened here? Here was something incomprehensible, the feeling of the unknown. His great desire to leave was offset by a compulsion to stay. He had the need to know death, to taste death without actually becoming dead.

His heart pounded, emphasizing life in this place where not even the wind blew—in this place avoided by all. Suddenly he had a great revulsion for archaeology, for the prying into ancient lives, for the discussion and handling of artifacts. It was life which mattered.

He hurried back, up the path by which he had come, by the shell craters and the rusting equipment, toward the dark opening of the alley between the stone buildings. As he rapidly found his way back over the barbed wire in the alley, he could hear a jeep and the sound of men talking. A woman's laughter came from an upper window, rolling gently on the air—the pleasantest sound in the world.

He could smell onions cooking; and when the children came toward him, he emptied his pockets of candy for them, all the time saying heartily, "Here, take these! These are for you!" He wanted to talk to someone, anyone, and feel that he was still living, still breathing, still active, still thinking, still in possession of a future.

XXI

Lucia d'Alenzo regretted her sudden departure during the call of Colonel Spaulding. It seemed to her, looking back on it, that her action had been rude; and her loneliness in the villa with only the old count and Maria for company made her, in retrospect, wish that she had hidden her feelings for the sake of enjoying the visitors. She cared little who came, but she longed now for diversion, anything to interrupt the silent monotony of her present life.

Rather tentatively, the count had suggested that they might invite the colonel for dinner. She had concurred and the invitation, in which Chivington was also included, was sent off.

When it reached Spaulding, his own reaction puzzled him. He found himself eager to go to this dinner party. He had his orderly polish everything, allowed plenty of time to dress, and again the jeep left the olive grove to climb the steep drive to the villa.

Chivington was delighted. He heartily disliked the officers' mess. He planned tonight to charm the sad woman and to enjoy himself over the count's wine. Again the officers brought gifts, this time canned fruits and sweet cookies.

The two men eyed each other and grinned like school boys. It was so long since either of them had been invited to dinner that a simple invitation had become a party to them.

Again the jeep stopped before the weathered door and again they rang the bell and waited until Maria came shuffling through the halls to open the massive door. She led them directly to the large hall where tonight a small fire burned on the large hearth. The distinctive and pleasant odor of the old building was now familiar to the two officers.

The count sat in the same chair, but tonight he wore a jacket of deep blue velvet with worn satin lapels and across his chest hung a gold watch chain which shone in the firelight. The lean hound lay at his feet but rose to growl as Spaulding and Chivington entered.

Opposite sat Lucia in a long dress of dark green silk, her hands quiet in her lap, waiting.

Polite greetings were exchanged; Maria brought wine and the evening mellowed.

The count grew expansive. Tonight he was entertaining again after a long period through which they had merely existed. In an attempt to cheer Lucia, he found himself in his old role of host and patron.

When the wine was finished, he led them to the dining hall where two candles gleamed in silver holders on the old polished table. It was scarcely enough light for the room, but the enormous chandelier which hung over the table was without candles. The carved beams of the old ceiling vaulted the room giving a feeling of great security and strength. Places for four were laid on openwork mats marking bright accents in the dusky room. They sat with enormous spaces of dark table separating them, stiffly upright in high-backed chairs.

Chivington looked about him. For the first time since he had come to Italy, he felt truly happy. The old villa seemed to him a haven from the gaucheries and lack of perfection with which he felt himself each day surrounded.

He wondered who, in former days, had banqueted at this table and pictured the room with the chandelier glowing with dozens of candles and an atmosphere of restrained dignity in which distinguished men and beautiful women dined in the high-backed chairs. He felt great sympathy for his host, reduced to the worn dinner jacket and only two candles.

Maria shuffled around the table serving Spam and canned peas on ornate silver platters. It startled Spaulding to see the rations which had been part of the initial gift to the count served with such distinction. It occurred to him that, for all their possessions, these people were almost without food and that he should see that gifts came this way regularly. Chivington hardly realized that he was eating Spam. The old Italian woman had prepared it with herbs and a sauce of pasta.

Spaulding looked carefully at the contessa. She met his eye directly and without embarrassment, in such a way that her sadness seemed somehow touching to him. He attempted to amuse her with stories of some of the difficulties his men had encountered with the local citizens. He was rewarded finally with a smile which crinkled the little lines around her eyes. He judged her to be about thirty-five, although it was hard to guess. He wondered whom she had been close to and seen killed, and the sharp prick of his curiosity tempted him on to further success with her. The count beamed at him benevolently.

Once she had smiled, both Chivington and Spaulding thought her a beautiful woman; but still the languid air of aimlessness hung over her, and they strove to repeat the success. They carried the conversation, each vying with the other good-naturedly for her approval and the reinforcement of his own ego until Chivington recognized in Spaulding's eye that spark of masculine competition which made him remember that Spaulding was a colonel and he only a first lieutenant. Chivington withdrew, leaving Spaulding the conversational field. Soon she laughed.

The count was delighted. As they left the dining room, he took the silent Chivington by the arm and said, "You must see my books. You have sympathy. I felt it on your first visit."

Lucia turned. "My father rarely shows his books," she said. "You have pleased him."

Chivington was flattered. He felt that the count was one of the few people who had ever recognized his discrimination.

The count repeated his invitations until it became almost routine for the colonel's jeep to set out up the hill at dinner time. Usually Chivington went. Sometimes Van Tuyl, or a major from one of the other battalions, was included. Once Spaulding invited Captain MacRae but found him so silent and unsocial that the invitation was not repeated. Within ten days, headquarters was buzzing with stories of the contessa the colonel was chasing. As usual, the rumors were exaggerated, but he found her charming and his ability to amuse her made her grow in importance to him.

He found himself thinking of her as he did his paperwork; he found himself gathering little stories to tell her, thinking, as he tucked the details away in his mind, that perhaps this would please her. Her smiles, being rare, seemed to him of great value. He felt that he was important to her and therefore successful. It had been a long time since he had felt successful with a woman. It flattered his vanity. Occasionally he thought of Violet but without compassion. Violet didn't need him as Lucia did. Violet could take care of herself so well. He didn't want to think about Violet now. He wanted to help Lucia forget whatever terrible thing had happened when the Nazis had interrupted their trip south. He longed to know the whole story.

One night she seemed to him more silent and withdrawn than usual. He had tried to divert her; but after dinner, as the count and Chivington went into the library to look at some folio edition of which the count was particularly proud, she had sat in her chair staring moodily into the fire. Spaulding had seated himself, as usual, in the carved chair nearby. The clock ticked loudly.

"You are quiet tonight," he finally said.

"I do not mean to be," she said. "I was just thinking that you have become like an old friend and soon you will be gone. With old friends, it is not always necessary to be talking."

"That is true," he said, and they sat watching the fire.

Suddenly she turned her head, which rose on a slim neck from the folds of chiffon of her soft dress.

"Do you ever feel caged?" she asked with intensity.

"I have felt that way," he replied, startled.

"Sometimes I want to fling open the door and run away," she said, "but there is nowhere to run."

"You have had a hard year," he said struggling to comprehend this air of wildness and revolt which she was revealing to him for the first time.

"Come," she said, "we can see Vesuvius from the terrace." She hurried to the end of the long room and struggled impatiently with the bolt on the door. He had never seen her move so rapidly. She moved like a girl. He came quickly behind her taking her slim hands from the bolt and pulling it back himself. When the door was open, she ran across the terrace to the low wall beyond the colonnade.

"Look," she said, pointing through the dark. There to the south, where all day Vesuvius had belched smoke and ash, he could see the glow of red hot lava sputtering into the air and returning to cling to the crater sides in a livid flowing mass. It held him fascinated, glowing there in the night, seemingly suspended, almost supernatural. He felt Lucia's agitation beside him.

"Look," she said intensely. "Vesuvius is not caged. Look at it! You may never see it again!" She was shaking. He put his arm around her, steadying her against him; and she made no attempt to draw away. The whole scene seemed very unreal to him with the angry red glow of the volcano looming fantastic in the misty night and this emotional woman with him on an Italian terrace. Suddenly he pulled her closer and kissed her hard, trying to subdue the wildness which shook her.

She welcomed his kiss. Her lips were soft and full and sought his again until tears streamed down her cheeks.

"They were shot!" she sobbed. "They were shot! They killed my husband and my son!"

He held her by the shoulders wondering what to say. He was driven by the desire to quiet her, to force her to forget, to bring her back to the present and to him. He tried to think but could see only the fiery volcano lighting the night and the woman in his arms. The reserve between them was completely broken.

"They were shot!" she sobbed again. The incredulity and indignation in her voice seemed to come from long hidden depths. She was still shaking, almost hysterical, as she threw her head back and forth. He tried to steady her, to force her to see him standing here in the present while she struggled in the past. He grasped her by the shoulders, but still she sobbed. And beyond her far off in the darkness the lava boiled down the slopes of Vesuvius.

So this was her secret, her husband and son shot down while she and the count were allowed to proceed south through the lines. He felt an anger growing in him that this injustice had befallen her and that behind him on the ridges to the north those who had done this thing waited defiantly for him and for his battalion. For the first time the war became a personal issue to him rather than a professional challenge, and he felt a bitter resolve to even the score for her. As he looked down at her, she seemed to him so defenseless, so feminine, and a great tenderness for her

145

welled up in him as he realized the hopelessness of her great loneliness.

"Lucia," he said insistently. As she raised her dark eyes to his he heard himself saying, "Lucia, I love you! Do you understand? I love you!"

She stared at him through her tears. He kissed her again subduing the long gasping sobs which came rising up through the soft chiffon of her dress. As he held her, waiting for her response, slowly she relaxed. Her arms went around him; and as she clung to him, she ran her hand softly up the back of his neck above the stiff collar of his uniform. He put his lips against her neck feeling the throb and emotion within her. Her fingers found his ear, tracing its outline; and he felt the throb of his blood quicken.

By God, I will have her! he thought, tightening his arms about her. He took her head between his hands deliberately kissing her over and over again until she struggled against him for breath. As he ran his hands down and over the soft dress, she grasped his hand wildly and pulled him down through misty gardens to the summerhouse on the cliff.

XXII

General Steed's division moved up to the line, and now the men lay sprawled in foxholes vacated by the troops they had relieved on the western sector of a front which stretched from the Mediterranean across Italy south of Rome. Behind them, way to the south, lay smoking Vesuvius and battered Naples Harbor with its mountains of supplies. Before them lay German emplacements and mine fields protecting hardened battle veterans who would contest each acre of ground and exact its price in casualties. The rumble of artillery, low and rolling like distant thunder, was ominously present but, for the moment, ineffectual. This was known as the quiet front.

The organization of Spaulding's battalion had been tightened. Lieutenant Chivington had been promoted to captain and moved up to battalion headquarters where he worked closely with the colonel and Major Van Tuyl. Cutler, much to his surprise, was promoted to first lieutenant and made executive officer of C Company. MacRae was still C Company captain, but a strange change had come over him which none of his officers understood. Duval called him the mechanical man now, and the phrase was somewhat apt. Richard MacRae, who had always led his company by his own vitality and example, now repeated his orders almost by rote. He sat sometimes and just stared at nothing. He did his work; there could be no criticism there. It was just that he had done it so well before that the men had learned to expect more from him.

"What gives with the captain?" said Benard to Millen.

"Search me," said Millen shrugging his shoulders.

"What's the matter with MacRae?" asked Major Van Tuyl.

"Hard to say," said Chivington.

"Well, he better snap out of it," said Van Tuyl. "I thought he was one of the best men we had."

MacRae himself was confused. In his mind, he went over

and over the last weeks he had spent with Fran. He asked himself where and when things had started to go wrong. He asked himself whether she had ever really loved him, why she had not wanted his children. He puzzled over it, remembering bitterly. He worried about Diana. He wondered how Fran spent her time now that he was gone. He realized that her need for people and fun was stronger than any loyalty to him. He brooded over it, loving and hating her, hurt deep in his pride. He had not answered her letter.

As the days went by, he slowly became aware that his hard-built relationship with Colonel Spaulding had deteriorated. He didn't care. He felt it served Fran right.

Chaplain Rutherford, alert and on the job, tried genially several times to draw MacRae into conversation, but each time he was rebuffed. A shell was growing around MacRae. He let no one come close to him, and the men finally left him alone.

The little olive-drab observation plane was known as Iron Henry. Over the lines, it was a great favorite with the GIs since, while the plane was up on observation, the enemy artillery was silenced in order to conceal its location. As Iron Henry buzzed back and forth watching, photographing, mapping, the men below felt safer.

But to the pilot who flew it, Iron Henry was a sort of nightmare. He knew that the plane was watched from both lines, that at any given moment guns were trained on him waiting only an order to blow him out of the sky. Each day he left the relative security behind the lines for reconnaissance, wondering whether this would be the day the Germans decided to get him. The plane was slow. It had to be if information was to be gathered accurately. His job was to fly as low as possible but out of range of rifle fire from enemy troops.

As Lieutenant Cutler watched the plane taxi in down the small field, it looked to him flimsy and unsubstantial. He didn't want to go up in it, but it was an order. Colonel Spaulding had arranged reconnaissance flights for the officers of his command as preparation for a major push. As the plane came to a halt, Captain MacRae stumbled out looking slightly seasick.

"How was it?" asked Cutler.

"Go see for yourself," said MacRae.

Don climbed into the two-seated plane. The pilot, with his goggles up on his forehead, looked at him wearily.

"Cutler's my name," said Don extending his hand.

"Sure," said the pilot. "I'm Forster. Fasten that seat belt."

As Cutler fumbled with it, the engine roared, and they took off down the bumpy field with the smell of fumes and carbon in the cabin. Forster was intent on the plane as they wheeled into the air and turned north.

"Like to fly?" he asked.

"I guess so," said Cutler. "Like it better when the Jerries aren't down there."

"You can say that again," said Forster.

"Where are we now?" asked Cutler.

"There's the supply dump," said Forster, "and the hospital unit over there to the right. That road down there goes up north where you've come from. We'll follow it up and go over the lines at Hill 103."

Cutler nodded. Hill 103 was the German defensive position immediately facing his company. He thought he saw it ahead, but there were so many hills that he could not be sure. He was amazed at how pock-marked the land looked from the air. The later afternoon shadows rimmed one side of each hole making the bare fields look like the cratered surface of the moon.

"There's the hill," said Forster, and Don craned his neck trying to make out distinctive features of the land over which he would soon be fighting. Almost before he had a chance of orienting himself, Hill 103 was behind them. Below them the road wound north to a little town. He could see the artillery damage. All the roofs were caved in, but the landscape below them looked completely quiet.

"Lots of Jerries down there," said Forster.

"Only one way to get rid of them," said Cutler.

"That's right," said Forster, "but you know what that captain I just took up said? He said he didn't want to fight them. Said he didn't give a damn who won the war."

"He said that!" said Cutler startled.

"He sure did," said Forster. "Glad I don't have to go fighting with him."

149

Cutler thought it over. He watched as the little town slid by beneath the plane, and they turned west and then south again crossing several ridges. He tried to spot the location of the little boxes which were houses, knowing that each would have to be taken. He tried to fix firmly in his mind the relationship of Hill 103 to the ridges and road. He noticed a stubble field south of the town, bare of cover and gleaming wheat color in the late sunlight. As they swung back over the ridge, he noted a sunken trail leading over a spur to the right of the road near Hill 103.

"Seen enough?" asked Forster, anxious to return again to the safety of the field.

"Could you run back along that road again?" asked Cutler. "I want to spot those houses again."

"Okay," said the pilot turning the plane. He flew a zigzag course making it difficult for Cutler to keep his bearings.

"Come on," said Forster. "Let's get the hell out of here before Jerry throws something at us."

"Suits me," said Cutler.

They flew silently, following the road south. Cutler looked for his company but could see only an occasional figure, not the 185 men he knew to be in the area.

"Listen," he said to the pilot, "that captain you took up before me—do you think he's cracking up?"

"Hell," said Forster, "how do I know. Maybe he's just got indigestion, but I'd sure hate to have him giving me orders. Say," said the pilot, "do you know him?"

"I'm his exec officer," said Cutler.

"Oh, brother," said Forster, "forget I said anything."

"Did he take much interest in the terrain?" asked Cutler.

"Well," said Forster, "can't say that he did."

"Did he study those houses?" asked Cutler.

"I don't think so," said Forster. "Come to think of it, he just sat there like a Sunday afternoon passenger."

The plane taxied in again.

"Thanks," said Cutler as they came to a halt. Lieutenant Rusnick came up.

"Well," he said, "what did you see?"

"Trouble," said Cutler. "Go look at the placement of those houses just beyond Hill 103, and we'll talk it over tonight."

150

XXIII

An infantry attack is a curious thing. Into it come the combined efforts of many men and units. Out of it, there is success or failure, life or death. The object is the taking of a hill, a town, or any enemy position.

The complete attack, as planned, is rarely ever carried through to a satisfactory conclusion. More often it is a compromise or a series of compromises with destiny. When the attack is made at night, darkness conceals movement from the enemy. The most generally successful attack is made a few hours before dawn. Troops cross dangerous open ground in front of an enemy position and sometimes take the position itself before daylight. There is the additional advantage that enemy troops may be weary after a long night vigil. Then after the position is taken, the enemy must counterattack in daylight when the advantage of visibility rests with the defender. The Romans knew this 2,000 years ago as they fought over this same land.

First Lieutenant Donald Cutler looked to the northwest. The letter felt crisp in his fingers. Captain MacRae had handed it to him and then quietly gone away. He glanced at it once more.

> ...the main push that we have all been waiting for is at hand.... The object of the Fifth Army is to drive the Germans out of Italy.
>
> Mark Clark
> Lieutenant General, Commanding

His serious blue eyes watched the sun go down. Battalion headquarters had not yet sent the exact time of the jump off, but he knew that it would not be long now.

A fly buzzed around his helmet in the warm air that had the feeling of spring, a fragrance that held a taint of powder, of smat-

151

tered flesh dried in the sun, and of dust blown high by the occasional shell that drifted somewhat lazily over the lines and smacked into the ground short of an old Italian castle on the hill ahead.

Wherever Cutler looked he saw the marks which only explosions can leave. The shattered trees were without branches, without leaves. His thoughts centered on the fact that in these lines Germans, British, and now Americans had rested, fought, and rested again during the winter. From here patrols had gone out onto the rough terraced country—reconnaissance patrols, combat patrols, standing patrols, patrols to capture a prisoner, patrols for this, for that—all had gone out and only some had come back. Once the British had attacked the small town that lay a mile north, but the British soldiers had failed in their attempt. They had not tried again but contented themselves with patrolling until General Steed's division had relieved them.

Cutler himself had taken out his first patrol through the ditches and vineyards to the north. He realized what the ground was like and what effort he and the rifle company would have to make in order to seize the town from the enemy.

He looked to the east. Far ahead of him was a stone house. Above it the red rays of the sun stopped on the clouds formed by the smoke pots back where Via Appia crossed the river. Darkness crept slowly up the clouds as Cutler watched. He checked his pistol in the fading light.

A runner from battalion headquarters came. The communications sergeant signed for the message and handed it to Lieutenant Cutler, who opened the seal and read, "H-hour is 2300 tonight. Spaulding"

Cutler felt both relieved and anxious. The earlier anxiety about the time ceased. The larger anxiety about the battle which lay three hours ahead grew. The darkness to the north beckoned him, but first he must check the men, weapons, and ammunition. All four platoon lieutenants had inspected their men that day, but Cutler thought that small matters like batteries for the bazookas might need further checking. Attention to detail! Colonel Spaulding had hammered it into his officers. Attention to detail!

Cutler knew that the men were nervous with the closeness of their first battle. As he wandered through the area, he could feel the tension around him. There was no joking, only quiet words here and there as the men rested. Cutler wondered what had become of Captain MacRae.

Chaplain Rutherford worked through the area, speaking to the men and collecting letters to be mailed. There had been many last-minute letters written as the light had faded, and now Rutherford's pockets bristled with them. He had gained in influence since they had arrived in Italy. Men who in the States had said, "Tell it to the Padre!" meaning, "Go fly a kite!" had now a newfound respect for their chaplain. With the evidence of death around them, they knew that on any day it might be he who gathered their belongings together to send home or wrote that impossible letter from the company to follow a War Department telegram. Chaplain Rutherford knew, and the men knew too, that after this night there would be letters to write. It made a bond between them.

In the deep dusk, Private Benard came up to Lieutenant Cutler.

"Lieutenant," he said softly. Cutler could see his face, pale in the night under the clear sky.

"Could you do me a favor, Lieutenant?"

"What is it, Benard?"

"Could you keep this money for me till after the fight?"

"It's as safe on you as it is on me," said Cutler.

"You take it," said Benard. "I'll feel better that way."

"Okay," said Cutler, "I'll give you a receipt. How much is it?"

"Nine hundred dollars," said Benard proudly. The plate in his mouth clicked softly into place.

"You've done pretty well," said Cutler grinning. "Glad I haven't played poker with you."

"Yes, sir," said Benard grinning back. Then his tone changed. "Funny thing," he said. "I got more money than I ever had and it's no damn good to me out here."

"You're taking a chance," said Cutler. "I'll be right in the line with the rest of you. If anything happens to me, you turn in that receipt to the chaplain."

"Sure, Lieutenant," said Benard, "but you're smart. I figure you can outthink those Krauts up ahead better than I can."

Cutler watched Benard go, feeling somehow an added symbolic burden but pleased all the same by the man's trust in him. He returned to the dugout to wait. Private Covalos, the radio man, crouched on one side, his face streaked and his eyes somehow larger. His high-boned face reminded Cutler that Covalos was half Indian as he waited intently with the radio for orders which would determine the future of this company. Cutler wondered again what had become of MacRae, who should now, at this time, be with his men. As time went on, Captain MacRae still did not appear. Finally at 2230 hours, Lieutenant Cutler, as exec officer, ordered the men out of their holes toward the forward reserve position. Intent on the attack ahead, they went like silent animals on padded feet, dark shadows into the ominously quiet night. They went past trees that filled a small gully with dampness, around the slope of a ridge, all in single file stretched out. Somehow the front third of the column broke away. Cutler moved back along the lined soldiers, past the last man, and then farther back until he found dark shapes resting on the ground— men of the company held up because of doubt. As he led the broken segment toward the front and found the first man, Cutler felt the excitement of the night.

At 2300 hours, suddenly artillery pounded the night darkness behind them as Americans, British and French began firing simultaneously. The first rounds swished through the air over their heads, sounding like so many riderless horses rushing through the sky, all in the same direction. A moment later shells landed on the terraced hillsides to the north. The huge noise was behind at the guns' positions and forward where the shells exploded. Overhead shells screamed as they went by. The ground shook with the power of the heaviest barrage ever fired in Italy.

The darkness was no longer murky as it had been a halfhour earlier. The constant flare of the guns to the rear and the flashes of explosion to the north gave a permanent dull light to the entire area. Colored flares burst on the hillsides, overhead the streamers of tracers drifted in the air like the fantasies of a July 4th evening.

On and on went the barrage pounding into the night, thudding deeply within each man as the shock waves reverberated from the hillsides.

Cutler had given the order to dig in, and the men were again in foxholes leaning against the rumbling earth. Runners came in from each platoon to wait for further orders. Still Cutler waited for MacRae. Finally he left Lieutenant Rusnick in charge of the company and, jumping from the security of his hole, once more moved stealthily through the night. He wanted to know the situation. His feet, trained by many night marches, carried him across the rough slope. He went down a smooth path, climbed over two fallen trees, and found the stone farmhouse where battalion headquarters had been set up the day before. A sentry challenged him, but he gave the password and was allowed to approach the headquarters building.

He stepped through the outside blackout curtain into a darkened hall and then through the inside curtain into a candlelit room half full of uniformed men. The building was substantial, but its stone walls shook now with the reverberation of the barrage.

There in the room sat Captain Chivington on a folding chair with his feet on the table filing his nails.

"Hello," said Chivington coolly, looking up at Cutler. "What are you doing here?"

"Just checking up," said Cutler trying to appear as cool as Chivington but breathing rapidly in his excitement. He had never liked this "Old Mother Hubbard." "Where's the colonel?"

"He's out there now," said Chivington waving his nail file, "but Van Tuyl's in the back room."

"Anyone seen MacRae?" asked Cutler.

"Didn't you hear about that?" asked Chivington surprised. He swung his feet down to the floor and sat up abruptly.

"Hear what?" asked Cutler.

"Things got too much for him I guess," said Chivington. "When the barrage started, he went to pieces. Came in here like a wild man saying that we'd got to stop the attack. The colonel got the medics to send him back. C Company is all yours, Cutler. We sent a runner to tell you about it."

Cutler thought it over. He moved slowly through the men to the next room. In the far corner, Major Van Tuyl bent over a radio. Cutler went over to him and squatted down. As Van Tuyl turned quickly, the tight pock-marked skin of his face moved to a smile of recognition.

"Hello, boy," he said, "did you get the message?"

"Indirectly," said Cutler. "How's the attack going? I'm in position ready to move out."

Van Tuyl said, "A and B left on time. Spaulding and his group are right behind B Company on the right of the road near the spur. They should all be past the mine field now. You're going to follow B. They've laid white guide tape through the mines."

"Good," said Cutler. "Has the colonel said anything about using C Company yet?"

"Not yet," said Van Tuyl. "Why don't you hang around for a few minutes; and then if nothing comes in, you better get back to your company. Luck to you, boy."

Cutler went back to the other room.

"By the way," said Chivington, "has that Private Nolan checked in yet?"

"Not yet," said Cutler.

"Would you like a cup of tea?" asked Chivington. His lips broke readily into a smile, almost too readily.

"No, thanks," said Cutler hurriedly. He would have choked on it. "Have you got an extra message-blank book?"

Chivington mulled this problem over in his large mouth for a moment and then slowly went to his field desk and fumbled with both of his large hands. Finally he pulled out a small yellow-sided message book. "Here's one," he said handing it to Cutler. Then he sat down again and, clasping his large fingers around one knee, rocked back and forth on the bench.

Cutler watched his mouth that smiled too easily. "Thanks," he said. "Hope I didn't short you." He moved toward the blackout curtain.

"No, no," said Chivington quickly. "Glad I had one. Good luck to you." His eyes followed Cutler. Cutler had the strange feeling that at this moment Chivington envied him.

Delaney, his runner, came toward him out of the dark.

"Got a message for you," he said holding out an envelope.

"So I hear," said Cutler. "Thanks, Delaney." He read the message slowly:

. . . take command of Company C. . . .

He folded it thoughtfully and placed it in his pocket.

"Everything all right, Lieutenant?"

"Yes," he said quietly. "How has everything been around here tonight?"

"Okay, sir. They say Colonel Spaulding took a hot bath, shaved, and put on a clean, pressed uniform. He even gave his orderly ten bucks!"

"Is that right!" said Cutler. "I guess that's the way a good West Pointer does it. Anything else go on around here tonight?"

"You heard about Captain MacRae?"

"Yes," said Cutler quickly. He didn't want to talk about it now. "I'm going back to the company. I'll be in the place I showed you until the colonel orders the company up."

"Yes, sir," said Delaney. "Good luck, Lieutenant."

Cutler went back the way he had come and soon arrived at his old foxhole. The men were still dug in, waiting.

"What's happening?" asked Rusnick. Cutler told him about MacRae and showed him the orders to take over the company.

"Swell time to fade out," said Rusnick wryly. "Well, what do you want me to do?"

"Everything seems to be on schedule so far," said Cutler. "When we move out, you'd better follow your platoon so that you can keep the men moving when we leave. I don't know how long we'll be here now."

"Okay, see you. Good luck," said Rusnick.

Cutler wondered how many men were wishing him good luck now. Everyone he had talked with in the last half-hour had said those words almost mechanically. Well, he wished them all good luck too. No one could have too much good luck in the hours ahead of them. They would all need all the luck they could find. *God,* he thought, *let me make the right decisions!*

XXIV

In the rumbling security of an earthen hole, Cutler waited for the order which would start his one hundred eighty-five men across the unfriendly territory beyond the ridge. As he waited, he felt a lessening of the Allied barrage. The sharp firing of a German zipper pistol filled one of the silences between shell bursts and told Cutler that B Company had made contact. There was another burst nearby. As the moon started over the horizon to add its light to the battle, several shells burst with an asthmatic whine in the company area. Cutler was glad that his men were dug in. The radio called his code.

"Blue-white six to blue-white three, over." It was Colonel Spaulding's voice.

"Blue-white three to blue-white six, go ahead."

"Move your walnuts to Hill 103 and then stand by for orders. Over."

"Roger," said Cutler. He wondered how well the press in Spaulding's uniform looked now.

Cutler tried to get his platoons on the walkie-talkie but static garbled his words. He shouted for the platoon runners.

"Tell your platoons we are moving right away."

The runners silently left as the men around Cutler gathered rifles, packs, and ammunition onto their shoulders. Cutler climbed out of his hole and turned to First Sergeant Pulska, who waited his orders.

"Pulska," he said, "keep the headquarters group behind the two leading platoons. I'm going up ahead to get things started in the right direction."

The sergeant nodded silently.

Cutler started up the slope with Covalos and the radio trailing him. They went past a rusting German antitank gun knocked out when the British had made their attack several months before. He found Lieutenant Jensen lying near the crest of the slope ready with his platoon. Cutler told him about Captain MacRae.

"You all set?" he asked.

"Yes, Sir," said Jensen emphasizing the "Sir."

"I'll lead your men down to the white tape that goes through the mine field," said Cutler.

"I'll be right behind you," said Jensen.

Cutler climbed quickly and, crawling over the top of the ridge, looked out onto the moonlit terraced country. Hill 103 loomed to the left beyond the draw, and he could see the road to the town winding over the flank of the hill toward the houses which he had spotted from the plane. On the road a tank's motors whirred as its treads clanked in the dark like some monster from an old myth, relentlessly moving north. The excitement of the coming conflict was in him as he moved down the north slope with Jensen and the platoon zig-zagging behind him. Down, down they went, Cutler looking for the white tape.

"There it is," he said finally to Jensen. "Hold up at Hill 103 until I give you the word and don't shoot up any of B Company. They're out here somewhere."

"Okay," said Jensen. "Thanks for finding the tape."

As the men went silently through the mine field toward the Germans, Cutler waited and rejoined headquarters group as it came by. He sent Pulska up ahead to help Jensen. The Allied artillery had stopped falling on the town ahead. He hoped that this meant that the plan was working and that A and B Companies were up there now. The ground became rougher and rougher as they advanced, and the men went more slowly. The gullies offered protection from incoming artillery fire. Each time a shell landed near the column, the men dropped abruptly to the ground; and after each barrage, it was more difficult to start them forward again for now men were being wounded.

In the confusion and whine of the shrapnel could be heard the cry, "Medic, medic" in thick agony searching for help in the darkness. In one close blast First Sergeant Pulska had his arm torn off above the elbow; and his crumpled form against a tree, groaning as the men went by, did not help to move the men faster. Aid men came up quickly in the dark and fumbled over him with morphine and bandages before carrying him back.

At Hill 103 a German machine gun fired on the First Platoon. The men lay flat on the ground while half a squad went up toward the road and stopped the gun's firing with grenades.

Cutler stared at his watch as he lay by the radio waiting for Spaulding's orders. No message came. He tried to reach Battalion on the radio but no one answered his call signal. The noise of machine guns and rifle firing drifted back through the night mists lit now by flares on the spur. It sounded to Cutler as if the Germans must be burning up their machine gun barrels as burst after burst followed viciously.

From the rear, a lieutenant from Battalion came out of the mists looking for Cutler.

"Van Tuyl wants to know what's going on," he said. "Regiment is putting on the pressure. Says things are going too slowly."

"I'm getting orders from Spaulding," said Cutler. "I don't want to confuse things up there. B Company's up ahead; and if I get in there now, my men are liable to shoot up Americans."

"Okay," said the lieutenant. "I'll give them the word. The Krauts' mines knocked out two of our tanks," he added. "Their machine guns are covering the road so we can't get the tanks or the mines out."

"That's a hell of a note," said Cutler. "What does Van Tuyl want me to do?"

"He sent me up to check your situation," said the lieutenant. "Have you heard from Spaulding yet?"

Cutler looked over toward the ridge.

"No," he said, "haven't heard a word. It's been quieter up there too."

The lieutenant shook his head. "We've got to clear those machine guns out of there. Otherwise our tanks are useless."

Cutler said, "I'll move ahead and try to contact B Company. Anything else you want?"

"No, I'll tell Van Tuyl what you are doing."

Cutler looked around. "First Platoon runner," he called. The soldier came up to him. "Tell Lieutenant Rusnick to move forward and to watch out for B Company men. The rest of us will be right behind him."

Reluctantly the men stumbled forward in the moonlight. Cutler was up and down the column repairing several breaks.

The single file formation was the only way he had of controlling the men in the night while crossing the rough country over the side of Hill 103. He did not want to release any of his men until after Colonel Spaulding had given him a plan.

The night was fast disappearing and still his column had not come up with B Company. He wondered where they could be. As the first morning glow broke through the smoke and mist which overflowed the gullies and ravines, an American came over the rocky ground ahead past the silhouette of a leafless and branch-less tree.

The man moved faster toward him. "Have you seen any of B Company?" he asked. It was the sandy-haired Third Platoon leader of Company B.

"No, we haven't," said Cutler. "We're looking for it now. When did you last see the rest of them?"

"We got into a fire fight in the spur ahead and had to pull back. The others were up there then. It was terrible. The Krauts had machine guns all over the place. Crossfires everywhere. I lost about half my platoon in a few minutes. The rest of them are in the next draw. The company commander got hit on the hand and went back. Everything in B Company is confused. Nobody knows who's supposed to be in charge or where the rest of the company is.

"Where's Spaulding?" asked Cutler.

"Colonel Spaulding's dead. Machine gun bullets got him in the chest. I saw it," said the lieutenant lifting his shoulders as though to protect himself from the picture.

"What was he doing up that far?" asked Cutler.

"Oh, he came up and took over a squad. They were trying to get by one of those stone houses. The damn flares those Krauts put up made the whole hill bright as day. We didn't have a chance."

"Well," said Cutler, "I'm going ahead with my company. Why don't you take your men down on my right flank and parallel us. We'll probably run into the rest of your company soon."

The lieutenant did not want to go back up to the spur. Cutler saw dimly the determination in the man's red stubbled chin overcome the fear in his eyes. He watched the man's face closely while he talked.

"Okay," said the lieutenant. "You had any casualties yet?"

"Some," said Cutler. "Let's move out now. This morning mist will give us a good cover if we go fast. We won't be able to do much after daylight comes and the mist goes. You guide on me, and we'll try for the spur." He turned to Corporal Delaney, his runner, and said, "Delaney, you go with the lieutenant and stay with him. Find me if he needs anything."

"Okay, sir."

The lieutenant and Delaney disappeared down the slope into the dark mist which still filled the low places.

The news of Colonel Spaulding's death troubled Cutler. He wondered how it would affect the outcome of this day.

He went ahead of the column past two dead Americans, past a shattered rifle and scattered ammunition, past more trees that no longer lived. No artillery came in. Nothing moved save the fog that occasionally opened to show the black mass of the low ridge ahead.

The steep sides of a large ravine directly in his path forced him over closer to the road, forced him too much. He thought, *The Krauts are probably near the road. They've got this thing spotted here.*

The broken masonry of a house beside the road was visible just beyond the narrow part of the path. Looking back, he could see his men in the light of day now. They were moving slowly; some had stopped. All were wary, bewildered after the sleepless night of waiting and moving, after the weary hours of expecting combat at any moment. The men were like a mule that did not want to go. They were stubbornly, carefully, moving forward at their own speed. Cutler shouted back to them, "Come on! Don't leave me out here. Come on!"

The men came on, but their movement now was of animals hunting and being hunted. They sensed the situation.

Cutler moved slowly ahead watching, listening. Another and even deeper ravine with steeply pitching sides lay in front of him. This one made him hug the road even closer than the other had. The smoke of powder and the mist of the land filled his breathing and quickened his thinking. Two buildings, one on either side of the road, lay around the contour he must follow. The sunken terrace road of the spur was to the right of the houses. He didn't like the situation at all. His body crowded lower as he quietly moved forward. He became more and more aware of the buildings with their hollow window eyes. Finally, he could bear the greater tension no longer. His voice sounded distant to him, but he knew it was in a long shout, "Come out of there or we're coming in!"

No sound answered him. The men behind had paused with him. They moved as he did, listening to his voice.

"You sons of bitches, come on out of there! Come on out! We know you're in there. *Kommen sie heraus mit den Händen hoch! Heraus! Heraus kommen!*"

No one answered. The column was thirty yards behind him now, watching him. His men were not his men but an audience sensing his mood. He shouted back to them, "Come on! Don't leave me out here. Keep spread out, but come on!"

The mist rose to reveal the spur blackened with artillery burns. The narrow terrace road scarred away from him halfway up the hill. He noted quickly that the bank of that terrace would offer protection for his men. But first he had to clear the two houses.

He reached the terrace road through a stone-sided gate close to the houses. He shouted back to the column, "Second Platoon, come up on the right, quickly."

Almost before he finished, a grenade burst close beside him followed quickly by another that lifted his whole body and cut like a whip into the back of his arm. Some of his men bunched close around him now. A sergeant to the right of him had two dark green figures ten feet from his tommy-gun. When the gun jammed, the Krauts disappeared. Cutler tossed one of his grenades across the main road up onto the top of the bank that rose steeply on the other side. He dared not go into the road for two of his men already lay there dead from a machine gun that covered it.

"Get a bazooka up here! Shoot it into that wall." He pointed to the house as he shouted.

A potato-masher grenade turned end over end as Cutler watched it fall. Fragments of its shrapnel struck his forehead and brought forth blood which ran down over his eyes. Suddenly he couldn't see. He called to Rusnick.

"Take over," he said.

"Okay," said Rusnick. And then to the men he shouted, "All you men, get down along this terrace road and dig in."

Cutler lay down in the hollow of a small gully. He held his hand to his forehead to slow the flow of blood, feeling it trickle through his fingers and run down his arm to the bend of his elbow. He felt weak and dazed but was afraid that if he passed out, the bleeding would be uncontrolled. Gradually it slowed and he could look out through his sticky fingers. It was minutes before he had the courage to explore the wound with his fingers; but as he felt more and faster, he found that he was not badly hurt. Several small steel fragments stuck into the bone just above his right eye.

As he lay there, he thought that this could not be, that he had not even begun to fight. The Krauts could not knock him out of the war before he even had a chance to fight back. He could not quit now. He must stay, must go forward. The men needed him. There must be some way to get past those houses just ahead.

Out of the smoke came Lieutenant Rusnick. A bullet had gone through his helmet hinging a piece of steel so that it stood up above his head like a small flag. If he had been two inches taller, the bullet would have killed him. His shirt was ripped open. Blood streaked his undershirt. He was a half-comic, half-tragic figure.

"You go on back to the aid station," said Cutler getting shakily to his feet. "You look funny as hell with that helmet of yours!"

Cutler stumbled forward again to taste the rock powder and the smoke of explosions and dirt. The men were still where he had left them half an hour ago. They were trying to go over the terrace, but each path they tried caused a casualty. His men could make no more ground through the crossfire of German weapons. He said to them, "Get back alongside the bank there. We'll see what our mortars can do. Fourth Platoon, set up down the hill and get your telephone wire back here quickly."

The men moved.

Barely had the mortar section reached its new position when an enemy mortar barrage skimmed over the top of the ridge, hugged the ground, and landed. Cutler thought that the barrage had finished the whole section, but minutes later a wireman came up the slope reeling out wire.

Cutler asked him, "Did you get many hurt from the Kraut mortars?"

The wireman said, "One man got it in the arm. That's all. It shook us up some though." He clipped the telephone to the wire as he talked.

"Here's the phone, sir," he said handing it to Cutler with a flourish.

Cutler called Van Tuyl, now the acting battalion commander with Colonel Spaulding gone.

"Blue-white three to blue-white six, over."

"Blue-white six to blue-white three, go ahead."

"We're dug in out here to hold what we've got. I guess you can see where we are."

"Yes, we've been watching you. Have you seen anything of B Company?"

"Not much. Some of them are on my right though."

"What do you need out there?"

"We need ten sows, also mercury and popcorn." Sows were litter bearers for the wounded; mercury was water, and popcorn meant grenades.

"Roger. We'll try to get them to you as soon as we can."

"Roger—out."

It was quiet on the terrace. The sound of artillery and machine guns echoed down from the hills; but here on the terrace, the men waited cautiously and ahead the Germans, knowing that they were there, waited for them to make the first move. Cutler felt his head clearing. The bleeding had stopped completely.

Cutler dug his feet into the soft dirt and, grasping a rifle, raised it until his helmet on the other end was above the edge of the bank. He held it there for ten seconds, fifteen seconds. Suddenly bullets knocked not only the helmet from the rifle, but also the rifle from his hands. He shook his numb fingers, replaced the helmet, and moved down the terrace road about twenty feet to where there was a small bush at the top of the bank. Again the helmet moved above the edge and remained there. This time no one fired at it. He lowered it and, putting it on, raised his head to look across the ridge.

165

He could see no movement. Everything was motionless wherever he looked. Around the houses close by, further along the road, and out in a saddle of the spur nothing moved nor were any Germans visible, but he knew that their weapons covered the level ground ahead. He called back, "Raise another helmet in the same place I did a minute ago."

Benard pushed his helmet up to the same spot. Nothing happened. He raised it higher and wiggled it from side to side. Still no bullets came.

"These Krauts are playing it smart," said Cutler. Then to the men to his left, "Try two helmets about thirty yards further along."

When the helmets appeared above the ridge, many bullets scored the dirt but did not touch them. By projecting back the line of dust, Cutler spotted an opening in a low wall near the road.

Cutler, with his wound, had not intended to stay long on the terrace with his men, but the more he thought of remaining, the more it seemed the thing that he should do. He would hold the ground he had and let Battalion try to mount another attack. His men had already dug deep holes in the brown loam close to the slope. He knew that he could save them from casualties by staying. He had already spotted the machine gun emplacement behind the wall and he would find out more.

He left his hole carefully and walked quietly past his men until he came to a turn in the terrace. He wanted a better look at the houses of which the Krauts were still in strong control. An artillery shell landed close by. A steel fragment grooved deeply the top front of his left combat boot. His whole body fell back where he had come. The blow made him limp as he scrambled into a hole. The fragment had torn the leather completely through and had bruised, without breaking, the skin. He held no doubt that the Krauts could hit him, but so far, they had not hurt him seriously.

At noontime Cutler asked for volunteers to clean out the houses. Ten minutes later Lieutenant Duval came up with only two men.

"If it's all right with you, I'll go with these two men," said Duval.

"This is a tough nut to crack here," said Cutler thoughtfully. "They've got the houses well organized, but you might catch them off guard. Take it easy. If you need more men, come back and get them. We'll try to cover you from here. Good luck."

Cutler watched them go down the trail. It was quiet on the terrace as the men waited straining their ears for some hint of what was happening at the houses. Cutler wondered whether he should have let Duval go with only two men, but then, he knew that often a few men could accomplish by surprise what a larger group could not. He briefly pondered his own responsibility for the casualties in his command looking about at the badly wounded, dying, and dead men who shared the terrace with the others.

Twenty minutes later Duval stumbled back with one man. A grenade had split open the whole side of his face starting at the outside of his eye.

"Mac's dead," he said.

"Lie down in that hole," said Cutler calling for an aid man. We'll get you out of here as soon as we can. What did you find out about the Krauts?"

"Not much," said Duval stiffly. "There are at least two groups of Krauts out there and they're wide awake. We didn't get too close. Mac shot one in a window before the others got him. They saw us coming. We couldn't get at them. Have you any water?" His breath came with difficulty. Cutler gave him a drink from his canteen. Duval swallowed it gratefully but grimaced as he moved his jaw. Then he lay back and closed his eyes.

They spent a long day. Holed up, the men were reasonably safe; but the strain told on them until they felt somehow suspended between life and death, waiting patiently for an inevitable finale either this day or on some other. As they waited, the past lost meaning and so did the future. There was only this day with the sky disarmingly blue above them and the distant sounds of conflict and the warm sun baking them into a lazy desire to sleep there in their holes. If it had not been for the wounded among them, they might perhaps have been able to enjoy moments of this present time—but not with Duval lying there, his wound crusted in the sun, oozing if he moved; not with a crumpled corporal twisted around a jagged tree just as a shell

167

had left him; not with the lack of food and water and the flies buzzing endlessly.

Finally the sun began its slow descent into the West dropping down behind the hills where the Mediterranean lay hidden. The dusk fell about them bringing its own quiet. The coming of night was a soft and gentle thing with no hint of the violence hanging over the men who now stirred in their holes.

When the moon rose again, soldiers came up bringing food and water, mortar ammunition and bazooka rounds. It encouraged the men to realize that a link still existed between them and the army's supplies; but most important, medics carried back the wounded, relieving those left of the groaning anxiety and weight of their presence.

The men crawled briefly from the safety of their holes, ate K rations, filled their canteens.

Cutler, in his advanced position, waited radio orders. By trying to move forward without reinforcements, he would gain nothing; and as long as his men remained here, they held this ground.

The artillery continued, but the shells from both sides whistled high over their heads toward targets behind the lines. Here in the ominous night was peace like that in the eye of the hurricane, deceptive peace, lasting, as Cutler well knew, for only a little time.

Next morning Cutler, with his men, expecting adjacent units to move abreast of him, still waited for orders. Artillery shells continued overhead. At 1400 hours, three rounds from American artillery fell too close. Cutler grabbed for a green smoke grenade, the signal that friendly troops were present, and pulled the pin. The green cloud floated upward while he called battalion.

"Blue-white three to blue-white five, over."

"Blue-white five to blue-white three, go ahead."

"Friendly artillery is falling on my position. Get it raised, will you?"

"Roger—out."

The men waited anxiously until the shelling stopped. An hour passed. No more shells had come into the area. A runner from battalion crawled up and gave him a message. He read:

> We attack at 1630 hours. Your company will move around the east end of the spur and over the top. Get there and hold. Chivington will take over B Company and attack across the ground near the road where you are now. First Battalion will attack on the other side of the road at the same time. Good luck.

> Van Tuyl

"Platoon runners! Tell your officers to get on up here right away," Cutler said quickly.

The runners left and soon Cutler saw the lieutenants coming. As they squeezed into nearby holes Cutler said, "We are going to attack at 1630. We'll move around the spur. Second Platoon will lead followed by First, Third, Fourth and Headquarters. Be careful of any B Company men who may be around there. I'm going out now to check on their location. Any questions?"

The men shook their heads.

"Rusnick will start the attack," said Cutler. "I'll join you when you come by. Good luck."

As the platoon leaders returned to their men, Cutler called Major Van Tuyl. "I have your idea. Anything new?"

"No, nothing new."

"Roger—out."

Lieutenant Cutler, still in his hole, wondered about B Company. He could not see how its scattered men were going to be much help in the coming attack. He felt that he could not ask any of his men to try to contact Company B across the open ground to the east. Duval's torn face was the result of sending someone else on a bad job. This job he would do himself.

Sheltered by the terrace wall, he walked past his men in their holes down the narrow terrace road and edged out onto the flatter open ground to the east, his .45 in his hand. The men watched as he moved quickly, listening carefully, all his senses alert.

He heard a sound coming faintly, very faintly, like the rustling of budding leaves in the wind; but he knew the sound of a mortar shell. He flung himself on the ground as the first round burst close, scattering dirt and wood over him. He rolled turning and twisting erratically to get away. As he floundered, a mortar shell fell where he had just been. He tasted the powder. He continued his twistings as the bursts followed him. Finally the firing stopped, and he lay still behind ten inches of green grass. His lungs breathed rapidly while the dust blew away.

He knew a German mortar crew had spotted him. By now, perhaps they thought he was dead. They must have a small knee-type weapon, he thought, as he lay still in the grass pondering his next move. It was still important to find B Company before the attack. He wondered how much of it could still be left.

Suddenly he rose and went ahead. He had not taken five steps when again he heard the rustling noise. Once more he fell to the ground and rolled over and over as shells exploded where he had just been. A heavy fragment creased his left leg in the calf. Blood came rapidly, but still he rolled. He squirmed into a large artillery shell hole welcoming the protective walls around him. Here he dug in the sun-dried earth. He scraped with his fingers flinging dirt in every direction. The mortar fire stopped. The shells had burst very close but upward over him. His ears rang with the echoes of the explosions. He realized now the impossibility of contacting B Company before the attack.

He was still digging in when the men of the company started toward him moving fast. As the men came by, the shelling started again, but Cutler jumped from the hole. He saw Lieutenant Rusnick coming. He had on a new helmet. Cutler wondered what had become of the one with the hinged flag on top as he called out to the men, "First Platoon, cut back on top after you get around the end." A moment later he repeated the order for the Second Platoon. To the Third Platoon leader he shouted, "Swing clear around the hill lower down and hold when you get to the north bottom." He waved his arms to show the direction he meant. The Fourth Platoon he sent up behind the First and Second.

Up where the First Platoon was, rifles and machine guns started firing. The noise of the fight grew stronger as he moved ahead around the spur. Below him on the hill the Third Platoon also started firing rapidly, and the Germans returned the fire from a house. Behind him tank destroyers supported the attack with direct fire which skimmed over the spur and plunged savagely into the German bunkers.

The men crossed rapidly. Covalos, with the radio, rejoined him as the others went by. Cutler's leg bothered him so much that he sat down to bandage it. He tore the metal strip from his first aid packet to find the sterile bandage inside. He wrapped it quickly around his wounded muscle and tied it snugly. I hope that holds, he thought, limping after the fast moving platoons.

The hill echoed with the noise and confusion. Clouds of dust from the mortar bursts hid the moving men who advanced, bayonets fixed, shouting as they went. One by one the German positions were silenced, but not without a cost in casualties. It was as Spaulding had predicted—ground was bought with men and for this reason must be held.

When darkness came, Cutler inspected the positions they had won. He checked with the platoon leaders and found that each needed ammunition and food. Runners from the platoons accompanied him to the east slope. He told one of his men to go to the Third Platoon to get an exchange runner. He sent one of his best men back to Battalion to help bring forward the needed ammunition and food.

Again Cutler waited the night through. Occasionally artillery fire or a long burst from a machine gun combined with a brilliant flare to disturb the soft breeze coming from the moonlit Mediterranean. Just when the morning light showed on the horizon, the carrying party from Battalion came with the supplies. With the group was Corporal Delaney, whom Cutler had not seen since he sent him with the B Company lieutenant two nights before.

The corporal said, "Captain Chivington sent me over from B Company to check in with you."

"Hello, corporal. How's it been going?"

"Okay, sir. A little bit rough though."

"How did the attack go last night? How in the devil did B get past those houses? Were you with Chivington then?"

"I was pretty close to him. We was supposed t'go when you guys did at 1630 so over we went. There were about forty of us, I guess. We didn't make twenty yards when the Krauts cut loose at us with machine guns, mortars and the works. Everybody hit the ground. It was a bad deal, right then. Them mortars was a splashin' all around us and the machine guns was keepin' our heads down. Guys was cryin' 'medic' around there plenty. Captain Chivington was over near the buildings. Well, he rose up and went toward where the machine gun was firin' from near the corner of the house. The Krauts spun him around once, and he fell down with the bullets. But then Captain Chivington heaved a smoke grenade at them and crawled toward them. He stood up and went right at them runnin' and a hollerin'. When the Krauts see him through the smoke comin' a second time at them, I reckon they knew the jig was up. He threw another grenade and fired at 'em with his pistol. Then some of us went over there where he was, and we got a bunch of them Krauts and another machine gun. We had the houses then. The Krauts had boxes of grenades all over the place. They could have held out for a week."

"Well, I'll be darned," said Cutler. He could not believe that "Old Mother Hubbard" had done it, and yet here was one of his best runners telling him that he had seen the thing happen. Chivington had fooled him completely. He said to the corporal, "What color was the smoke grenade?"

"Green, sir."

"Green, eh. Why that old son-of-a-gun!" Cutler said.

Before the men completed the supply, daylight had come; but the light brought no enemy fire. The morning mists rose from the hills to show the shapes of men lying in slit trenches on the flat slope that was the top of the spur. The men did not move, but Cutler knew that they were awake and alert to any nearby enemy. They covered the visible parts of the road and the houses with their weapons. The mortars pointed upward from close behind the riflemen. Cutler waited for further Battalion orders. He sat eating his ration with the radio operator. As Major Van Tuyl's voice called his code, he picked up the radiophone.

"Come in blue-white five."

"Move your walnuts forward right away to the east side of the town."

"Roger."

"Part of D Company will support your move. They should be near you now. Can you see them?"

Cutler stepped to the edge of the terrace and looked back. He saw two sections of men walking toward him along the terrace road where he had been pinned down the day before—men with large tripods and machine guns. He returned to the radio.

"Yes, I see them coming. I'll move up right away."

"Roger—out."

As he turned to his runners, he said, "Tell your platoon leaders to get their men ready to move right away. Third Platoon runner, you tell Lieutenant Jensen to hold where he is and cover us until he sees us ahead in the flat. Then have him join us. Okay? Move out." He fastened his pistol belt as the runners left.

When they had had time to reach their platoons, he started toward the men on the slope. He stumbled across the shell-pocked earth that artillery and mortars had beaten badly until he came to the waiting men. "Okay, now. Keep well spread out as we move forward. First and Second Platoons move out on line. Fourth follow in behind the First. Keep spread out and watch yourselves."

Lieutenant Walker came up with the two machine gun sections. "Where do you want me?" he asked.

"You set up on this ridge and cover us as we move out across the field," said Cutler. "Keep your guns spread out. I don't know what we're getting into but we'll soon find out."

His men moved rapidly before him down the steep forward slope into the small valley where tree stumps smoldered—evidence of American artillery's strength. On the far side, broken stone buildings rose in a steep wall at the top of the ridge, but between lay the yellow stubble field Cutler had seen from the plane. No one spoke. All moved toward the silent buildings. The radio called Cutler. "Hold your men where they are! Hold your men where they are!"

"Roger."

"Out."

Then to the men about him, he shouted, "Hold up! Hold up where you are. Keep spread out." Cutler did not like the order. His men were in the open valley surrounded by higher ground which the night before had been alive with Germans. He could not understand why they were not fired on. His men certainly offered targets treacherously outlined by the yellow stubble.

As he sat down to rest, he said, "Send an aid man over here."

The man came over. "What's the deal, Lieutenant?"

"Say, fix up this leg of mine, will you? Just put a bandage on it." He pulled up his pant leg to show a two-inch gash on the outside of his leg. The bandage that he had put on the night before had slipped down. The woolen pant leg had chafed the edges of the wound making it burn. The aid man sprinkled cool powder over the wound and then wrapped white gauze around the leg. "How's that, Lieutenant?"

He stepped on the leg to feel that it stood stronger because the bandage held it in. "Fine," said Cutler.

"You had better get that fixed up in the hospital pretty soon. It's already infected, and it'll get worse."

"Yes, I'm going pretty soon, I guess."

He called Battalion on the radio but received no answer. He tried Regiment and immediately raised the S-3. "What's going on. I'm sitting out here in the open waiting for orders. I don't like this spot a bit."

"Hold where you are. I'll check and call you back in a couple of minutes."

Cutler leaned back against a rock and tipped his helmet forward to shade his eyes.

Lieutenant Walker of the weapons platoon shouted down from the hill behind, "What in the hell's going on down there?"

"I don't know right now. Battalion wants me to hold up. I'm waiting. Sit tight there and cover us. We may need it. Cover us."

He called Battalion once more. This time he got through to Van Tuyl. "What's going on?" he asked impatiently. "This is liable to be a hot seat any minute."

"Anyone firing at you now, boy?"

"No, no one has fired at us yet."

"We think the Krauts have pulled out. We're not sure yet. I'll call you back inside of fifteen minutes and have something definite for you then."

"Roger—out."

Cutler turned to the men nearest him and said, "They think the Krauts have pulled out."

This traveled rapidly among the men as "The Krauts have pulled out."

174

Cutler shouted back, "They think the Krauts have pulled out, but they're not sure yet. They're not sure yet."

The ground seemed to breathe hot, dry air from the scorched stubble of grass. Smoke smouldered quietly upward from a log near by. Other logs gave off an occasional spark while the sun, almost at its peak, beat upon the men in their dusty valley without shade.

The Third Platoon moved toward Cutler. He waved his arm for them to hold up where they were. The men sank to the ground.

"Blue-white six to blue-white three, over." It was Van Tuyl's voice again. "Move your walnuts across the road into an assembly area at the large culvert in the road bend. The Germans have moved out. Watch for snipers though. We're going to try to feed hot chow. Give me a count on your walnuts, and also tell me what equipment you need. Get me this as soon as you can."

"Roger. Anything else?"

"No, that's all. Out."

As Cutler gave the phone back to Covalos, he shouted to the First Platoon leader. "Swing your men toward the road. Keep spread out. We're going into an assembly area. The Krauts have moved out."

Most of the men were too weary to cheer.

Back to the D Company sections, he called, "Fall in behind my last platoon. Watch out for snipers."

"Okay," yelled Walker.

The men climbed rapidly to the top of the ridge, then down a steep bank to the road. Cutler guided them. As he felt the hard-packed earth under his feet, he saw two Americans coming toward him. One of them he recognized as Captain Chivington. He had never seen Chivington so disheveled. His face was blackened and streaked. His uniform was torn and spotted. Moving to meet him, Cutler shook his hand strongly.

"Congratulations," he said meaning it heartily.

Chivington smiled. "I didn't do much. Couldn't let you win the war by yourself, Cutler."

Don Cutler felt all the weight of the last three days fall from him while he stood there. He had been in all the blackness of the burnt grass, the shattered bodies, the torn earth, and the smashed trees. He had been torn himself in several places, but he was still alive. Blood stains were on the side of his lightly-bearded face. The sleeve of his shirt was dried brown from blood from the cut on his head. From the gash in his leg, the ragged pant leg hung stiffly above a combat boot that showed the scar of an artillery fragment. In spite of the scratches, he stood on the road shaking Chivington's hand.

"Did they get you very badly?" asked Cutler looking at a white bandage that showed through a rent in Chivington's shirt.

"No, two bullets just creased the skin, not deep at all. Rather uncomfortable though," Chivington said as he stood in the road wiping his face on one of his handkerchiefs.

"I've got to put my company in the assembly area," said Cutler. "Where is it, do you know?"

"Just down the road. Part of A Company is already there. You should find plenty of room. Say, have you seen any B Company men?"

"Just a few. I'll send them over when we get in."

Cutler moved the men along the road and down onto the terraces which were now the assembly area. "Keep spread out now and dig in right away. We may get artillery fire in here at any time."

He sat down and leaned against the cool earth of the terrace nearest the road. He looked over the north country. The Arunci Mountains rose high and rocky several miles away. The Mediterranean Sea lay far, far off to the west. The water looked hazy and refreshing. Two flies bothered his vision as he crossed his legs. Green sprouts grew out from the trunk of a smashed tree. He rolled onto his side and saw ants struggling over the loose ground climbing the little hummocks, struggling over pebbles.

On his message book he wrote four carbons:

Give me a count of the number of men you have effective. Also, a list of equipment needed. If the hot chow gets here, we'll eat in order—First, Second, Third, Fourth and Headquarters Platoons.

Cutler

He called the runners and gave each a copy.

A jeep stopped on the road. Mess kits rattled in a mattress cover as it was lifted out. The men cheered wearily.

"Bring the food down on this terrace. A few of you men give them a hand," said Cutler.

The big metal pots were steaming. As the cooks set them down ten yards apart, the men of the First Platoon formed a double line with five paces between men. The cooks sat between the two columns and served first to one side and then to the other. The battalion doctor stood at the end of the line and asked each man as he came through, "Any wounds?"

Cutler went through last. While the doctor looked over his wounds, he chewed a large piece of slightly salty ham.

The doctor said, "You're going back to the hospital for a while."

"Okay," said Cutler, "but first I'm going to give Major Van Tuyl my report of casualties."

The medic tied a tag through a buttonhole of his shirt.

XXV

When the report was in, Cutler looked around him once more before climbing into the waiting jeep. The men, fed and exhausted, were resting quietly on the ground. Lieutenant Jensen came with him to the jeep while the cooks packed up the kitchen equipment. There was an air of ease in the area. For the moment, the war was stopped. They had come through, acquitted themselves well.

"Take care of yourself," said Jensen to Cutler. "We'll miss you."

"Sure," said Cutler. "A week ought to do it." His strength seemed to be leaving him rapidly. The blood had stiffened on his face and seemed to make it difficult for him to talk. His arm ached in his shirt sleeve. His leg throbbed under the bandage. He wanted very much to lie down like the men under the wrecked trees and doze in the sun with his full stomach. He wanted to enjoy this peace which, for a little while, they had won. The breeze flapped at the medic tag tied to his shirt.

"So long, fellas. Keep your heads down," he said.

"We'll be looking for you back," said Rusnick. "Take it easy."

The driver was waiting impatiently. As Cutler settled wearily onto the hard seat beside him, he gunned the jeep forward with a jerk and left the area enveloped in a cloud of dust.

"The front is a good place to get the hell out of," said the driver intently.

As they drove south along the road, Cutler sleepily noticed a group of German prisoners moving toward the rear. They were weary and dispirited, shuffling their feet up and down methodically as they moved back. These men were not the husky men of the elite Afrika Korps he had seen in the States but rather the dregs in the barrel—young men, slight and bewildered; older men with graying hair and lined faces. He also saw Allied men and supplies moving up to reinforce the division. He wondered whether that Private Nolan who had never yet showed up was among them. There was organization here. The men and supplies would keep coming even though he was going back. There were others to take over, to carry on, to hold the ground they had taken and to go on to take the town ahead.

The jeep drew up at a collecting station. Cutler roused himself and looked around. There were three tents set up to one side and on the ground men on stretchers lay waiting. Aid men were moving back and forth giving plasma, morphine, talking with wounded. Cutler climbed slowly down to the ground. He hated to move his leg for when he did the hurt came back. As he stood hesitating, Chaplain Rutherford walked up and shook his hand.

"How are you, Cutler?" he asked.

"Cut up a bit," said Cutler, "nothing very bad."

"That's good," said Rutherford.

"Over here," said an aid man and Cutler went obediently. The aid man reached for his tag and looked into his face only after he had read it.

"You'll have to wait," he said. "We've got to take care of some of the stretcher cases first. What's going on up there now?" he asked.

"The Krauts have pulled out," said Cutler.

"That's a swell piece of news," said the aid man. "They've kept us too busy the last three days."

Cutler nodded. He sat down against a small tree, and leaning his head against it, went to sleep.

When he woke, the sun was much lower. The aid man was shaking him by the shoulder.

"Come on," he said, "you're next."

Cutler stumbled to his feet and let himself be led into one of the tents. He was still half asleep.

In the tent a lantern hung from the ridge pole over a pair of tables. A doctor in field khakis glanced up, reached for his tag reading it silently. They had Cutler sit on a table and removed his helmet. The doctor peered at the mass of blood and grime stuck to his forehead. When it was washed clean, tweezers were brought and one by one the doctor lifted three fragments of steel and dropped them in a pan. Cutler stared at them dully.

"Were those in the bone?" he asked.

179

"That's right," said the doctor. "This was your lucky day."

They went to work on his arm, cleaning, prying, dropping more steel in the pan. Then they unbound his leg and pried in the open gash. Cutler saw red flashes of pain before they sprinkled on more cool powder and rebandaged it.

"Consider yourself lucky," said the medic holding out the pan to show him the fragments of steel.

"Thanks," said Cutler starting to get down from the table.

"Not so fast," said the doctor. "You're not walking on that leg for a few days." The doctor reached under the table and pulled out a bottle of whiskey. "Here's what you need now," he said with a grin. He gave Cutler a drink.

They brought a stretcher and as he was carried out Cutler could feel the whiskey warming him all through his body and out into his toes and fingers. He pulled in a long breath and relaxed. He was carried to a waiting ambulance. There were two men already there with their stretchers buckled in when he was loaded. One was pale and either asleep or unconscious. His face looked almost waxen against the olive-drab blanket, but the other one managed a weak smile.

"How's it going?" asked Cutler feeling great need for any human contact, but the man only smiled again without answering and then shut his eyes. Cutler watched the blanket over the man's chest rise and fall and slowly realized that he was much better off than either of them. It gave him a feeling of elation. He, Donald Cutler, lived in a body which had not been badly hurt. The steel had peppered into this body he lived in but not enough to drag him down to the balance line where the decision rested. He was well this side of that balance line. He thought of the pieces of shrapnel in the medic's pan knowing that any of them could have ended his life out there as he had twisted and turned from the mortar fire. He was lucky. The conviction filled him. The relief to him was inexpressible. He wanted to shout or sing or talk with someone, anyone, about how lucky he had been up there—to tell them of his narrow escapes, of the ground they had taken.

The aid men came up with a fourth stretcher. Cutler was surprised to see Private Benard's broad face. He suddenly remembered the roll of money which he had buttoned into his pocket three days ago. He wanted to joke.

"Well," he said almost gaily, "look what a man will do to keep track of his money."

Benard grinned toothlessly at him.

"What's the matter with you?" asked Cutler.

"Through the shoulder," said Benard with a strange lisp.

The ambulance started down the road.

"Much pain?" asked Cutler.

"Naw," said Benard. "They shot me full of something makes my head thick. Worst thing is that somewhere I lost my plate. Must have jumped clear out of my mouth when that damn Kraut spun me around. Can't hardly eat without it."

"They'll get you another one," said Cutler.

"Sure," said Benard, "but that takes a long time."

Cutler fumbled in his pocket. "Here's your money," he said.

"Gee, Lieutenant," said Benard, "if I'd a known what you was going to do, I'd a carried it myself. I sure thought you was a gonna out there with them mortars playing tag with you."

"Oh," said Cutler echoing Chivington, "it wasn't much."

"Jeez," said Benard, "a man wouldn't want much more than you got."

Cutler handed him the roll of money, and Benard handed back the receipt. It somehow seemed to be a very formal transaction here in an ambulance.

They were silent for a while listening to the sound of the motor and the indistinct hum of the voices of the aid men up in front. The waxen-faced man started to groan. The jouncing over the rough road gave him pain. The ambulance was a heavy, cumbersome vehicle which hit almost every hole in the twisting road. Cutler wanted to help him, but there was nothing he could do but lie on his own stretcher. He wondered whether the man was going to make it. He found himself waiting for the next groan. At least as long as the man groaned he was alive.

Outside, night came and the men in the ambulance rode in almost complete darkness. Only a little reflected glow came through the glass window of the cab. Cutler slept again sinking gratefully through the warm whiskey into deep sleep.

When he woke, the doors of the ambulance were open. He turned his head slowly and saw that they seemed to have

181

stopped in a tent camp. Slowly he remembered. This must be the hospital. Aid men were lifting Benard's stretcher out.

"So long, Lieutenant," said Benard.

"See you," said Cutler. "Good luck." He felt his own stretcher lifted and braced his good elbow against it to lift his head and look around.

The men carried him into a tent and put the stretcher down across a table. Again medics looked at his tag and assigned him a tent number. Cutler thought how nice it was to have someone else making the decisions for him. All he had to do was lie back and rest.

The tent was huge. Men in cots lay sleeping on either side and, under a lantern, two nurses sat at a table making out reports. One of them spoke quietly to him.

"Hello, fella," she said and smiled at him.

"Hello," said Cutler. He looked at the bright lipstick and at the brown curls which stuck out under her cap. He began to feel that he liked it here.

An aid man helped him into bed. To Cutler, it was amazing to be once again in a bed with clean sheets. He twisted under the covers enjoying the freshness and incredible cleanness. To him, this was the ultimate in luxury. The nurse came over and smiled at him again as she stuck a thermometer in his mouth. He watched while she took his pulse. He wondered how any man could have a normal pulse under these circumstances. She smoothed his pillow and straightened the crisp sheet across his chest.

"Now," she said, "you just get some sleep, and in the morning we'll bring you some breakfast." She smiled again and gently patted the back of his hand before she went to the table under the light. Cutler watched her. He felt that if he allowed himself to go to sleep, he would wake again crouched in a foxhole. If this were a dream, he wanted to enjoy it a little longer.

Gradually he became aware of the men around him—the breathing, snoring noises, the creaking noises as a man turned over in his cot, the soft calls to an aid man. Outside in the distance he could hear vehicles coming and going, ambulances he supposed, or supply trucks whose business could not stop just because the deep night had come. The two nurses talked quietly to each other under the light, but they were too far away for him to hear what they were saying.

Suddenly he realized why it seemed so quiet here. There was no artillery. Though he strained his ears, he was too far away from the war to hear it. A feeling of sheer exuberance grew in him. He was no longer sleepy. He wished that morning were here. He wanted the daily routine to begin so that he could enjoy this outing. He wanted the nurse to come back and take his pulse again and smile at him. He began to think quietly of home and of his old room in his father's house and of the gentleness of his mother. It had been a long time since he had had leisure to think of these things. They came back to him with great reality and intensity. He lingered over the details—the comfortable old bed in his room with the place in the footboard where he had tried out a new jackknife at the age of ten, the curve of the banister in the hall, the slant of the sun through the dining room windows, the smell of fresh pies in the kitchen.

Gradually he let himself think of Helen, remembering not to think too deeply and lose himself in his longing for her. He had done that once and it had been hard to find his way back to the responsibilities of the job when his longing for her dominated him. Far better, he had decided, to shut out that side of his life which softened him. She was there waiting for him. He wondered whether the baby had been born, if it was a son and if he would ever see them.

He thought that now that he was wounded, he might be sent home, but he knew that it was wishful thinking. His wounds were not bad enough for that. The medics would patch him up and send him back to his company in a week or a month. Somewhere out there the war continued. He longed with his whole being for peace.

He turned over and watched the nurse. He wished that he could think of some way to get her to come back. Perhaps if he pretended to choke? He grinned to himself as he discarded the idea and, watching her, finally fell asleep.

XXVI

When the telephone rang, Violet Spaulding was still asleep. She reached out with one manicured hand, groping for the phone, and looked at the clock, wondering who would call her at 8:30 in the morning.

"Hello," she said flatly.

"Violet," said an excited voice in her ear. "It's Bea. Have you seen the paper?"

"What paper?" she asked with annoyance.

"The morning paper, dear! There's a write-up about Malcolm's battalion. It's just so exciting!"

"What did you say?" asked Violet.

"Read your morning paper, dear. Hutchins' column is all about Malcolm and his battalion."

"What has he done now?" asked Violet, pulling herself up against the pillows to force herself awake.

"It only says he's got the best-trained outfit in Italy, Vi, and is well organized and going to fight all the way to Berlin."

"Well," said Violet, "that sounds like Malcolm playing soldier all right. What else does it say?"

"Oh, a lot about the privates getting mail from home and how they live—you know—the usual, darling, but I thought you'd want to know about Malcolm. He might even get his promotion on top of all this."

"Well, thanks for letting me know," said Violet. "I'll have a look at it. How about lunch?" she asked.

"Love to, darling. At the Bluebonnet?"

"Make it 1:30," said Violet.

When she hung up, Violet rested against the pillows a moment. *Imagine Malcolm bragging to a war correspondent,* she thought, *and then getting in all the papers. How ridiculous of him.*

She pulled on her pink robe and stepped into a pair of satin scuffs which were beside the bed. The glow through the venetian blind showed her that it would be another warm day. She wished that Bea had not called her so early.

The paper was just outside the door, rolled into itself like a small log. She took it to the kitchen and started the coffee before opening to Hutchins' column.

With the Fifth Army—Somewhere in Italy

For two days I have been living with a battalion preparing to enter the lines in the near future. The aggressive leader of this fighting force is Lieutenant Colonel Malcolm Spaulding, a West Pointer, who told me personally in an exclusive interview that his battalion is now completely ready to meet the enemy and awaits only the order from division headquarters. I interviewed him in a tent set up in an olive grove where the rumble of artillery at the front could be distinctly heard. He sat before a folding field table covered with well-organized papers and gave the impression of being on top of his job.

Lieutenant Colonel Spaulding hails originally from Missouri but now calls San Antonio his home. He explained to me that the men of his command had been given special training to make them the best fighting force in Italy. Soon he will have a chance to prove this.

It was a pleasure to meet Colonel Spaulding. He reflects the best traditions of the U.S. Army. He told me personally that he expects to march these men to Berlin and then go to the Pacific; and I'd like to state here and now that if any outfit does that, it will be Colonel Spaulding's. He has a great fighting battalion here, a real pace setter.

It was down in the companies that I met the men that make up this great battalion. I lived two days with these men sharing their lives, getting to know them, listening to what they had to say; and I'd like to report to you folks back home that they're great Americans, all of them, and with men like these we'll win the war.

It was also my privilege to witness the distribution of mail. . . .

Violet was extremely amused. She took the paper and

185

walked into Alice's room.

"Look what your father has done now," she said.

Alice sat up in bed. "What time is it?" she asked.

"Only 8:30," said Violet, "but your father is in the papers this morning."

"Let's see," said Alice.

Violet stood over her while Alice hurriedly scanned the article.

"Well," said Alice, "it sounds like Daddy all right. At least he's still safe."

"Of course he's safe," said Violet. "Why do you always worry about him. He's a big boy now. He can take care of himself."

"I hope you're right," said Alice, "but sometimes he acts so aggressive."

"It's all just bluff, honey," said Violet. "I've been married to him twenty-two years and I know."

"What do we do today?" asked Alice.

"How about shopping?" asked her mother.

"What for?" asked Alice.

"Well," said Violet, "let's try on hats. I've got a lunch date with Bea at 1:30 but you can come along."

"Thanks," said Alice wryly.

"Wear your navy blue, dear," said Violet. "Maybe you'll find a hat to go with it. It needs something with a little sparkle."

"It isn't the dress that needs the sparkle," said Alice, "it's me. I get so bored sometimes."

"Well," said Violet, "don't blame me. You would run off and get married at the last minute. Alice Spaulding would have had a fun year here in San Antone, but as Mrs. Van Tuyl, you sit home."

"Sometimes I think I'll get a job," said Alice.

"Whatever would you do, dear?" asked her mother. "Just be glad you don't have to work."

"I think I'd like to have something definite to do," said Alice.

"You'd tire of it very rapidly," said Violet, "Besides," she said "who do you know that works?"

"Well, nobody," said Alice, "but if I worked, I'd get to know them."

"Really, dear," said Violet, "you don't seem to know when you are well off."

It was almost 11:30 before they found their way downtown. They spent the rest of the morning shopping leisurely. For some women, this is a form of entertainment. They tried on hats sitting at little tables before mirrors, and Alice finally found a little pink feathered cap which Violet told her was stunning on her. Alice bought it half-heartedly and carried it up the sidewalk in a smartly striped box.

San Antonio was full of soldiers—both Infantry and Air Corps from the Fields filled the sidewalks and lingered in the square about the Alamo. Sometimes Alice wondered where they all came from, these alert young soldiers in summer uniform who made San Antonio a military town. To Violet, it was touching to see these naïve young men whose lives would be determined by men like her husband. She felt sharp pity for them.

By 1:30 Violet and Alice were waiting in the lobby of the Bluebonnet Hotel. Bea Whiting bustled in hot and hurried.

"My dear," she gushed, "isn't it exciting! Imagine Malcolm in all the papers. He's so flamboyant."

"That's the last thing I'd call him," said Violet. "He's just playing soldier and had a new audience."

"Now, Vi, I should think you'd be thrilled to have him in the papers like that."

"Oh, I am," said Violet.

"Hello, dear," said Bea to Alice. "What's in the box?"

"A hat with sparkle," said Alice morosely.

"You mean sequins?" asked Bea.

"Oh, no," said Violet. "Show Bea the hat, dear."

Alice opened the box.

"Yes," said Bea, "that's quite nice. Reminds me of a little feathered hat I had when we lived in New York. I used to wear it with a beige dress and shoes. I always liked that hat. It had a little whirl of feathers in the back, and I always had my hairdresser swirl my hair in the same direction so it would blend."

"Quite chic," said Violet.

They lingered over lunch and then found their way to an afternoon movie. The hat box was very much in the way. The show diverted them for almost three hours. When they were again on the sidewalk, it was the end of the afternoon so they dropped in again at the hotel and lingered through dinner. They sat at a table for three—an island of lonely women in the busy life of San Antonio.

Violet, looking around her, saw the young officers, splendid in their tailored uniforms and polished insignia. She was acutely aware of being outside of their world. With Malcolm away, she was no longer in a political position. There was nothing anyone wanted from her. Like Alice, she lacked "sparkle," but unlike Alice, this fading had gone further than mere boredom and lethargy and become part of a relentless aging process. Her skin sagged, her face looked made up, the lines which had been hinted before were becoming prominent. As she gazed out across the room, she had the look of defeat. Her longing to be desirable to the splendid young men, tall and strong, broad-shouldered and tanned, rose again in her bitterly unfulfilled heart. She was a woman who lived with the constant belief that somehow she had not yet found a happiness which was quite near if she could only open the right door, meet the right person, be in the right place at the right time. But the thing she sought continually had eluded her, and the years had gone by leaving a longing which embittered her.

Finally Violet pulled on her gloves. "Bea," she said, "we've got to get home. It's been good to see you. Call me tomorrow."

"All right," said Bea, "and when you write Malcolm, be sure to tell him how thrilled I was to see his name in the paper."

"Oh, Bea," said Violet, "you know how those war correspondents are."

"Well, anyway," said Bea, "it will make Malcolm feel good to know we were impressed."

"Men are such egotists," said Violet, "why add to it."

"My dear," said Bea, "you must be very sure of him."

"Let's just say that I can see through him," said Violet, "and predict his dull behavior every time."

Violet and Alice rode back in a taxi. They unlocked the door and went into the little hall walking over the mail which had been pushed through the slot in the door. Violet snapped on a light.

"Get it, will you?" she said to Alice taking a cigarette out of the box on the coffee table.

Alice brought in the handful of mail. "There's a telegram for you, Mother," she said unsteadily.

Violet turned abruptly to look at the yellow envelope in Alice's hand. "Well, let's open it," she said, but Alice just stood there holding it away from herself as though it were contaminated.

"Give it to me," said Violet shrilly, somehow sensing disaster. She opened it carefully and read it slowly, Alice at her shoulder.

The War Department regrets to inform you of the death of your husband, Colonel Malcolm Spaulding, in line of duty...

"No," she said unsteadily. "No! No!" She stared at Alice. "He can't be," she said, but Alice was already in tears. "Stop that," she said as though stopping Alice from crying would negate the telegram.

"Oh, my God," she sobbed, "I love him so much. I do. I do."

XXVII

For two weeks Lieutenant Donald Cutler stayed on his cot in a convalescent tent enjoying the sense of being cared for, of being very lucky. The other men lay about with bandages or plaster casts. Some wandered about in bathrobes and heavy boots. They read, played cards, or talked. There was no rank here, just men needing attention. Each day their wounds were dressed, at first by the doctors, later by nurses. Cutler enjoyed a real sense of well-being after days and nights of living on the ground. He often thought of the company. He wondered where the men were, whether they had taken the town beyond Hill 103, what casualties they were getting. He knew that the Fifth Army was just below Rome now.

The day came when the doctor said he could get up. He tried out his shaky legs and soon was allowed to walk to meals at the officers' mess. This was a particular treat to him since the nurses and Red Cross girls ate there too, and the atmosphere was much friendlier than a stateside officers' club. Cutler noted a particular sense of dedication in the medical personnel. He would very much have liked to have known some of the doctors better, to have sat with them and talked; but as a patient in a bathrobe, he was at a disadvantage. He retained a particular fondness for the nurse who had treated him on the night he arrived. Her last name was Jones and everyone called her "Jonesie." It had been rather a shock to Cutler to find that she smoothed the pillows and patted the hands of other men besides himself, but after an hour or two of jealousy he forgave her.

When he was on his feet, he was able to look up Benard who lay quietly in a tent of more seriously wounded. Benard's shoulder was shattered. X-rays showed a collection of bone splinters around the joint. It was too soon to know how much use he would have eventually of his arm. Cutler found him weak but happy.

"Guess what, Lieutenant?" he said, "I'm going home on the next boat!"

"That's fine," said Cutler, struggling against his own wish to be going home. Would he change places if he could with Benard? He didn't know.

"Still got your money?" asked Cutler grinning.

"Sure," said Benard, "but you tell me what the hell it's good for now."

"Cheer up," said Cutler, "once you get home and out of the hospital, you can use it for a real vacation."

"Yea," said Benard, "maybe I'll do just that. Find me a chicken to help spend it."

"It won't last long that way," said Cutler grinning at him.

"What the hell," said Benard. "A short life and a merry one."

Cutler wandered about asking for Captain MacRae. He found that MacRae was still at the hospital and had been given the part-time job of Graves Registration Officer. He found MacRae sitting at a table with a long checklist. He seemed glad to see Cutler but was very subdued and gentle.

"How are things going?" Cutler asked him.

"So-so," said MacRae. "I keep track of the graves now." He dropped his eyes shyly.

"So I hear," said Cutler.

"Thousands of them," said MacRae.

"Are they going to send you home?" asked Cutler.

"I don't want to go home," said MacRae staring at the table.

"Well, what do you hear from Fran?" asked Cutler trying to be pleasant.

Captain MacRae looked at him intently. "Diana has night-mares," he said. "She's afraid of big birds and every night the birds frighten her."

"That's too bad," said Cutler. "She'll outgrow it after a while. How's Fran?"

MacRae looked right at him and beckoned him to come closer. Cutler, puzzled, leaned down wondering just how sick MacRae still was. "Fran's having a baby," he said.

"Why that's fine," said Cutler.

"Fran wants a divorce," he whispered. "What do you think of that?"

"Why," said Cutler, "Fran can't divorce you while you're overseas."

"I know it," said MacRae. "But it's not my baby and that's why I'm not going home. They can't make me!"

Cutler didn't know what to say. "Well, Rich," he said finally, "when you go back you can see Diana."

"I'm straightening things out for Diana," said MacRae confidentially. "Every night I shoot down the big birds so that she can sleep."

Cutler stood back confused.

One day Cutler received a handful of mail which had been sent back from the company. He spent several hours opening it, reading and rereading, digesting the contents. There were several letters from Helen. She still waited for the baby, but it would be soon now. He thought of her tenderly and wondered how she looked now big with child, his child. He wished that he could be with her while they waited. Again he longed for peace. It occurred to him that right now as he read the letters the child might already have been born, and he would not know of it. How strange that would be, he thought.

The day that the Fifth Army took Rome was a day of celebration at the hospital. The men in the tents cheered as the news was brought. Cutler cheered with the others, thinking of Colonel Spaulding and of Duval and Benard, of First Sergeant Pulska and the many others who had paid hard for this advance. He wondered whether all victories were colored by their cost.

His restlessness grew as he roamed about in his boots and bathrobe trying to strengthen his leg. He signed up to go to a USO show and was driven out at night with the others to be entertained. The show was full of laughs and they were an appreciative audience, but the things he remembered best afterwards about the show was how lonely he had been for Helen, and the way that the English, French, and Americans had sung the three national anthems.

When the medics came through next day, Cutler asked when he could be discharged.

"Why," said the doctor with mock surprise, "here's a man that doesn't like our hotel. How about giving it a little more time," he added. "We don't want that leg opening up the first time you have to depend on it."

"OK," said Cutler, "you're the doc." From then on his attention was focused on getting back to the company.

Now that he was up and wandering about, he got to know other officers. There was a good-natured captain from Pennsylvania that he talked with. One morning the captain said, "Ever hear of the Orange Club?"

"Sure," said Cutler, "in Naples?"

"That's right," said the captain.

"Some of us are going down there tonight. Want to come along?"

"Sure," said Cutler pleased to be asked.

"We'll go right after chow," said the captain.

The Orange Club hung high on a cliff above Naples and the harbor. Afterwards, when he had had time to think it over, Cutler decided that the only possible way to enjoy the Orange Club was to have been very drunk. There had been one drunk Canadian there who could hardly walk, and on his face had been the benign look of complete happiness.

The club was terribly crowded, hot and noisy. Cutler stood to the side of the dance floor noticing the uniforms of the Allied Command—American, Canadian, British, French, Australian, Brazilian—he was not sure of some of them. Men ringed the dance floor, far outnumbering the women who wore the uniforms of the WAAC, Red Cross, and Nurses Corps. The orchestra beat out the rhythms. The others, struggling to get the most out of every minute in this festive atmosphere, seemed to Cutler to be looking in the wrong place. He wasn't sure what it was that a soldier on leave wanted, but it was more than women and whiskey and it wasn't here in the club. The artificial gaiety repelled him. He wondered whether it was because he was tired and wounded that he felt this way. His leg throbbed. He felt disoriented away from his company. He found a seat in a corner where, by turning his head, he could look out over Naples to the bay.

In the bright moonlight, he could see the dark land mass spreading left and right, and beyond lay the Mediterranean, deceptively quiet and peaceful. At the water's edge lights burned where the unloading continued day and night. A large white ship, completely lighted, lay in the harbor, *a hospital ship—the one Benard goes home on,* thought Cutler. He remembered when they had first come to Italy and, looking back at night from their first bivouac area, had seen the blossoming trails of tracer bullets searching the skies for German planes over a blacked-out Naples.

As he had on the first day he had seen Naples, he thought of the history of this bay, of the Etruscans who had sailed their small boats up and down this coast four thousand years ago leaving fragments of a language still to be deciphered and handsome sculptures, strong and simple. He thought again of the sibyl cave at Cumae. How could he see this place of ancient prophecy? Again he wondered about his impenetrable future. What lay ahead of him to the north?

The Pennsylvanian captain grabbed his arm.

"Hells bells!" he said, "what's the matter with you. Get up and dance, man!"

Cutler resented the grip on his arm. "Maybe later," he said.

"What's the matter with now?" said the captain cutting in on a little blond WAAC and waving as he danced off.

Later, when he was back with the company, he heard the men looking forward to three day passes to Rome, Cutler remembered the Orange Club and wondered how many of the men would find there what they looked for.

XXVIII

When Cutler was discharged from the hospital, he no longer needed bandages; but the newly mended flesh showed dark scars and was still tender to the touch. He went to the message center to wait for transportation north to join his company, which was now resting in the Alban Hills after the taking of Rome. When he had the chance, he climbed into a truck which was going by way of Anzio. It was good to be headed back. He couldn't quite explain his eagerness. It seemed contrary to reason to want to get back to the line which he had for so long been very eager to leave. He wondered whether it was because life behind the lines seemed pale in comparison with the constant threat to life in the line which gave a zest he had come to depend on.

During the first half-hour of his ride, Cutler saw more supplies and organization than he had thought existed. The truck drove through fields of stacked shells, through gasoline depots, through tank-repair yards. He saw salvaged scrap being loaded onto ships. He was amazed to see the number of men busy moving supplies this far behind the front. He felt that the dread of running out of supplies, which always hounded him in a forward position, would ease now that he had seen all this activity.

They headed out into flat, open country passing a wrecked German tank lying on its side in a ditch. Grass grew up around it and already it was starting to rust in streaks. They crossed a Bailey bridge, drove through a completely demolished town, and passed an old German airfield where broken planes still sat behind dirt embankments—the old slim fighters fragile, deadly, but silenced now.

The lines were still moving north. The truck sped toward them over the winding Italian roads. The driver paused at an intersection where the signs were completely blotted out with dust to ask directions of a swarthy Brazilian M.P. His face and uniform were covered with the most delicate layer of dust. It was in the air and on everything in the vicinity. It had trailed the truck sifting up through the floor as they came to a halt. The M.P. pointed out the way, and they were off again, heavily grinding their way toward the front through the loose dirt.

These roads were not meant for convoys but rather for the easy motion of a mule or burro pulling an old cart in which might be riding a sleepy Italian, or strong-legged women carrying heavy burdens on their heads. All such, the convoys, by their presence, ruled off the road.

They passed crossroad graves marked with helmets hung on German crosses. The grass spread out, but Cutler knew from the sickly odor which came faintly on the wind that these growing grasses hid bodies as yet unburied. His trained eye saw the difficulties of fighting here without cover. It was good tank ground, he thought. They went slowly north through flooded sections of the marshes, north toward rolling hills, north toward the rumble of artillery and the men he knew.

He rejoined his company in another olive grove where they rested now while being re-equipped. Some of the old trees were snapped off and broken. Down the slope were courtyards and stables and the remains of terraced vineyards. He arrived at the end of the afternoon. The men were relaxed, unshaven, lying around waiting for mess call; they greeted him heartily.

"Hey, look who's here!"

"Hi ya, Lieutenant Cutler."

"We thought you'd gone home!"

"Hey, you should have taken Rome with us."

"Now we can start the war again."

Cutler grinned.

"How are you, fellas?" he asked.

Lieutenant Rusnick came up and shook his hand. "Glad to have you back, Captain," he said.

"Captain?" said Cutler.

"Sure," said Rusnick. "You got promoted. Congratulations!"

"Well," said Cutler pleased and looking around. "Where's everybody?"

"Well," said Rusnick, "Jensen has B Company now. You'll see him later. Duval's gone back to the States. That wound of his infected his eye. Chivington's up at battalion headquarters, and you're stuck with me as exec officer."

"That suits me fine," said Cutler.

"We've got a new colonel," said Rusnick. "Colonel Horace Galvin."

"Any good?" asked Cutler.

"Well," said Rusnick reluctantly, "perhaps you had better make up your own mind on that."

Cutler raised his eyebrows.

"Hard for anyone to replace Spaulding," said Rusnick.

"Surprises me," said Cutler, "that Van Tuyl wasn't moved up."

"It probably surprises Van Tuyl too," said Rusnick with a grin.

"Who else have we got?" asked Cutler.

"Couple of new second lieutenants," said Rusnick. "Ninety-day wonders fresh out of Benning. Nice kids but no experience."

"Been doing any training here?" asked Cutler.

"Not yet," said Rusnick. "We only got here the day before yesterday, and the men were so tired that I've just let them rest. The replacements came in today. That Private Nolan was supposed to be with them but is on P.O.W. report."

"Well," said Cutler, "guess I'd better check in with the new colonel. What did you say his name was?"

"Galvin," said Rusnick, "Colonel Horace Galvin."

Cutler turned to leave.

"Hey, wait a minute," said Rusnick, "you've got a telegram or cable or something. I almost forgot. I've been carrying it around for two days." He fished in his pocket and brought out a crumbled envelope.

Cutler looked at it and then ripped it open. His fingers were clumsy, slippery and sticky at the same time. There was a stab of realization as he read: "Donald Cutler, Jr. arrived safely. Both well."

He read it again and looked up at Rusnick. "I've got a boy," he said huskily through the lump which was rising in his throat.

"Well, congratulations again," said Rusnick slapping him on the back.

Cutler wiped his face. His hand was shaking. He was still weak. He wanted to sit down and realize this thing which had

197

happened to him. Suddenly the image of Helen was clear and real to him for the first time since he had come to Italy. All his defenses were down. He wanted to tell her he loved her.

"Take it easy, man," said Rusnick.

Cutler collected himself. "Still weak, I guess," he said by way of explanation.

"You better sit down before you faint," said Rusnick. He grinned at Cutler.

"I haven't any cigars," said Cutler, "or I'd give you the first one."

"Tonight," said Rusnick, "we'll get hold of Jensen and have a celebration, just the three of us."

"That's a great idea," said Cutler. He felt as though he was finally in the right place for the first time since he had left.

"I'll show you company headquarters," said Rusnick, "and you can take over."

"Not much to do tonight," said Cutler.

Chow call sounded and the disheveled men got to their feet and formed ragged lines. Cutler, in the headquarters tent, could hear the clatter of mess kits and the jovial calling back and forth.

"They sound good," he said to Rusnick.

"You should have seen them forty-eight hours ago," said Rusnick.

"You were right to let them rest a day or two," said Cutler, "but we better get them shaved and pick up the area tomorrow."

There was a commotion, an argument, outside. The MPs were trying to move back the Italians who now had gathered hungrily near the eating men.

"Oh, my God," said Rusnick, "it's those pitiful people again. It's like being haunted."

Cutler looked out. A crowd of Italians were backing off, quarreling noisily with the MPs who ordered them away. There were old women with black shawls over their heads and black-coated men and dark-eyed children carrying pails.

"Almost be good to get back in the line again," said Rusnick.

"The sooner we finish up this war the better," said Cutler.

The next morning, Cutler woke sleepily and, for a moment, wondered where he was. Then he remembered. He was back with his company as captain now, and he also had a son named Donald Cutler, Jr., whose health he had drunk several times last night with Jensen and Rusnick. They had also drunk to his return, and several times to his promotion. He got up, wishing that his head were a little clearer. This was the morning he was going to take over the company.

As the men gathered for breakfast, he looked them over. He decided that they looked like a bunch of pirates. They were downright sloppy with their stubbled chins and shirts unbuttoned, sleeves rolled up, boots dusty. Some wore helmets, some not. They were thoroughly enjoying the lack of discipline after several rigorous weeks.

As he watched, there was a sudden stir among the men—a whispering, an excitement. He wondered what could possibly have happened. He stepped out of the tent for a better look.

Walking into the area, followed by a group of officers, was Major General Steed from division headquarters. He wore a chestful of ribbons, his leather gleamed, he wore gloves and carried a swagger stick.

Cutler managed to tuck in his shirt tail while the general bellowed, "Who's in charge here?"

"Captain Cutler," said a sergeant.

"Where is Captain Cutler," demanded the general.

"Here, sir," said Cutler acutely aware of his situation.

"Captain," said the general, "this company is a disgrace. Why aren't those men shaved? Why aren't they in proper uniform? Do you know what uniform means? It means all alike—u-ni-form. Major," he bellowed, "take notes on this!"

A major with a clipboard stepped forward.

"Men unshaved," said the general, "men out of uniform, dirty boots. Soldier," he bellowed at Millen, "take off your shirt!"

Millen looked as though he would collapse, but he fumbled with the buttons and removed his shirt to reveal dog tags on a hairy chest.

"No undershirt," yelled the general triumphantly. "All you men, take off your shirts!"

There was a rapid peeling off of shirts.

"Aha," said the general looking about, "three men with no dog tags! Don't you know that's against army regulation, Captain," said the general, "This is a serious breach of military discipline. When were the rifles cleaned last?"

"I don't know, sir," said Cutler.

"He doesn't know," said the general to the major. "He's a company commander and he doesn't know when the rifles were last cleaned. He is also not in full uniform. Are these men getting calisthenics?" asked the general.

"Not at present, sir," said Cutler.

The major wrote it all down while the men stood rigidly at attention. Cutler stood there with his chin stuck out. He'd be damned if he'd make excuses or blame it on Rusnick. He wondered whether he could be court-martialed for this.

The general looked at him scathingly. "I trust, Captain," he said, "that you will remedy these oversights immediately."

"Yes, sir," said Cutler glaring back at him.

The general turned to go. He swung his swagger stick jauntily, but arrested it in mid-air as he noticed a bush full of white chicken feathers near an old wellhead. For just a moment, Cutler was sure that he was going to be asked to explain the presence of the chicken feathers. The general turned back.

"And police this whole area, too," he barked.

"Yes, sir," said Cutler again.

As the general disappeared, Rusnick caught Cutler's eye. "The old bastard," he said, "giving it to you when you're just back from the hospital. Why didn't you tell him you just got back?"

"Forget it, Rusnick," said Cutler. "Let's get this outfit cleaned up."

"You took it for me," said Rusnick, "but you shouldn't have. It's me he should have bawled out. Boy, I'd sure like to have him up in the line someday to show him how we live up there."

"Come on, Rusnick," said Cutler, "get the men through breakfast and shaves and then start them policing the area."

Three hours later the area was immaculate. All the men were shaved and their boots were clean. They all wore undershirts and dog tags and almost looked like an outfit which had never seen action. Almost, but not quite, for on the faces of these men lingered the strain and weariness of combat, and there was about them an air of listening alertness, of being prepared at any moment for the unexpected.

The pup tents were in neat rows and the litter of candy papers, cigarette butts and feathers had disappeared down the old well. The army had its own water points and left old wells strictly alone. A great many things had disappeared down the old well. It was a gigantic wastebasket conveniently nearby. Into it had gone scraps of old lumber, spare boulders, remains of campfires, bottles of Skat, extra equipment, an old tire, the breakfast dishwater, torn comic-book pages, several broken combs, worn-out boots, old letters, chicken bones, and odds and ends too numerous to mention. Cutler was well pleased. It amused him to think of some future generation of archaeologists trying to figure out the conglomeration in that well.

When the job was done, Cutler had the soldiers lined up at ease. "You've done a good job, men," he said. "I hope the general doesn't come back; but if he does, let's be ready for him. Anyone lucky enough to catch another chicken better eat the feathers too."

The men roared.

XXIX

As the rest period came to an end, orders came down from regiment for three-day passes to Rome for the officers and men. Cutler and Rusnick could not both be absent from C Company at the same time, but Cutler found that Jensen had drawn the same leave time as he and was glad that they could go together. Cutler's leg still bothered him some, but he felt much stronger and almost himself again. He was glad that the company had been out of the line when he returned. It would have been difficult, he was sure, to go right from the hospital into action.

The day they were to leave, Jensen, Captain of B Company now, came by in a jeep almost before Cutler had finished breakfast.

"Let's get a move on," said Jensen. "Three days is hardly enough time to see Rome!"

They headed north again, over land in this rolling hill country.

"Was it tough fighting through here?" asked Cutler.

"More of the same," said Jensen grinning, "but you should have seen the welcome we had in Rome. Really made it seem worthwhile."

"Wish I'd been with you," said Cutler.

"They can welcome you today," said Jensen. "Wait till you see those Italian beauties on every street corner."

"I'm going to be a real tourist," said Cutler. "I've wanted to see Rome for a long time and today's the day."

"What do you want to see?" asked Jensen.

"Well, the Colosseum for one thing," said Cutler, "and maybe a museum or two."

"Ugh," said Jensen, "my feet are flat already."

"What you need, my boy," said Cutler grinning, "is more culture. Don't you want to improve yourself?"

"The hell I do," said Jensen. "What I want is some good

wine and a beautiful gal."

As they came into the outskirts of Rome, Cutler felt his excitement rising. He wished that he had some sort of guidebook with him, and said so to Jensen.

"We'll get you one at the Excelsior," said Jensen. "They have everything, and I do mean *everything,* at the Excelsior."

The Excelsior Hotel was one of Rome's finest. With the Allied occupation of the city, it was reserved for officers on leave; and as Cutler and Jensen walked past the MPs into the lobby, it was swarming with officers in uniform.

"Hallelujah," said Jensen, "let's start with a drink."

They each downed a vermouth and juice. There was no other choice unless they had their own bottle.

"Now," said Jensen after they had left the bags in their room, "let's see Rome."

"Sure you want to go?" asked Cutler. "We can split up and meet again later if you want."

"Naw," said Jensen, "I'll give it a chance."

They bought tickets for a sightseeing tour and climbed into a bus in front of the Excelsior. The seats were crowded with jovial men in uniform calling back and forth between the seats. Cutler and Jensen found seats together and looked over the guide book which Cutler now carried.

"OK, professor," said Jensen as the bus started, "educate me."

It was late afternoon before they were back at the hotel. Cutler was elated and frustrated by what he had seen. He had stood in the Colosseum, seen the Roman Forum, the Baths of Caracalla, the Quirinal Palace, the Pantheon, St. Peters, the Sistine Chapel. They had been herded through the tour like sheep standing patiently while the guide whined through his memorized spiel. Cutler had been impatient to be done with the explanations and frustrated by the fact that he was hurried away from things which interested him. There had not been time to see, to evaluate, to remember detail. His total impression was one of confusion.

When he and Jensen finally went back to their room they were both weary. They flipped a coin for the first bath in the large marble tub. Through the wall they could hear the soft provocative laughter of a woman.

"Lead me to it," said Jensen gaily. "It's been a long time. I make it a policy," he explained to Cutler, "never to miss an opportunity." He was in a buoyant mood when they finally went down in the elevator, both wearing fresh uniforms and hungry after the long day.

In the lobby, Jensen ran into a friend from Montana, and they stood there, pumping the other's hand, elated to see a familiar face in the crowd. They celebrated with vermouth and juice; the lieutenant introduced them to two friends of his, and they celebrated this meeting also, and before they knew it, they were members of a group. The lieutenant's friends each had a girl in tow.

"Go get your own," they bellowed at Jensen when he tried to get friendly.

"Where?" asked Jensen.

"Walk around the block," roared the lieutenant.

"I'll just do that," said Jensen draining his glass and adjusting his hat at a rakish angle.

He was gone ten minutes. When he came back, he had a girl on each arm. He came into the dining room like a conqueror, extremely pleased by the reaction at the table.

"It's my personal magnetism," he explained to the astonished Cutler. "You may talk to one of them," he said grandly. The girls giggled. One was dark-eyed with black hair and olive skin. She was thin but not unattractively so. The other was blond, bleached dull, plumper and shorter than the other.

"Do they speak English?" asked Cutler.

"Who cares," said Jensen, "this is going to be a real night out."

They had more vermouth and watched the floor show. Cutler found it a carnival atmosphere. The vermouth made him bleary as he watched the tap dancers and the impersonator and the plastic people who seemed to turn themselves inside out in their contortions. When the show was over, the orchestra played for dancing; looking on, Cutler began to feel the same detachment and depression he had felt at the Orange Club. The music was nostalgic—perhaps, he thought, the same that had been played on that other night—and it brought out poignantly the need of a man for a woman.

He looked at the women—ringlets against skin; lips moist, provocative; breasts roundly ripe just below the veil of cloth. The women enticed him, dragged at his imagination with their laughter and knowing eyes.

He looked about at the uniformed men gathered over the tables. There was everywhere in the room a sense of tension and expectation. His mind flashed the old phrase—"See Rome and die."

Knowing well the need of these men to find, for a time, a passion in which death was inconsequential, Cutler wished there could have been here for them real women of compassion rather than these exploiters. He felt that man's need of woman was too basic to play with, too perceptive to be satisfied with commercialization, too demanding to be satisfied by substitution. He had sometimes wondered whether the greater part of the bravado and bragging among men hid the disappointments of half satisfaction, the knowledge of having been cheated by circumstances into searching in the wrong place. He felt the depression he had felt at the Orange Club growing in him again.

The hell with philosophy, he thought. A man tortured himself with scruples here where the taking was so easy. Perhaps all women were the same. The vermouth twisted in him. He felt a little wild with the blaring music and the lights and the swirling mass of dancers going by. He would not let himself be depressed. He made up his mind to dance and looked around the table. What did it matter which one. He chose the little blond. The men said that they bleached it with hot sea water, but what did it matter.

He put his arm around her and curled his fingers around her waist. He crushed his chin down into the straw-blond hair and took off with the music. She was pliant, following well his relentless tour about the floor. When the music stopped for a moment, he stayed on the floor with his arm around her and then they danced again. It would be easy, he thought, to take her up to the room. A man needed whatever woman was available. Helen couldn't know the need of a man and the strain of war in a strange country.

He tried to feel angry with Helen, but all he could think of was that she had borne him his son. The knowledge trapped him. He looked down at the little blond twisting to follow his steps. She had a dimple on her cheek and tossed her mane of hair back over her shoulder. Whose sons would she bear?

Suddenly he wanted to get rid of her. He felt defeated, but he knew that he could not take her or any other like her to his bed. There were more wars than big wars, he thought, hating this awareness in himself. He went back to the table counting the hours until they could return to the company where life seemed relatively uncomplicated. He sat quietly. Even the vermouth and juice seemed to have lost its flavor as his depression gathered about him like a cloak.

The party went on around him while he sat moody and alone. If he could just get back home everything would be all right again. If he could just get away from this world of death and wounding, of mud and greasy mess kits, of yearning and expediency. It was the enemy that kept him here in Italy, using up these days of his manhood in endless waiting, fighting, and waiting again. He hated them now, hated them for the attrition of his company, hated them for the wounds which were still tender, hated them for being there, well-entrenched above Rome, waiting for the battalion to come after them.

XXX

Captain Cutler's company had been moved up with the rest of the battalion to go into the lines in the open rolling country south of the Arno River. Across the wide American sector of the front, battalions were to be on line with no reserve. Each was to be largely independent. Much pressure would be placed on the enemy in order to move the war northward during the good weather or the troops would spend another bitter winter in the mud and chilling cold of the Appennine Mountains.

Lieutenant Colonel Galvin remembered the harangue which the colonels had received from Major General Steed.

"On to the Arno. Push your men and put pressure on the enemy at all points. Find the soft spot that must exist in any line, break the line, and exploit the hole. Knock the German off balance and never let him recover. Push on, organize, attack, reorganize, move, move, move. Don't worry too much about casualties. The individual companies of each battalion must be coordinated in their movements by you so that each may be in position to strike the enemy hard. Push the companies forward. They're always holding back. Keep driving them. There are many replacements for the soldiers. Gain the objective. Expend the soldiers, if necessary, for time is all important. A few lives now will save many more later. Above all, coordinate and control your units. Keep control."

Colonel Galvin thought of the more than twenty years he had studied his reserve officers' manuals for just this opportunity. His was the job of commanding and directing a battalion of infantry—over nine hundred men. It was quite a change for a high school principal. At forty-four his dreams demanded recognition for himself, and he felt that he did not have much time left to gain distinction.

Two weeks in the rest area had gone by rapidly. Colonel Galvin thought that this short time of training with his new battalion had been hardly enough for an officer as new as he to the actual conditions of warfare. He tried not to show his bewilderment but, at times, things happened too rapidly. There were many things which did not match his earlier ideas. He did what he could and welcomed the opinions of others. He found the battalion ran itself very well. He felt competent to handle the job.

Late afternoon was turning into night when the battalion moved into the outskirts of a small town. The men moved up to a tree-covered slope behind the buildings. They were preparing to dig foxholes and take a few hours of rest when a heavy concentration of artillery fell on them. High on the slope cries of "medic, medic" floated down to those in B and C Companies lower on the hill. Colonel Galvin looked over the slope and saw the quick flashes of yellow and orange light spread out close to the ground; he heard the whine of the flying steel fragments in the air. In the few minutes of the barrage, all the outer covers of protection and indifference seemed to leave him. He felt naked as a skinned rabbit. This was what he was to be up against. He did not know these men, these wounded, and did not feel a personal loss. They were units in the larger picture, and the regimental commander had told him there were many replacements available. He shrugged his shoulders, rubbing his closely-cropped hair vigorously, as he turned his head to call the runners. He replaced the heavy steel helmet, to which he had not yet become accustomed, and said, "Tell your company commanders to meet here at 1930 hours."

The men saluted and quietly returned to their companies from which they had come a few minutes earlier. Delaney and his exchange runner went quickly down the road. Leaving it, they descended a narrow, winding path, a short distance alone which they heard a faint whisper, "Lost!"

"Chord," said Delaney just as quietly. A little further along the path he found Captain Cutler and gave him the colonel's message. The exchange runner immediately went back to battalion headquarters leaving Delaney with Cutler at the C Company command post.

Cutler thought over the past two hours. The fire on B Company above him on the hill could only have come from a German observer's close direction. His combat knowledge of the past month told him that the artillery giving the fire was not too far distant from where he now lay propped on his right elbow, chewing a piece of fresh green grass. Tomorrow would probably see contact with the enemy infantry. His company was in fair condition. The men were ready for this again—as ready as they ever were—after two weeks' rest. He wondered if he would come to know the replacements as he knew the older men, as he had known those others who were no longer available.

Cutler missed Spaulding. He realized that Spaulding had thoroughly understood the running of a battalion and the handling of men. He wished that Van Tuyl had been given the battalion. It seemed to Cutler that Colonel Galvin became too excited at times. He recalled their first meeting. He had noticed then a strange light in Galvin's small, black eyes, set in the face of a man who had denied himself many things. That skin had not much flesh beneath it. The lips were thinly drawn beneath a long, well-shaped nose. But the eyes overshadowed the other features of this slight but active man. The eyes burned their way through things in an attempt to find answers. The eyes showed a forceful man behind them, one whose potential obstinacy Cutler feared. He wished that Galvin played poker so that he might learn more about the man. The game had taught him much about other battalion officers. Money was always secondary in his poker games. When he played, he watched the other players, like a man stalking a horse. He learned how the wind blew with each one and knew how to stay on the leeward side of each.

The next morning, at 0300 hours, the battalion moved out with Cutler commanding the reserved company. All moved down the moonlit, shell-pocked road, the men in one file on either side, down past a badly twisted bridge and into the darkness to the north.

When daylight came, Cutler found himself in open, rolling country. Located just behind his two lead platoons, he could see the men spread out with the scouts far in front and to the sides of the battalion. A and B Companies were abreast. The whole battalion appeared to flow forward covering the ground as a blowtorch with its wide sweep up one rise and down the other side toward the next. At this rate they would soon reach the Arno

River, but Cutler knew such rapid movement could not, would not, last.

Another hill, more like a ridge, lay ahead. An electric high-line halfway up distinguished it from the others. In the quiet, clear air Cutler saw the front scouts far ahead go silently upwards. The other men followed more slowly now on the pull of the slope. Higher and higher they went until they disappeared over the tree-covered ridge. C Company followed close behind the last men of B Company.

As Cutler went over the crest of the ridge, he saw that its forward slope also had trees, but that the next, a smaller ridge, and the rolling country beyond, was land from which a wheat crop had been recently harvested. The men of the forward companies had crossed over this smaller ridge and were moving more quickly now. The downward pitch of the slope hurried his own men. Ahead, coming up through the trees, he saw six German soldiers guarded by two B Company men on their way to the rear. The enemy was not far away now.

When Cutler reached the crest of the small, stubble-covered ridge, his eyes met another ridge far ahead. This new one swept around to the west and extended parallel to the line of march at some distance. A slightly lower hill mass stretched along the right side of the battalion. Cutler continued with his company down to the flatter ground of this huge cirque-like basin. His watch told him that it was 1000 hours. The battalion pushed quickly forward in the open country.

All at once an orange flare shot high into the air on the ridge far ahead. Two more quickly followed, and their faint trails of smoke mingled with that of the first. Artillery shells started to fall on the battalion. The column ahead disappeared instantly as the men threw themselves to the ground. Rifle and machine-gun fire from the ridge on the left intensified the danger. Cutler heard the whine of a bullet. Shrapnel from the artillery shells was increasing. The singing and whirring noises of the fragments seemed all around, punctuated as they were by the whacking of pieces on the ground. Only about ten of his own men were still visible. He scrambled into a shallow ditch. Confusion was everywhere. He estimated that more than two-thirds of his company were with him. The rest had not yet come over the top

210

of the ridge. He knew he was in a bad situation. Just then a prolonged buzz called him to his radioman.

Lieutenant Colonel Galvin's voice was high pitched, excited. "Sky-blue fox to green rabbit. Over."

Captain Cutler answered in a voice as steady as he could make it, "Green rabbit to sky-blue fox. Go ahead."

"Take your unit around the left and clear that ridge with the two houses on it."

Cutler paused before answering to lower his head quickly as a shell burst too close. His cheek felt the impress of the wheat stubble as he again spoke, "I'm in the same fire you are. I'll do what I can. Over." He struggled closer to the ground as another burst threw dirt over him.

Galvin's voice came in again shrilly with, "You've got to start immediately. We're getting heavy casualties and can't move!" Its tone was demanding and rose almost to a whine.

Cutler wondered at Galvin speaking of casualties over the radio. He knew German intelligence worked rapidly. "OK," he said. "It's going to take a little time though. Moving out."

Cutler looked around for his scattered men. One mortar squad was firing on a house silhouetted against the sky on the ridge to the west. The first round had gone through the roof of the house. The corporal wanted to know how many rounds to fire.

"Save them, Corporal. We're going to need all of them." Then in a much louder tone, he shouted, "Everyone get back over the hill." He repeated it even more loudly, but the bursting of shells distorted his words.

As he rose to go, a fragment of a branch dropped from a small tree and lay beside him. A sniper's bullet, he thought. He crawled, stumbled, ran, and lay flat, breathing with difficulty. He crawled again when the shellfire diminished. He urged the others to move, but many were more reluctant. He finally reached the far side of the hill. His radio operator, Covalos, joined him followed soon by twelve others. He led them to the tree-covered slope of the next hill where he could observe the situation and make his plans. Ten other men of his company were there behind a house. He immediately sent out two runners to points where he thought others might have gathered. The radio came in again.

"Sky-blue fox to green rabbit. For God's sake hurry, hurry!" said Galvin. "What's the matter? What's holding you up? We're afraid of enemy tanks."

"Green rabbit to sky-blue fox. We are progressing slowly. Have few walnuts. Over and out." He signed off abruptly.

Cutler checked to see what men and weapons he had. He found three machine-gun men with one light machine gun and five boxes of ammunition, three mortar men with one light mortar and nine rounds, and sixteen riflemen including the two he had sent to look for more of his men. These were what he had to work with of the one hundred seventy one who had marched down this same slope an hour before. He knew that the company should have been kept further back, but the colonel had wanted the reassurance of many men close to him. Now he would have to clear the ridge with the men he had. He needed more. It was amazing how rapidly they could disappear. At the end of fifteen minutes, he had rounded up nine more riflemen for the group. He could delay no longer. He sent one scout ahead as far as another scout could see him and then followed with his other men.

All moved slowly, cautiously, through the shattered trees, skirting the open places, following ditches, aiming for the highest point on the ridge. Each man was quietly alert. Cutler was suddenly alive. His eyes were keenly aware of the position of everything around him; his ears listened more carefully, awaiting the unexpected noise. He looked at the ridge ahead through an opening in the foliage. Nothing moved.

Through his binoculars, he had seen that the highest point of the ridge was the end nearest him and that, once he was on it, he could move down through an olive grove very close to the large farmhouse without overly exposing his men. His idea was to go to the high part of the ridge and complete his plans for attack there once he had seen the situation.

Cutler watched his nearest scout intently. He saw him raise his rifle horizontally over his head and move it up and down three times; three Germans ahead. He sent four men up to the nearest scout and then to the lead scout. When they were out of his sight, he sat and waited with the others behind a long terrace. Ten minutes, then fifteen minutes passed. Cutler watched the scout clasp both hands together and shake them over his shoulder, at the same time smiling back at the group. The scout waved them forward.

Five Germans without rifles stood on the empty road. "Fall in at the rear with your prisoners and bring them with us," said Cutler to the three men guarding them.

The group followed the scouts over the top of the ridge to a small, empty shed. Cutler directed the five prisoners into the one room leaving two men to guard them, one inside, the other outside hidden in the trees 20 yards away.

Cutler gave his orders quickly now, "Set the machine gun and mortar on the edge of the olive grove and cover the rest of us as we move out on the double to that house." He pointed through the trees to the large farmhouse on the bare ridge. It was a bluff, a greater bluff than he had ever made in poker. Should the enemy resist, they would kill most of the advancing men. He hoped to surprise them.

The first eight riflemen left the grove running and shouting as loudly as they could. Thirty seconds later a second eight moved down the gentle slope, followed almost immediately by the remaining riflemen. Captain Cutler ran with them. He saw one German come out of the open door of the house, stop surprised, throw down his rifle and raise his hands above his head crying, "*Kamerad, Kamerad.*"

Others came out of the house, still others from behind the haystack. All threw down their rifles and surrendered. By the time Cutler reached the house, his men had lined up and disarmed the prisoners. Eighteen he counted, including one German wounded earlier by the mortar round. He left two of his men to guard them as before and moved toward the next farmhouse further down the ridge. Again the weapons group covered their attack, this time from the first farmhouse and a haystack nearby. The men moved rapidly across the open ground, well dispersed, shouting as before. No machine-gun burst disturbed the hot summer air. Cutler listened and wondered as he ran if the Germans would fire on them. It seemed a long time until his leading men reached the house. The Germans once more gave up readily. There were twenty-five in this group. He appointed two men to guard the new prisoners and said to them hurriedly, "Get these back to that other bunch at the last house and then take all of them to the rear." As the men moved out, he shouted after them, "Be sure and get receipts for them."

His one thought now was to get his men away from this farmhouse. Other Germans on the hills to the north had probably watched his progress over the treeless ridge. His audience would be throwing artillery shells very soon.

With some difficulty, he persuaded the men to leave the water well. They needed to fill their canteens, he knew, but they had to get away from the house for it was too much of a target. He moved the group forward down the slope further to the left to where there was a draw filled with bushes and small trees, where the mass of a hill waited to protect them. No sooner were they safely behind this hill mass than many shells splattered around the house. The men looked back and saw bursting holes in the red tile roof as shells smashed into the stone building. As they watched, one of the men offered a narrow-necked bottle of reddish-golden wine to Captain Cutler. The captain took a good drink of it as he stood watching the shells strike the empty house. The wine felt warm to his stomach and, in a moment, to his arms, his legs. The eyes of the owner of the bottle winked as he remarked loudly, "Don't take much, Captain. We don't want you getting too brave on us."

Cutler smiled as he reached for the radio to call the colonel.

Colonel Galvin had been unable to move his battalion for several hours. At the time of the first barrage, he had seen what he thought was the end of his command. The possibility of the enemy's using tanks had worried him from the moment of the first casualties. He had wanted to move all the men back over the hill, but Chivington pointed out the dangers of this. Galvin could see that there were few casualties after the initial surprise barrage. The men had immediately flung themselves into drainage ditches and dug deep holes under the threat of continued heavy fire. It was better to wait for Cutler to clear the snipers and machine gunners from the ridge to the left than to re-expose the men on the bare crest of the hill. It was a long delay, an eternity for Galvin but he managed it somehow. The radio call from Cutler finally allowed him to swing the battalion to the west. By this time, he had a company of tanks with which to support his further attack.

With C Company leading the column of companies and with the tanks in close support, Galvin advanced with his battalion 2,000 yards. By the end of July, the general had said, they should be on the river. It was not going to be easy, he could see, unless Captain Cutler and the others were quicker about doing their jobs.

Just after dark each forward platoon established a listening post on the north side of the hill. Halfway up the back slope of a treeless ridge, Cutler directed the men of two platoons to dig foxholes. The others dug in further down. Cutler was glad to again have a full company. He had acted the part of platoon leader on the recent operation, but a company could do so much more. Casualties had been less than he expected—ten wounded, three killed and six missing.

Darkness enshrouded the company. While half of Cutler's command slept, the men in the forward positions were especially vigilant to warn of an attack. The noise of distant shell fire, and the many flashes along the horizon to the east and west, made Cutler realize the extent of the war. He could hear the rumbling of enemy tanks and the clanking of their treads not far away.

The night air was pleasantly cool on his face as he stood watching, listening. Suddenly a phosphorus shell splashed not far in front of him near a haystack, and a large fire lit up the area. The fire burned for several hours consuming a nearby house until at 0230 the embers' glow was all that remained. At that time Covalos awakened Cutler and handed him the telephone.

In a low voice, he said, "Cutler talking."

Through the earphone he heard the rapid, shrill, too-wide-awake voice of the colonel say, "How's everything in your area? Can you hear those tanks any more?"

Cutler replied slowly, "Everything's quiet now. The tanks moved off to the left front. I believe there's a road over there."

Galvin answered less rapidly than before, "That's fine. That's fine. Say, I want you to send four men to that town up ahead. Tell them to get a prisoner if they can. Otherwise whatever information they can find. Send them out at 0400 hours and be ready with your company to move with the battalion just before dawn."

215

Cutler wanted to argue about the value of the patrol's leaving that much ahead of the battalion, but he swallowed once and replied, "Yes, sir."

Galvin said, "B and C will move out on line, A will follow C, and D will follow B. I'll be between you and A Company. See you at daylight. Out."

Cutler thought of the next day. Galvin would be close to him. He did not relish the nearness of his colonel, knowing the rapid changes in orders that he would receive. Cutler hoped that Van Tuyl and Chivington would be with the colonel.

As the battalion moved closer and closer to the enemy's main line, the resistance became greater and greater. After making three daylight attacks on the fourth day and taking no ground, Cutler thought that Colonel Galvin would surely realize that the next ridge was the enemy's main line. In each of the three attacks Cutler had known that as soon as his men started over the bare crest of the hill the enemy artillery and small-arms fire would envelop them. Each time it had happened. The men had dropped quickly to the ground, and he had pulled them back to the reverse slope of the hill before the German fire became most intense. B and A Companies had done the same. Captain Cutler realized that to cross 1,000 yards of open stubble wheat field in the daytime was an outright impossibility. As he sat in a small ditch cleaning the bore of his pistol, a runner from battalion headquarters handed him a yellow note. It read:

> There will be a meeting of all company commanders at 1945 hours at the farmhouse behind this ridge.

The farmhouse was like many others Captain Cutler had seen during the struggle up the Italian peninsula. He arrived a few minutes early, and for these few minutes, he went underneath the stone house where the farmer ordinarily had his stable. Here there were no animals, but the wounded of the battalion. They lay close together on clean straw, safe from the further searching of artillery shrapnel. Many were asleep with morphine; others were receiving blood plasma. Cutler spoke quietly to the medic in charge.

"How're you getting along?"

The answer was in a low voice. "Waiting for ambulances. Too much business. You looking for someone?"

"Yes, Private Edwards, one of my runners."

"Down there on the left."

Cutler went down the line speaking to several of his men as he looked for Edwards. He recognized him sleeping on the straw with a face so pale and colorless that it startled him. Cutler had seen that look before. He shook his head and quietly went out into the dusk of another night.

XXXI

When Cutler stepped through the blackout curtains into the main room of the old farmhouse, which was now battalion headquarters, he saw in the candlelight a large, black-stained table on which lay a few aerial photographs. He nodded to the men sitting around the table. Colonel Galvin was there with Major Van Tuyl and Captain Chivington as well as Rusnick and the company commanders of A, B, D, and Headquarters Company. Lieutenant Walker was there as artillery liaison officer. Cutler seated himself and glanced about the room. The fireplace opposite was unusual, he thought, because it was in the middle of a wall instead of in a corner. On the mantel over the hearth was part of a loaf of dark bread and two wine bottles. There were faded religious pictures on the walls.

Colonel Galvin nodded to Major Van Tuyl, who explained the situation of the battalion.

"We know," he said, "that the enemy is on the ridge 1,200 yards ahead. Their lines run before the town which is 700 yards back along this ridge here." He pointed to the aerial photograph with his red pencil as they all leaned forward in the candlelight to look.

"The Germans are well entrenched. They have good artillery support and excellent observation in the daytime, as you all know only too well. We have orders to attack at 0300 hours. The whole regiment will go forward at that time."

The others shifted in their chairs and cleared their throats. They waited for Van Tuyl to speak further. The clock by the fireplace ticked relentlessly, its hands at 2000 hours.

Van Tuyl continued, "Supposing them to be well entrenched, our only chance of knocking them out, as I see it, is to throw artillery fire at them and follow up very closely with the men."

The Captain of A Company interrupted to agree. "I believe you're right there. I'd give about twenty minutes to get the troops

218

to the bottom of the hill." He said this before the colonel could speak a word even though the latter already had his mouth open.

Cutler realized that the colonel did not want the artillery fire but preferred to try to surprise the enemy again. He agreed quickly saying, "The artillery suits me fine. I suggest starting the troops at the same time. Twenty minutes sounds reasonable."

"Any other comments before we go ahead?" Van Tuyl asked, looking around. Galvin looked puzzled, but the others all nodded agreement.

"I believe that shellfire should also be placed on the town, in this draw and on this house." Van Tuyl again pointed to the aerial photos as he watched the others questioningly.

Cutler spoke again, "I agree, but the artillery should be directed from the ridge when we get there."

Van Tuyl said, "That's a good idea. We'll let you direct it." He looked at Galvin, who nodded agreement. He went on, "We are going to divide the attack into two phases. The first will have as its objective the ridge in front of our troops. Once we take that, we'll reorganize and go on to the town, the second objective. We'll go through the town and hold up on the north side."

Cutler knew the rest of the order before Van Tuyl spoke. Two companies would move out abreast, each with two platoons on line. He would be the company on the right; B would be on the left. The rest of the battalion would follow. He would go to the right of town and B would go to the left. The only thing for him to do now was to talk to Walker, the artillery officer, and get the numbers of the concentrations on the three targets. Smoking a cigarette, he leaned back while the meeting continued until all questions were settled.

As Cutler was starting toward the door with the others, Brigadier General Josephs, the Assistant Division Commander, came through the black-out curtains and greeted the group cheerfully with his usual, "What's going on here?"

Colonel Galvin explained the attack plan briefly.

The general nodded at each point. "No reason why it shouldn't work. No reason at all. I'm glad you plan to use artillery while the troops are moving. We have tried too often to surprise the Krauts by jumping off without softening them up.

How are the radios working?"

All in the group answered simultaneously, "OK, sir."

The general shook hands around the group. Then, as he went out, he said, "Well, good luck and for God's sake be aggressive."

Captain Cutler always had to struggle with the excitement he felt just before an attack. It was 0258 hours—almost time. His men were ready. They had taken their positions noiselessly in the cool night air. The whole battalion was vulnerable to artillery fire now as they lay on the surface of the ground in the deceptive moonlight like so many rocks. Cutler walked over to a lone tree that separated his company from B Company. There he met Captain Rusnick.

"You all set, Bill?" Cutler asked quietly.

"All set. My men are in position. They'll guide on your company. Good luck, fella."

Cutler returned to his company. As the artillery started, they moved out. He was in the middle of his men, two platoons on line before him and two platoons similarly distributed behind. The rude square of running men was all around him. His feet seemed to move by themselves they were so light. The ground felt different, somewhat spongy and soft. Perhaps the root stubble of that wheat pushed his combat boots upward in these bare fields, which were worse than a curse to advancing troops in the daytime, but now, at night, allowed for rapid movement. The men's fast pace slowed to a jog. All were spread out, five or ten yards from one another. They seemed to Cutler to glide forward effortlessly in the dim moonlight. Ahead the flash and splash of bursting phosphorus shells mingled with the night. Smoke drifted back to give added concealment to the advancing men.

The company was veering to the right. Cutler sensed this and spoke out, cursing and muttering to himself, for he knew that nothing but a draw with steep walls awaited them in that direction.

He called out, "Give way to the left! Give way to the left! Pass it on! Give way to the left!" He knew the enemy could not hear him above the noise of the exploding shells. Once more he shouted, "Give way to the left!" They were edging over a little now. The men had heard him and passed his words forward.

Now they were approaching the hill. The first of the troops were too close to the exploding phosphorus. Cutler spoke quickly to his radio operator. As Covalos handed him the receiver, Cutler called, "Green rabbit to XYZ. Over."

"XYZ to green rabbit. Go ahead," came back immediately.

Delighted at the quick response, Cutler shouted, "Lift the fire. My men are approaching it now."

"Roger—out," was the answer almost before he had finished speaking.

He gave the receiver back to Covalos and continued forward, watching. He saw the fire lift and come down again further back on the ridge. Two minutes later it stopped completely.

As Cutler went up through the vineyards from one terrace to another, glancing back, he saw a spurt of flame in a staccato of noise. One more burst and the flash was covered, muffled, and then ceased. The men were doing their work, bayonets fixed. He paused with Covalos. The whole company was on the hill. The next move was to get the prepared artillery fires onto their targets losing as little time as possible. His flashlight had broken several days before when it struck a rock as he hit the ground to avoid shrapnel. Out of the sight of the enemy, he scratched matches in the shelter of a tree near the slope of the hill in order to read from his small notebook the numbers of the proposed fires. He would not trust his memory. With the second match, he found the page and spoke the numbers over the radio.

Shells came down almost immediately over on the draw with steep sides, on the town further north, and around a house up ahead. Very little time had elapsed from the moment of the first barrage to the landing of the shells on these other three areas—possibly five minutes, perhaps ten, certainly no more.

The smell of smoke was everywhere. A building smouldered to the left, higher on the hill. Since the climb had slowed the progress of the men, Cutler sat and waited with Covalos for a few minutes. He was there when Colonel Galvin came up and, in a voice mixed with worry and excitement, said, "How are you getting along?"

Cutler replied, "Fine. We made the hill all right. I'm waiting now. The men are busy."

"Well, we don't want to wait. We want to move and attack

the town as soon as possible."

"I believe we'll make it all right. Artillery is softening it up now. You can hear it. I called it down as we arranged at the meeting. We ought to let that go thirty minutes anyway."

"We don't want to waste all that time," said Galvin. "Strike while the iron is hot, I always say. Get organized for the move on the town."

"Yes, sir," said Cutler, "but I think that for the next few minutes the best thing we can do is leave everything alone and let things develop. We've done our job for the moment. Let's think out the next move carefully." Cutler did not want any interference now. Things seemed to be going too well as they were.

"Well, all right," said the colonel moving closer to Cutler. "Send out two patrols right away to look around a little and see what's happening. I want to know what's happening. And then, after you do that, you. . . . "

Here he was interrupted by the approach of running Germans silhouetted against the gray morning sky. Germans came quickly toward them, single file, with their hands above their heads. Americans were moving them along.

Both Cutler and Galvin stood up quickly. Still more prisoners came from another direction. Surrendering Germans were everywhere. There were more Germans than Cutler had ever seen, except at the prisoner-of-war camp back at Camp Carver. Cutler immediately ordered five of his men to continue to the rear with the group of about seventy prisoners. He wanted to prevent their recapture. He was afraid of a counterattack.

He questioned the men, and the platoon sergeant said that the Americans had caught them in caves where the Germans were waiting for the severe phosphorus artillery barrage to end. It was unbelievably good luck. This attack had succeeded.

The platoons quickly reorganized. The company moved on and through the town without anyone firing a shot. But not long after the men reached the far north edge of the buildings, German shells started landing in an ever-increasing number of rounds. Cutler found a wine cellar and ordered the men inside. The opposition seemed almost fanatical in intensity. The fire appeared to come from every direction except south. Captain Cutler distinguished several different types of shells from the sound each made in flight and the strength with which each exploded outside.

The walls of the large wine cellar were of brown hard-packed earth. The marks of shovels were on the walls made many years before. In a deep-set cubicle, a small lamp fitted easily and burned steadily, away from the disturbing draft that moved coolly between the two entrances. A wooden door of heavy two-inch planks blocked the main outlet but swung easily on large hinges which needed oil to drown their rasping squeak. The wine cellar could easily hold a company of men without much crowding. It was like the inside of a bank vault. Here was a refuge such as the company had not known since arriving in Italy. Here was safety from all artillery fire.

The sergeant of the squad which Cutler had placed on the north slope of the town came into the wine cellar and reported, "Captain, the artillery fire has killed two of my men and wounded six more in the last hour. The three men I have left are with me now. Nothing can live out there."

Captain Cutler noticed his bewilderment and the exhaustion of the men with him, "OK, Sergeant," he said, "I'll try to have some men observe from another point. We can't let the Germans take us by surprise. You get some rest. When the barrage eases up, we'll bring those wounded back."

They heard a commotion in the street outside. A tank's motors added to the noise of the exploding shells. The tank moved down the street toward the wine cellar and passed within two feet of the entrance. Opening the door a crack, Cutler smelled the hot oil and saw Americans in the turret take up a position blocking the road to the northeast. He felt relieved. The tank would be a great help in combating a counterattack. He knew, however, that its presence in the town would draw additional fire from the enemy.

Suddenly there was a squeaking of the door. Colonel Galvin and two men peered into the dim light.

"Where's Captain Cutler?" he said.

"Here I am, sir. Come in."

"Thanks," Galvin said sitting down wearily on an old chair. "It's pretty bad out there."

"I have all the men I could find right here," said Cutler.

"There are about eighty of them and a few more scattered around outside observing. How did B Company make out?" He whittled on a slat fragment of the wooden door as he waited for the reply.

"B Company is scattered through the town. So is A. The men are in every building," the Colonel replied breathing less rapidly than when he entered.

Cutler stopped whittling; and looking at the piece of smooth wood critically, he said, "Well, if the men are scattered around that way, we have the town secured."

Three heavy shells crashed, one after another, not far from the shaking door. WHOOM! ZARBROUT! TA PLUSH! Rocks and mortar tumbled to the street gradually diminishing in amount until one last piece struck the ground.

Colonel Galvin sneezed and mopped from his face dust which had fallen from the ceiling. He cleaned his glasses as he thought aloud, "I want to move out to the northeast as soon as possible. We must go forward. We can't waste time sitting here. We'll never get to the Arno at this rate. Get your men ready to move out."

There was a murmur among the men as this news spread to the back. It rose higher to a grumble. Outside two more rounds landed. UMMPHT! DA BLAM!

Cutler found himself wondering what to say. His sharp trench knife bit deeply into the wood. He knew that such a move would be bad for some of his men. He answered by questioning, "What about B and A Companies? We can't coordinate a battalion move because we don't have the control."

Galvin answered without hesitation, "Well, we'll see what we can do with your men. We can get well out there and dig in. At least, we can see something more than we can from here."

Cutler paused in his whittling and said in a wondering voice, "We won't get very far out there with that artillery coming in. They've got us pinned down now. The enemy's watching this town closely, and I'm afraid we'll get heavy casualties and not accomplish a thing." As he finished saying this, several large stones thumped to the street and banged against the thick door causing more dust to jump into the air.

Galvin answered defensively now. "Well, we're going to try it anyhow. Get your men ready, Captain!" His small black eyes flashed as he finished with the look of obstinacy Cutler had noticed at their first meeting.

Cutler answered, "Yes, sir." Then, putting his knife in its case and the stick in his pocket, he turned to the men in the cave. "You heard what . . ." Shells interrupted him. "You heard what the colonel said. We're going to move out. Get your packs on. Third Platoon, follow me out."

He waited, breathing quickly, while the men sullenly put on their gear and picked up their rifles. Then he swung the door wide, jumped out into the street and dodged around the tank. The men started after him. They had to pass a twenty-yard open space before they could gain the protection of a few buildings. Cutler reached this shelter safely and stopped there to wave his men on. He saw the Sherman tank move up to a firing position. Twenty-five men had come out of the cellar, Galvin among them, when artillery shells smashed nearby. One piece of shrapnel whirred past Cutler's head and dropped to the ground three feet away. He reached over to pick it up. The jagged steel fragment was hot to his touch. The cry of "medic" mingled with the noise of exploding shells. Corporal Delaney lay crumbled in a heap in the middle of the street. Men near the cellar entrance rapidly stumbled inside. The barrage increased.

Colonel Galvin crawled on his hands and knees toward Cutler. Behind him, through the dust and din, Cutler could see the whole inside of the village church blown wide open. Wall paintings glowed blue and gold and red, incongruous in the smoke. He could see a crucifix dangling to one side. The face looked as resigned to death as Delaney's.

Colonel Galvin shouted from behind a culvert, "Better get back. They've got better observation than I thought."

Cutler called to the men, "Get back when you can." He tasted the rock powder and the smoke of the shells. The fumes bit into his lips. He was furious. Delaney lay dead and some of his men had serious wounds because Galvin had not known when to attack. *This colonel may get to the Arno River*, thought Cutler, *but he won't have many men with him.*

In the cellar again Colonel Galvin mopped his face with his handkerchief. The remaining soldiers muttered among themselves. Sensing their mood, Galvin waited silently for a lull.

It was not until midnight that the battalion left the town. C
Company led the single file that was the inevitable method of
moving forward at night in rough country. The column of men
moved slowly at first; but as soon as Cutler realized that the Germans had again withdrawn, they moved more rapidly.

All night they moved north searching for a retreating
enemy. Artillery slowed their progress, but they continued forward toward the Arno.

XXXII

Helen lifted her small son from his crib, gently cradling his head in the palm of her hand. His small blue eyes stared blandly at her. She was tender with pride. He seemed the most perfect, incredible entity to her as she let her eyes linger on his fuzz of dark hair, on the tilt of his nose, on the little balled fists red with the exertion of trying to wave his arms about. She put him on her shoulder letting his head rest against her cheek and feeling the soft hair and the warmth of his skin against her.

It was a warm, dark summer night. She had come in quietly in nightgown and slippers to give him his last feeding of the day. It was a time which she particularly enjoyed when, in the stillness of late evening, she could hold him quietly and watch his greedy eagerness give way slowly to satisfaction and sleepiness. She gently pried open one of his fists with her finger which he grasped while she examined again the tiny fingers with the paper-thin nails.

He fit so perfectly into the angle of her arm, she thought. Already he seemed to have grown, to have become more wakeful and alert. She wished that Don could see him tonight. She wanted Don to see his son while he was still little and helpless and dependent, but so complete. It was a wonderous thing to her, unspeakable, indescribable. She wondered how she could write to Don to make him understand.

Thinking of Don brought back the feeling of melancholy which hung above her these days descending like a net to trap her when she least wished it. It seemed to her that Don had been gone a very long time. She was losing her ability to project the vitality of him into his pictures. It had been a frightening thing to her until she had his son and saw, or thought she could, flashes of Don in him.

A slight breeze ruffled the white curtain gently bringing with it the sound of leaves rustling and the odor of the flowering bush in the border beyond. Somewhere, far off, a whippoorwill called; over and over again the notes of his song went up and down in her mind as though she were struggling to put them accurately on a staff in proper intervals. She had listened in this way before and come to the conclusion that different whippoorwills sang different intervals. She wondered whether there were whippoorwills in Italy. Perhaps not, she thought. Perhaps there were no birds over battlegrounds. Perhaps they disappeared leaving the area as birdless as the ancient entrance to Hades about which Don had once told her.

She wondered whether Don was seeing any of the old buildings and sites. He had written that he had been to Rome, but it was a short letter and more full of questions about the baby and herself than about what he had seen. He had written that one day they would see Rome together. She hoped so. How could he be sure when he knew that he would fight again. *Perhaps,* she thought, *he is fighting tonight. Perhaps . . .* She stopped herself quickly as a pang of anxiety went through her; she looked down at the baby who slept in her arms. His little head was turned in against her and she could watch and hear his soft breathing.

She put him again on her shoulder and steadied his sleepy head, rubbing her cheek against his hair. He was groggy with sleep as she rubbed his back gently, feeling the solid little mass of his back and rib case where it curved away from the backbone.

She sat there for a long time thinking of Don. Finally she put the baby back in the crib and turned off the light.

XXXIII

Cutler dreaded Colonel Galvin's orders, fearing each day that he would be ordered into an impossible position in this relentless march north. He knew that the ground must be taken and yet the cost to his company appalled him. Replacements arrived almost every day. He found that he was leading men whose names he did not even know. Control became much more difficult. He kept the casualties as small as possible by trying to anticipate enemy moves, by keeping hill masses between his company and the Germans whenever possible, by keeping his men off paths which might be mined, by keeping the men well spaced whenever possible.

One cloudy morning in September, he found himself with about twenty-five of his infantry men dug in along a road flanked by high banks. Generations of passing carts had dropped the road below the level of the steep slope. Galvin had ordered him forward at 0400. He had expected A and B Companies to move up to cover him in the forward position; but when gray light of morning came, Cutler knew that he must hold the position until night with the men he had.

As they waited there, he had the ominous feeling that the enemy had waited for him to reach this place, that all his past moves and decisions had led him here.

German machine-gun fire swept overhead sealing off escape. The sky was oppressive. Great masses of cloud hung low over the hills promising rain soon with its attendant mud. He could not go to the left down the path. Small-arms fire blocked that direction. The other end of the path led up level with the ridge top. He could not move forward.

Cutler wondered where the two missing companies were, whether Colonel Galvin had changed his mind and called them back or whether they had run into trouble on the far slope on the way up. He wished that he had brought more rations. He had counted on supplies reaching them before this. He knew that the men were hungry.

Enemy mortar fire began to search out his position. He could hear the bursts coming closer and closer. He huddled close to the radio trying to get through to battalion.

As he sat there bent over the phone, he saw one of the new replacement lieutenants rise quickly, start across the road, stop abruptly, spin around and fall twitching to the ground. A moment later, the observer on the bank above rolled down with bullets in his arm and hip.

Van Tuyl's voice came through on the radio, and Cutler asked for mortar support from D Company. He realized that their position was serious. The men's eyes were on him watching, waiting for him to give the orders which would spring them from this trap. The mortar support from D Company was not enough to slow the German fire.

Something struck the bank above Cutler and bounced down to stop beside his outstretched leg. He looked at it for a fraction of a second fascinated. He knew what it was. He had seen a German rifle grenade before. Six inches of orange steel three-quarters of an inch in diameter lay among the rocks and twigs. He knew it was useless to run. Automatically he moved to pick it up and throw it away. The grenade, as if to escape the oncoming hand, exploded in a flash of dirt, smoke, powder, and steel. Pieces of metal tore into Cutler, and he lay crumpled on the ground. While he looked around dazedly, another grenade fell close by. His radio disappeared and Covalos lay dead—not apparently hurt, but dead in the smoke.

Cutler felt no pain, just an extreme dullness as though his head were on a wooden body. Through the split leather of his combat boot, he could see the bare tendons frayed like torn ropes just behind the toes. Pieces of ragged flesh lay piled on the outside of the boot. The leg was scored with long red gashes which were bleeding hard. He knew that he must stop the bleeding.

He reached down with his right hand towards the scraps of cloth which had been his pant leg and found that his hand also was badly cut. Carefully he tore a strip of the cloth and, with great exertion, tied it around his knee. He reached out and pulled a bayonet free from the case of one of the dead soldiers and inserted it slowly and deliberately through the loop in the cloth to form a tourniquet, twisting the cloth with it in order to stop the flow of blood from his boot. When it was tight, he pushed the pointed end of the bayonet into the ground and lay back breathing hard to rest for a few minutes. His head felt like a balloon bobbing in the wind on the end of a string.

The pressure of the tourniquet soon caused a pulsating throb. He felt the fullness of blood in his knee. He remembered his first aid packet and scattered sulfanilamide powder over the shattered foot, which seemed so far away from him, and over his useless hand. Sharp steel fragments had ripped the skin between the middle fingers, had dug deeply at the base of the thumb on the front of the palm, and had grooved strangely the top of the longest finger as if to chastise it for sticking above the others. Dirt, steel, wood, and cloth—all were in the hand.

He could not see very well. His whole face beneath his steel helmet felt as though it had been too close to a hot fire. He knew that he was through with fighting, but the Germans were still nearby. He felt them coming slowly. To hold out now he realized would be to murder the men who were still unhurt. He could not let more men be doomed in this impossible situation. Men could not fight their way out of this open-air coffin. Cutler had been in serious situations before but never when he was so badly wounded.

He gave the order to surrender.

Germans came over the crest quickly. Thirty or forty of them jumped into the road and disarmed the Americans. The hands of his men stretching high in the air looked unnatural to Cutler from his position on the ground. The whole scene appeared unreal. His eyes blurred. Never before had he seen Americans with their hands up. He was silent, stupefied by the shock. This was the end of his command. He was broken and beaten.

A German took Cutler's pistol from him and stepped back as an *oberlautenant* approached and stood above Cutler looking down. Cutler sat up and showed his concealed captain's bars beneath his jacket's wool collar. He said to the man in broken German, *"Ich bin capitano."*

The German was probably twenty-two years old. The eyebrows and the hair beneath the helmet were black. The lips lay tight set in a straight line above a tense chin. The black eyes flashed as his voice excitedly gave orders to take the American prisoners able to walk over the ridge. Cutler watched them go. He looked at the Luger waving in the young *oberlautenant's* hand, and a small Italian rifle under his other arm. He struggled to speak again, but he could think of only one fragment of German poetry that his father used to sing. He spoke softly, almost to himself, remembering. *"Ich weiss nicht was soll es bedeuten, das ich so traurig bin."*

The German *oberlautenant* was the only standing man left among the dead and wounded. Cutler could think of no words with which to speak to him. He sensed the *oberlautenant* aim the small rifle at his head. He tried to turn, to twist away from the bullet. The sudden explosion collapsed him forward on his face. Echoes of the shot reverberated through his brain. He lay still, waiting, expecting another shot. The German's feet moved away in the dirt, then stopped. Another shot interrupted the stillness. He moved further away from Cutler. Another shot. Another and another and another, each separated by footsteps. Bullet after bullet tore into the wounded men and echoed through the vast chambers of Cutler's head. He remained motionless, breathing as quietly and as little as possible. He dared not move to look up. He thought that this was the end of him. His life flashed by like the shuffling of cards, each card a person or episode.

The explosion had been like the blow of a club. His head creaked as its parts readjusted themselves. His right shoulder felt as if the bullet had lodged there. He continued motionless while his ears tried to detect some nearby sound. He waited a very long time. All was still.

His helmet rested on the ground supporting his head. Without stirring, he strained his eyes to see. Then, very carefully, he lifted his head. Crumpled men lay everywhere. Nothing moved between the banks of the road-way. He rested again on the ground sleepily.

As moment after moment went by, Cutler became more aware of his neck. The skin burned from the flash of powder. Blood oozed down inside his collar. He wondered what he should do about his neck. He certainly could not use a tourniquet there. That is the way the neck is.

232

He lay resting. Finally he hitched himself forward a few feet off the road into a small gully and lay still. He breathed heavily, partly from sharp twinges of pain and partly from the effort of dragging himself by his one good arm and leg.

He rested again. As the low gray clouds began to drop light rain, he languidly pulled a canvas shelter half over himself after first forcing the blade of the bayonet firmly in the ground again. He listened, thinking and waiting.

Occasionally Germans hurried along the road, but not one bothered Cutler as he lay silently in the gully. Just before dark footsteps stopped a few feet from him. He stopped breathing and peered through a small rent in the canvas. Two Germans were bending over Covalos' crumpled body in the rain trying to remove the combat boots. Cutler heard them unbuckle the boots, unlace, and pull; but the dead man's feet had stiffened at right angles to the legs. The shoes would not come off. The Germans grunted with their efforts. In the dusk of the coming night Cutler saw the forms of the men less distinctly. He heard a rifle stock twice thud strangely against something. A few minutes later the two forms disappeared into the mist.

Lying in the darkness alone, Cutler thought of many things. The fighting that his company had done during the past six months blurred into one continuous effort. They had taken one Italian hill after another until it seemed to him that each new hill was in reality the same hill, that the whole campaign was a ghastly nightmare trick on him. He had been wounded before and had spent a month in the hospital, but the other wounds had been mere scratches compared with his present ones. He thought of the company he had started with from the rest camp two weeks before. Two weeks had seen the end of that company—two weeks. No fighting in the south had been as bad. Before, he had lost less than half of his company, but now all of it was gone. His regiment had moved swiftly and quietly into this part of the line in the Northern Appennine mountains to take advantage of a reported weakness in the German defenses. Like a wooden pencil pushed against a grindstone, the regiment had become smaller and smaller. Cutler had told Colonel Galvin that he could get to the top of the ridge but that he could not hold it with his few men. The colonel had answered, "We'll try to reinforce you. I have my orders, Captain; you have yours. That's the way it is."

Cutler's thoughts blurred with his vision. Both cleared when the distant American searchlights shot their beams horizontally over the ground through the rain. Yet, again his mind and eyes dimmed in the diffuse light.

Toward midnight he was roused from his stupor by a hand lifting the canvas. It was a German who must have heard him breathing. Cutler showed the man his bandaged hand and leg. The German answered by a quiet question, *"Cigaretten?"*

Captain Cutler fumbled at the button on his shirt pocket and found his green plastic case half full of cigarettes. He gave them all to the soldier, who took them eagerly and immediately lit one carefully concealing the flame of the match. In the flash of light Cutler saw the lined face of a man much older than the *oberlautenant*. As the German drew deeply on the cigarette, Cutler wondered what the man would do to him. He waited. The German asked him what time it was. Cutler showed him the luminous dial of his watch. The man wanted not only the time, but the watch. His fingers were rough on Cutler's wrist. Cutler smelled the sour sweat of the man close to him. The German took the watch and went away. Cutler covered himself over with the canvas once more, reflecting that the man would have killed him for the watch.

Cutler had reached the point of not worrying about what would happen next. What was, was. He dozed. His head felt very weary. Several times booted feet passed inches from his head, but no German disturbed him further that night. Just before daylight the searchlights went out.

Early morning showed a pool of rain water in a hollow of the olive-drab canvas. Cutler bent forward carefully until his dry lips were below the surface of the water. He tipped the canvas and sucked it in. The taste of the canvas puckered the roof of his mouth. He needed food to remove the rank taste. He had not had anything to eat in two days.

Suddenly he sensed a change. He did not know what it was. His hair bristled under his helmet. He looked around the road at the dead men lying motionless. The metal parts of their equipment glistened in the misty rain. Covalos looked very odd lying as he did on his belly with bare toes pointed into the muddy ground.

Further up the crest of the slope behind him Cutler saw a helmet move. He thought that his eyes must be blurring. It was an American helmet and it moved again.

"Who's there?" he asked finally. The man said he was a lookout for A Company on forward outpost. Cutler asked him if he had anything to eat, and the American threw down a K ration which Cutler slowly and painfully opened. Between bites of cheese and biscuit, Cutler told the man that he was badly wounded. The man said quietly that he would go back for help as soon as he could get relief. His helmet disappeared behind the bank.

Cutler felt very weak. His hands and feet were cold and the blurring of his eyes played so many tricks on him that he shut them wearily.

It was not until the middle of the afternoon that Cutler heard the three volunteers coming for him. One of them was Private Millen. They carried a white flag and a stretcher and crawled over the bank of the sunken road. Cutler groaned as they lifted him onto the stretcher. Dizzy and sick, he begged to be put down. The cold rainy wind flapped a white flag over the silent soldiers. They stumbled with him up over the crest of the roadside then down the slope, the stretcher swaying.

Cutler fought to stay conscious. The weakness in him aggravated him. He felt that if he relaxed he would slide off the stretcher and roll over and over down the steep rocky hill. The dizziness sickened him. He wondered whether he was bleeding again. He felt that he must help the soldiers so that they would not drop the stretcher. He wished that they would keep his head higher than his feet on this uncertain ride which seemed to go on and on in the light rain. The slippery mud made their progress treacherous.

As the cold rain fell on his face, Cutler knew that the whole world was here in the throbbing of his head. His strength felt almost gone. He tried to rest, to breath deeply, to find somewhere a little more energy. And still they went on steadying the stretcher down through the shattered half-dead trees.

"Water," he said finally after thinking about it for a long

time. They rested the stretcher on the ground, and Millen opened his canteen and put it to Cutler's lips. Cutler felt it trickle over his tongue, which seemed to fill his whole mouth.

"Thanks," said Cutler weakly. "Lion and mouse," he said with effort.

"What, Sir?" asked Millen puzzled.

"Thanks for coming," said Cutler.

"Captain," said Millen, "we couldn't leave you out there."

Cutler smiled wanly. He began to wonder how far they must go. The men were panting now. It took all their strength to hold back the stretcher on the down slope. It seemed such a long, long way. He closed his eyes and saw the *oberlautenant* standing uniformed before him aiming the rifle. He twisted on the stretcher. The men stumbled but did not drop him.

"Take it easy, Captain," said Millen. His knuckles were white with the strain of the stretcher. "We'll be there pretty soon."

Cutler wondered where they were going on this rainy night. It seemed a strange night to go on a trip. He looked up into the blurry night and saw shooting stars. *Just like the funny papers,* thought Cutler; and then everything blacked out.

There was a man there, a friendly man. For some reason he seemed to be holding Cutler's head.

"Drink this," said the doctor holding the warm rim of a canteen cup against his lips.

Cutler swallowed. It was warm bouillon. He felt it in his mouth and then in his throat and then the flavor went down and radiated out. He gulped at it. He couldn't get enough.

"Easy," said the doctor, "we've got plenty of it."

Cutler felt his head clear as the doctor came into focus, and he saw the walls of a small farmhouse room.

"Where am I?" he asked bewildered by the lantern which hung over his head.

"Battalion Aid Station," said the doctor. "We've been looking you over."

Cutler drank more bouillon. Then he remembered. "A German shot me through the neck," he said.

"We've already seen it," said the doctor.

Cutler looked up. He found that he was attached to a plasma bottle.

"What's that for?" he asked sleepily.

"Make you feel better," said the doctor. "You're going to have a ride in an ambulance."

"I've already had one," said Cutler. Then he thought of something else. "How's my leg?" he asked.

"You've got a serious wound there," said the doctor, "but they'll fix it up for you further back."

Suddenly Cutler tried to sit up on the stretcher. "I've got to talk to Colonel Galvin," he said excitedly as a sharp pain twinged through his neck and shoulder.

"Not now," said the doctor. "Let's not bother him now."

"Got to see him," said Cutler. "There's a damn Kraut up there that shot all my wounded men!"

"What do you mean?" asked the doctor.

"*Oberlautenant*," said Cutler. He felt wide awake now. "— tried to kill me, coup de grace, shot all the others! We've got to get him." He would have climbed off the stretcher if they hadn't stopped him.

"I'll let the colonel know," said the doctor. An aid man brought a hypodermic.

"Hey," said Cutler, "I don't need that. I'm all right now."

"Sure you are," said the doctor, "but this will keep you from hurting while you're in the ambulance."

Cutler relaxed on the stretcher. It was nice that they would tell the colonel for him because now he was very tired and it would be good to relax for just a little while. He wondered whether he was dying. Somehow the idea did not seem strange to him anymore.

He was in the dark. He felt he was in a vault like a coffin with no air and something very heavy was on his head. He knew that Helen would not know where he was. He called to her and someone kept trying to stop him by telling him that he was all right; but he wasn't all right in this dark place with that weight on his head. He thought that he saw her coming but it wasn't Helen. It was a fat old woman with streaming knotted hair and deep eyes that looked through him like an x-ray. He looked closely and saw that it was the Cumaean sibyl. She took him by the hand and tried to lead him away into the clouds of smoke. He looked about him into the broken trees. There were no birds here and the grass was burned and scorched beneath his feet.

He saw a soldier coming through the smoke. Somehow the soldier was Hannibal. He wanted Cutler to help him get elephants over the mountains. It was exhausting work and when they had struggled to the top, there in the pass was the *oberlautenant* with his pistol and the *oberlautenant* shot all the elephants one by one. They sank in heaps around Cutler, trapping him in the center.

Again the sibyl came and took his hand to lead him away. They walked through a field of Etruscan sculptures. Cutler admired them very much; but while he watched, they came to life and marched in circles around him faster and faster until his head whirled and he marched off with them down the Via Appia. They marched and marched until Cutler, dragging his boots in and out of the mud, could no longer keep up with them and fell behind.

He was so very tired. He wanted Helen, but again the old sibyl came. She called him Aeneas, but Cutler wasn't fooled. He knew that the sibyl had led Aeneas into Hades. They had gone through the birdless Lago d'Averno to the shore where Charon, dread boatman, ferried Aeneas to the land of shades. Cutler tried to remember whether Aeneas had returned, but his head was too tired.

"You must come for your prophesy," said the sibyl, and her eyes gleamed madly in her head. He tried to see, but it was getting darker and darker. It was hard to breathe. He tried to call again but he was choking.

And then he heard someone call to him. He pushed the mists back with his arms, pulling in big breaths as he left the angry sibyl. He came near the shore again and saw that it was Helen in the little boat. She pulled him aboard. He felt as though he were floating with her into some completely satisfying existence. She stroked his head and told him to rest and finally he slept quietly.

When Cutler woke, he came slowly out of sleep. At first there was only the awareness of being an entity. He lay very still with his eyes closed and enjoyed the lazy pleasure of breathing in and out, in and out, over and over again. What greater pleasure was there than this slow regular rhythm of breathing. He drew in one large breath and expelled it slowly. It was like a tremendous sigh. A voice near him said, "He's stirring now."

The meaning went echoing through his head. He wondered who that could be. He thought of opening his eyes but that seemed like a tremendous effort which was hardly worth while. He lay there listening to his own breathing for a long time.

Then somewhere in the back of his mind came a little glimmer. He tried to remember where he had gone to sleep, but it was no use. Finally he opened his eyes to find out.

Above him stretched yards and yards of canvas. He could not remember coming here. A nurse seemed to be trying to give him a drink. He took the straw in his mouth and sucked, but it made him so tired that he closed his eyes again and slept.

When he woke again, the nurse was still there.

"Feeling better?" she asked.

"Sure," he said languidly. He tried to raise his hand. "My hand's heavy," he said surprised.

"You have a cast on it," said the nurse. He looked down at it. The plaster was very white against the army blanket.

"How long have I been here?" he asked.

"Two days," said the nurse.

Cutler thought it over. How strange time was. Three days ago he had been leading men and yet it seemed years to him since Colonel Galvin had given the orders which had taken his company to the sunken road. He remembered the *oberlautenant* and the shots, but all that seemed now like fragments of an old nightmare drifting through his mind. He clearly remembered the sibyl with her knotted hair and keen eyes as she called him Aeneas and took him ominously by the hand. This seemed to him very real, even now, as he quietly rested from the turmoil of that struggle.

The nurse came back with warm food. She fed it to him slowly in spoonfuls which slid softly down his throat. It tasted good to him as he lay almost motionless, moving only his jaw to open his mouth and his throat muscles to swallow. The rest of him felt still asleep. He shut his eyes again drowsily. Just before he fell asleep, he remembered. He would be going back to Helen and to his son.

XXXIV

The hospital ship lay once again at anchor in Naples Harbor. In its white paint, it was shockingly conspicuous in the sunlight with the huge red cross painted brazenly on its side. Cutler saw it almost at once when his stretcher was unloaded from the ambulance. He raised himself on his good elbow to look around and was surprised to see how much of the twisted steel had been removed since the day he had first seen the harbor six months before. And now he was going home, leaving Italy. He wondered whether he would ever come back to this blue harbor, which shimmered now in the lazy light of early autumn. Vesuvius stood off in the haze, immovable and imperious in lonely grandeur. He was going home, but he had not seen Pompeii, he thought, or even the cave of the Cumaean sibyl. He still remembered that dark sibyl. She had led him to the brink of hell but he, like Aeneas, was returning. He suspected that the path was long and still full of obstacles, but at least he would not remain behind like Colonel Spaulding, like First Sergeant Pulska, like Covalos, Delaney, and the others, or even like MacRae in a private land of shades. The cost of this land to the Allies had been sobering. He wondered whether Colonel Galvin still said to company commanders, "I have my orders; you have yours," as he sent them north into the night.

His eye wandered down the slope of Vesuvius as he wondered how many wars and conflicts had skirted its base while it stood unperturbed. It occurred to him as he watched that the men who had come with him to Italy had taken a part in history. He wondered how large a part. Had their struggle been an epic in itself or would it perhaps be dismissed in a paragraph or even a sentence a hundred years from now? He wondered whether he would ever again read history objectively without seeing it in terms of men and mud, judgments and mistakes, exhaustion and sacrifice.

Stretcher bearers carried him aboard angling the narrow stretcher through the interior of the ship to a stateroom. Aid men lifted him into one of the four bunks. He rested back against the clean pillow. From where he lay, he could see a mass of masonry and buildings through the porthole but that was all.

Tired from the ambulance trip and loading, he slept. When he woke again he knew instantly that something had changed. It was night outside the porthole and in the cabin a dim light burned, but that wasn't what he sensed. It was more fundamental than that. And all at once he realized that the ship was moving. He was overcome by a feeling of thankfulness—they were on the way.

Helen's letter was still in his pocket. He took it out with his good hand and reread,

> ...I can't wait for you to get home. As soon as you dock, let me know and I will come wherever you are. I realize that you will be in a hospital for some time, but I will bring the baby and find a place to live nearby and we will visit you every day, and after a while you can be at home with us.

He tried to imagine it, a smile formed in the corners of his eyes and slowly spread over his face. They would find an apartment and they would play with the baby and she would cook the things he liked; at night she would be there, soft, happy and loving in his arms, and never again would he feel the loneliness he had felt in Rome. Going home! Going to the land of clean clothes and plenty to eat, away from the mud and the artillery and the wounded and the dead.

The doctors had said six months in the hospital would patch him up. Would it? He wondered.

Slowly the smile receded as he made his appraisals. He thought of Helen. He did not want her to see him like this. He wanted to be strong and whole and on his feet when he saw her again and when he saw his son; and instead he was returning in casts, torn, broken, helpless. He turned to the wall and felt the impact of his situation striking home, shattering the daydream of idyllic life. Somehow, now that he was actually on the way, now that their destination was only a matter of days ahead, now

241

that he was getting the thing he had most desired, a negative reaction set in. He felt that he would never belong again in a country of civilians who knew nothing of what the company had been through.

He saw again the crumpled bodies of the men of his last command lying as the *oberlautenant* had left them—Covalos-Perkins-March-Dalin-Mahoney-Bruce-Ramsey-Nessana-Fahey-Kruger-Stern-Tucker, and the others, some replacements he had not even known. He felt that he too should have died on that slope, sunk into oblivion when the *oberlautenant* pulled the trigger. By some torturous twist of fate he had been spared, but why? Did he somehow carry with him the necessity of living all those lives, of justifying his own existence. Why should he, Donald Cutler, be here and all the others lying now in shallow graves?

He remembered the leathery face of the first dead German he had seen on that afternoon when, fresh from the bathhouse, he had wandered in search of history. He had seen it now, seen history raw, seen it in all its lack of meaning, seen it in its perversity and destructiveness, seen that the armies of man were led blindly back and forth over the same areas, generation after generation. He had seen that history was not a polite intellectual game played by scholars. He, like all of us, had been caught in one of the great cycles and had played his part. Men build and men destroy, he thought. He wondered how long it would be before Italy could be rebuilt.

We have been wreckers, he thought, *and we did not ask to be wreckers. It is the builders who live good lives, who find joy in their work, who see whole before them the accomplishments of their hours and energy.* They had been wreckers leaving behind in that desolate land those whom fate selected as casualties. He had seen men cut down by one small piece of steel—dead—utterly and immediately dead and yet he lay alive throbbing with three major wounds, arm muscles torn, leg bones shattered, a hole through the neck. But his heart still beat and his breathing continued and slowly his mind searched for answers.

Somewhere in the back of his mind came the realization that the war could not be left behind, that in some unwelcome way, a burden traveled with him, weighing him down more than the heavy casts.

242

He felt closer to death than to life. Death he had seen and dreaded, but understood. Life was still the enigma; and the big question, the meaning of it all, still eluded him, still shimmered ahead like a mirage only to vanish as he approached.

A despair seized him, a futility seemed to overwhelm him as he realized that the gigantic task which lay behind him was only a part of his life. Now he would be expected to go on, to meet the expectations and impatience of those who did not understand this burden of soul which he carried with him, and would carry deep within him to the end of his days.

The Red Cross sent the telegram to Helen when the hospital ship docked. She felt a relief which left her weeping as she packed. He had come back alive. The dreads and fears of months seemed to drop from her as she gathered her things together and prepared to catch the next train to New York. She woke the sleeping baby and talked to him gaily as she dressed him, and he looked up at her happily, large-eyed and uncomprehending. She was early at the station and paced the platform restlessly all the time feeling an elation within which she could hardly contain. Today she would see Don and he would see his son.

She wondered how badly hurt he was but, in the happiness of his survival, found herself minimizing wounds. Whatever they were they would somehow heal and she would care for him, pour out to him all the affection which had been blocked within her for so long, somehow heal him with her love.

In New York the baby was sleeping in her arms, but she roused him again and found a taxi. On the trip downtown it seemed to her that the city was full of servicemen. There were uniforms everywhere, and she sensed a little the involvement of the whole country in the war effort. At home there were few uniforms to be seen but here in New York the sidewalks seethed with soldiers, sailors, marines, men and officers.

On the Staten Island ferry she stood by the rail with the baby. As the boat slipped away from the dock and into the river amid the jangling of bells and the toots of whistles, the soft wind caught them, blowing the curls back from her face and bringing again to her the indescribable elation she had felt when the telegram had arrived.

243

The ferry churned ponderously on its way down channel, past the lady with the torch in the harbor. As they passed, Helen, in her elation, saluted the statue—V for victory—the brave are home again, battered perhaps, weary perhaps, but home again to these shores. And you, bronze lady, have seen it all streaming by your imperturbable feet as you hold aloft a torch for those wise enough to love liberty.

The island shore loomed up ahead, creaky wharves—old docks—the bus, ordinary and unhurried, finding its lazy way to the receiving hospital. Questions and corridors and then a room.

Helen saw him then. He was sitting in a wheel chair with a blanket wrapped about him; and as he looked at her with the baby on her arm, she saw a smile light up his wan face.

XXXV

Letter from Donald Cutler to his father:

Albuquerque, N.M.
May 9th, 1947

Dear Dad,
  Your very welcome and interesting letter arrived yesterday. You have by now received my own brief note telling of my decision to stay out here for another year. I am delaying further study for several reasons, among which is a basic uncertainty as to the best direction in which to proceed. It is difficult to choose between several possible paths.

  My present job is adequate but not completely satisfying. Perhaps this is due to the possibility that I have not attained sufficient ability and knowledge in the profession of archaeology or perhaps I have not yet reached a position which will absorb all my interest, ability or energy. I do not know. However, I am sure that I might discover other jobs from which I could derive many different satisfactions.

  Neglected desires, even abilities, become tarnished with disuse. I am not exactly like the poor hungry man who went to the feast and could not decide what to eat of the good things before him, but I am close to this predicament. My energies have a tendency to exhaust themselves in determining what to do rather than in doing anything specific, other than my present job of course. I am much aware of the passage of time, and yet I am doing little but thinking. Probing history has fascinations that are difficult to find in other work.

  My army experience with its fighting and weary marches was exhausting. There was the constant necessity to think ahead con-

tinually, not for myself alone, but for a company of men. The men looked to me for orders which would place as few of them as possible on the casualty lists. In the rifle company, casualties were with us constantly. The responsibility is still with me. Week after week this went on. At any time I might have been hit myself. If an officer is hit, confusion rules for a while because the directing force is gone. What of this? What does it matter? What is it all about? When is the war to end? How many men do I have now? Where are we going to find food and water, especially water? What about ammunition? The colonel wants to attack again. Move out! Is he right? Why not attack at night? Too many attacks, too few men, no food, no sleep, ammunition getting low, men are getting weary. Control is not as good. Attack! Move out! The next hill and the next hill and the next hill. One more hill and we get relief. Not many men left, little ammunition, been raining for three days. Mud, mud, mud. The weapons need cleaning. One machine gun remains, for morale purposes. Open the bolt with your foot. Keep your rifle clean, soldier. We get relief after this one. More artillery and mortar fire falling on us. Move out! Are you crazy? Everyone's crazy in the Infantry. On your feet, men. Let's go—into the valley, through the trees and gullies, across streams. Water, there it is. Now, feel the pull of the slope. Keep spread out! The last hill. The last of the company. Get artillery on the radio! Three hundred yards right, 300 short. Let'er go. On the way. Splash. Here they come. Mortar fire on us, rifle grenades on us, machine-gun fire coming into us. Here they come. They got me with a rifle grenade. Handful of men. Less every minute. Throw in the towel!

Young oberlautenant—tough, hard. Short conversation. Then, through the back of the neck. In and out, no damage. Miraculous! Lie still. Taste the powder, feel it burn, eat the rock dust. Stay still! He's gone. Tourniquet on the knee; bandage the hand. How? No use anyway. Minute by minute, hour by hour, more rain; German takes watch; no particular pain.

Americans! Three volunteers with a white flag. Take it easy; I'm going out. Down the slope, down, down, shooting stars, hot bouillon, the stretcher, the friends, the field hospital. Plaster cast on leg, cast on hand. What about neck? No bandage; it sealed itself; leave it alone.

General Hospital two weeks. Maggots in bed with me. Angry pain twisting.

246

You're the doctor. Spinal injection, white sheet, always conscious.

Okay, nurse, all done. Now the hand.

Save the hand. Ether. . . .

Back in bed with plaster casts. What's going on inside? No bandage on the neck. Leave it alone. Hospital ship; the States; family; friends; time.

You see, Dad, the above is still with me. It colors my life, tempers my viewpoint on many matters. What bothers me now is, what am I living for? Why was I spared while so many others went? Is it in order that I may do what I am now doing? Is there something else that needs my attention? I have some of my old energy now, somewhat diluted, yes, but it is there. I am troubled often with the question of what to do next.

Sometimes I feel that I must read and write history until I have untangled the shadowy meanings of experience. I should like to write strongly and convincingly on many subjects, on war and men, on loyalty and death, on sacrifice and hope; let the words flow as in a torrent to wash away the dry rot which continually penetrates anything historical. The spirit of man needs a flood of understanding to clear away the pettiness of the times.

It is perhaps better to do nothing than to do a job poorly, but little would be done if everyone held this viewpoint. I dislike to do anything unless I can do a good job. I am not certain of my energy, but who is? It should suffice me in any undertaking, given time.

Lest this seem a completely gloomy letter, let me say that in many, many ways I am happy now with Helen and the children. They are growing rapidly. You must try to get out here for a visit soon. It is only at times that inwardly I still find uneasiness, dissatisfaction, restlessness, sometimes boredom. A man needs to know what it is all about.

This letter has dwelt too long on the personal side. I think, however, that you will understand.

Your son,
Don